Lost in her own [...]
current lecture on life, love and lust. Just as she turned
to ask her what she had been saying, the chimes over the
gallery's door signaled the arrival of a customer. The tail
end of Yanté's latest admonishment was carried off into
the stratosphere as both women turned toward the door
and laid eyes on an apparition from heaven.

At just under six feet tall, Amir Swift was breathtaking.
Azure regarded him with uncharacteristic interest, his
smooth skin bringing to mind a mug of warm buttermilk.
Thick, sun-kissed lips that wore a half smile as he
introduced himself were those of an African Adonis. She
found his bold features, including a powerful nose and
high, defined cheekbones, positioned ever so perfectly on
a slender face, to all be incredibly sexy. His light, dusty-
brown hair was laid in long dreadlocks, which hung
down to the center of his back and were tied back away
from his face with a black band. Unable to find a physical
comparison between him and any man either Azure or
Yanté had ever seen, they stood frozen, summarily blown
away.

to her own thoughts, Azure tuned out Yané's
chatter, letting the low-pitched hum increase to a mild
roar once again. It was only the latest in a series of
pulses connected to the arrival of a steamer. There
had probably been a dozen or more since noon. Back
there, at least, some work remained. Here in the quiet
end had crept a certain malaise from that time.

In just the last few days Azure Street was losing its
value, regarded as it was a useless, emptying precinct, far
enough that nobody cared about anyone's comings and
goings.

She saw no one in the street, but came to the
corner, where Yané went on ahead of her. Azure, who
preferred to be on her own, was walking a few steps
behind, along the shadowy street and across a square. A
breeze tossed scraps of... moonlike air. This half-empty
haven here was just a cheap functional depot, which had a
sleepy, deserted air that she still remembered had always
from her face with a childish hand. Up to try to find a physical
companion between hill and peak, where Azure or
Yané, had ever sensed any other beauty, mournfully drawn
away.

LOVE'S PORTRAIT

KIM SHAW

LOVE'S PORTRAIT

An Arabesque novel

ISBN 1-58314-699-7

© 2006 by Kim Shaw

All characters in this book have no existence outside the imagination of
the author and have no relation whatsoever to anyone bearing the same
name or names. They are not even distantly inspired by any individual
known or unknown to the author, and all incidents are pure invention.
Any resemblance to actual persons, living or dead, is entirely coincidental.

® and TM are trademarks. Trademarks indicated with ® are registered in
the United States Patent and Trademark Office, the Canadian Trade Marks
Office and/or other countries.

www.kimanipress.com

Printed in U.S.A.

This, my third novel, is dedicated entirely to my mother, Eugenia Sumpter. She has been, and continues to be, a beacon of support, encouragement and love for my brothers and I.

She is a testament to the strength, perseverance, humility and radiance of the black woman. Thank you Mommy.

Acknowledgments

I'd like to thank my husband, Donald. People always ask if the characters in my books are real and while each and every one of them is fictional, I have to admit that you were often on my mind when I wrote about Amir Swift. Like him, you have overcome many obstacles and directed your life in the manner in which you wanted it to go. As a result, you have become a role model for many and a motivator to me.

Once again I'd like to thank the wonderful staff at Kimani Press for taking such good care of me and my work. To Demetria Lucas, my first editor, I wish you the best in your future endeavors. I'd also like to thank my agent, Pattie Steele-Perkins. This is shaping up to be quite a career and your expertise and advice has been invaluable.

I would be remiss if I didn't thank a dear friend, Sue Sykes. For the many hours you spent proofreading, listening to me rant when a character just didn't fit right or brainstorming when a story line went limp, I am forever grateful. I promise to return the favor one day (so get going, girl!).

I'd like to acknowledge the work of some of the artists mentioned in this novel. While like Azure, I have a profound love and respect of artists of African descent, I must admit that I am not nearly as well-versed. In doing research for this story, I learned a great deal and developed an even deeper appreciation for the work of Essud Fungcap, Annie Lee, Jacob Lawrence and many others. I would also like to thank the people of Barbados for providing such a beautiful backdrop for part of the novel. I have enjoyed my visits there and have always found the people warm and inviting.

With this, my third novel, I have learned so much and am humbled by the experiences I have had. I appreciate the many talented authors who have shared their time and friendship with me. My final thank-you goes out to the readers who continue to demand good stories, which I intend to keep creating.

Chapter 1

"Azure, I'm serious. I don't know how you do it, but I can't function properly if I'm not getting some on the regular. It's like food, drugs or something," Yanté testified emphatically.

"It is not that serious, Yanté." Azure laughed.

"Humph, maybe to somebody like you who's not getting any. But the rest of the free world would agree with me."

Azure shook her head, knowing that it was pointless to argue with Yanté, who was now snapping her fingers to the new Anita Baker tune, which issued softly from the speakers mounted on the gallery's walls.

"Whatever. Hand me that white spray bottle over there," Azure said, pointing toward the floor next to the stool where Yanté was perched. "You could make yourself useful and help me with these."

Azure was standing on a step stool in front of a thirty-eight-by-thirty hand-embellished painting titled *Among*

Friends, by Essud Fungcap. She had been in the middle of her daily ritual of dusting the three dozen paintings on display in the gallery and polishing their frames when Yanté had dropped by and begun talking like a cat in heat.

Monroe Galleries was not simply a business for Azure—it was a dream come true. The small sole proprietorship located in the heart of Dupont Circle in the nation's capital city was her slice of heaven. Dupont Circle was home to a host of fine museums, ethnic restaurants—where one could find as many types of food as there are cultures represented in the country—and bookstores offering something for every reading palate. The largest concentration of private art galleries was located in the circle, and in that number was Monroe Galleries, Inc. They each showcased a different style of art and artist, with some specializing in the early Renaissance period and others featuring a more modern selection. Azure preferred to offer a wide range of art by Africans of the diaspora, all from various periods in history. Within its compact nine hundred and fifty square feet, surrounded by works of sublime grace, she was able to be just herself—Azure Monroe, lover and worshipper of the arts. Being an entrepreneur meant that she set her own hours and answered only to herself. Selling art was the piece that made the puzzle of her life fit together. The periods of the day, especially early in the morning before the door chimes rang out to signal the arrival of her first customer, when she reviewed inventory, organized new arrivals and placed orders, were the most peaceful times for her, her mind occupied by the business of running her gallery. Equally as enjoyable were the afternoons, when customers trickled in to shop or just to look around and admire the paintings on display. She loved every opportunity to discuss artists, varieties of styles and motifs. For Azure, this gallery was far from work. It was home.

"If I had wanted to work, I would have stayed at the hotel," Yanté said, picking a piece of lint from the lapel of the peach Barami suit that hugged her voluptuous size-eight frame sinfully. She smoothed her toned, stockinged thighs, sighing lazily when she realized that Azure was staring at her, one hand on her hip and the other extended as she waited for the bottle.

"Here," Yanté said, pouting as she thrust the solution into Azure's outstretched hand.

"Thank you." Azure smirked.

"Really, Ashes, you need to get out of this gallery sometime. Maybe meet yourself a nice guy…someone who could put some loving on you that would make you see there is more to life than selling paintings all day."

Yanté Lourde was beautiful; there was no denying that. Growing up, Azure had always been slightly envious of her. She had smooth, blemish-free skin and thick, natural hair which had never been chemically treated. By the time she entered her teens, she was curvaceous and graceful, which Azure was not. Yanté had been ladylike before she'd even become a woman. She was always at ease around boys and later men, self-assured and confident. Azure had learned much of what she knew about the opposite sex from Yanté. She watched her, emulated her and sometimes wanted to be her.

The most attractive thing about Yanté, however, was her sincerity. One could never be confused about where one stood with her because she was never fake or ambivalent about her likes or dislikes. If someone did something to her

that she didn't like, she made it known. She was never cruel
or malicious, but she did not take stuff off anyone. The one
thing which Azure found most irritating about Yanté, however, was her annoying habit of trying to run her cousin's
life.

"Why are you always trying to get me hooked up? I
would think you'd want to keep all of D.C.'s available men
for yourself," Azure teased.

"Oh, honey, please. You couldn't handle the tigers I
snag. No, you need something more along the PG line."

"What I need is for you to go back to work and leave
me alone," Azure replied.

She climbed off the ladder and stepped back to admire
the canvas. No matter how many times a day she looked
at that painting, it always brought a smile to her face. The
soothing colors and its casualness made her feel warm and
cozy. It reminded her of the home of her aunts Jeannie and
Janet, her father's older sisters. They were twins who had
lived together all of their lives, finishing one another's sen-
tences, one an extension of the other. Those women doted
on Azure, making her feel more loved and nurtured than
her own mother had ever managed to do. When Aunt
Jeannie had been diagnosed with cancer, it was almost as
if it didn't faze either of them because they had each other.
The disease progressed rapidly and within six months she'd
lost the fight. Ironically, exactly six months later, Aunt
Janet had passed away in her sleep. After a brief separa-
tion in which Aunt Janet seemed to age faster than she had
in her whole life, the twins were together once more.

Azure ran her hand through her medium-length cherry-
tinted hair, noting that she was close to being due for a
touch-up. She'd call her stylist, Michelle, later on and

make an appointment. Secretly, Azure had been toying with the idea of shaving her head completely bald, tired of the processing with chemicals that burned, the coloring which stained her scalp and the weekly wash and sets. She'd been wearing a bob for the past few months, which also meant a bimonthly trim to keep the style. Hair maintenance had become a hassle she could definitely live without. It all seemed so unnatural, and she felt as though it wasn't the person she truly was inside—although she couldn't quite put her finger on who that person actually was. She'd come close to taking that leap to shaving her head, but realized that her mother would probably drop dead on sighting her, certain that Azure had done it just to torture her further. Furthermore, Yanté would take the act as proof of her simmering suspicion that Azure was a card-carrying, bra-burning lesbian feminist. For the life of her, Azure never could understand why black women placed so much value on something as insignificant as hair.

Lost in her own thoughts, Azure tuned out Yanté's current lecture on life, love and lust. Just as she turned to ask her what she had been saying, the chimes over the gallery's door signaled the arrival of a customer. The tail end of Yanté's latest admonishment was carried off into the stratosphere as both women turned toward the door and laid eyes on an apparition from heaven.

At just under six feet tall, Amir Swift was breathtaking. Azure regarded him with uncharacteristic interest, his smooth skin bringing to mind a mug of warm buttermilk. Thick, sun-kissed lips wore a half smile as he introduced himself; he was an African Adonis. Azure found his bold features, his powerful nose and high, defined cheekbones positioned ever so perfectly on a slender face all incredibly sexy. His light dusty-brown hair was laid in long dread-locks that hung down to the center of his back and were tied back away from his face with a black band. Unable to find a physical comparison between him and any man either Azure or Yanté had ever seen, they stood frozen, summarily blown away.

Yanté recovered quickly, sashaying her way to the front of the gallery. Despite the fact that she neither worked there nor knew anything of value about art, she was quick to offer to assist this finely chiseled patron of the arts. Amir informed Yanté that he was looking for a painting for his sister, a housewarming present of sorts, and Yanté proceeded to show him around the gallery.

Azure almost burst out laughing as she listened to Yanté's ridiculous interpretation of an Annie Lee print. Her answers to Amir's questions were limited to the brief descriptions typed on the placards beneath each painting. Within minutes Yanté's ineptness became evident, and Amir turned to Azure with an imploring look. She wanted to respond, even imagined herself responding, but unfortunately, her feet had grown roots and she couldn't figure out how to move from the spot she seemed to be glued to. She became a mess of jumbled nerves; her stomach felt like a train wreck about to happen. Never in all of her twenty-four years, eleven months and thirteen days had she had feelings as overwhelming and all-encompassing as these, and she was at once astonished and embarrassed.

Finally, Azure forced herself into motion. She approached Amir, stopping within two feet of him, and was immediately lost in the pools of his gray eyes, speckled with brown, as they smiled openly into her own. Breathlessness took over, the spacious gallery suddenly as restrictive as a closet as his eyes held her captive like a fly caught in a spider's web. Unwillingly, and at great length, Azure broke the spell and with tremendous effort assumed a more professional stance. She wasted no time helping Amir to select a painting, giving him detailed descriptions based on the type of work he thought he wanted to purchase. She was unnerved by him and extremely eager to send him on his way.

It seemed his sister was a connoisseur of African-American history and was deeply interested in art which was reflective of that. He told them that she had done her college thesis on the black experience in America. The painting he eventually purchased, at Azure's suggestion, was *Daybreak—A Time to Rest,* the first part in a pricey series by Jacob Lawrence telling the story of Harriet Tubman and the Underground Railroad. Azure was taken by surprise when Amir paid for the painting in cash, with large bills.

Azure admired the smoothness of his penmanship as he filled out the sales register and mailing list which she asked all customers to complete. Even his name, Amir Swift, was as strong and commanding as the man who carried it.

While Azure clumsily wrapped the painting, still too much on edge to control her shaking, sweating hands, Yanté launched into flirtation overdrive. Amir's polite, engaging manner served to spur her on, inviting compliments on everything from his hair to his shoes to roll off her tongue. Azure listened intently as Amir remained as cool as a cup of flavored shaved ice in the summertime, taking it all in stride as if he experienced this type of adoration every day of his life. Before leaving, he extended a hand to Azure, wrapping strong, smooth fingers around hers and thanking her again for her assistance. From his jacket pocket he retrieved two passes for a club opening that night, insisting that both ladies come as his guests. Amir Swift's scent and aura lingered around the gallery for a long time after the door chimes rang out behind him.

Chapter 2

"Damn, that man is de-li-cious!" Yanté shouted as soon as the door closed behind Amir. "Is it me, or did it get really hot up in here?" she asked, fanning herself dramatically.

"You ought to be ashamed of yourself," Azure hissed, looking through the frosted windowpane on the door in the direction Amir had walked. Despite her admonishments to Yanté, she herself was quite taken by him.

"Uh-uh…no way. You're not going to tell me that that gorgeous brother didn't get your juices flowing, too! Even an ice princess like you had to melt under all that fineness," Yanté screeched.

"You are so nasty," Azure responded, shaking her head. "I swear I don't know how we're related."

"We, my dear, are related 'cause your mama is my daddy's baby sister. But that is not the point. You, Miss Thang, are either a greasy-tongued liar or you're as gay as the day is long if you refuse to admit that the brother who just walked out of your door was all that and then some!" Yanté said, as she joined Azure at the door, hoping to get a parting glance of Amir.

"All right, all right. I'll give you that one. Homeboy was something else." Azure smiled, a gentle shudder moving through her body. "But that doesn't excuse the way you drooled all over him. Have you no shame?" she scolded.

"Hell, no. Not when it comes to something that promising. I've told you a million times…while you're sitting back being cute and coy, the next chick will saddle up and ride away on your pony. Men don't want to always have to do the pursuing…sometimes you've got to be the pursuer. Feel me?"

Azure considered her cousin's solemn expression and realized that she was, indeed, very serious. She shook her head again and walked away, not answering. She retrieved her inventory log from the file cabinet at the rear of the gallery and sat down at her desk to record the sale into the book.

"So, what are you going to wear?" Yanté asked, resting her rear on the edge of the desk.

"What are you talking about?" Azure asked without looking up.

"Duh…to Amir's party. You've got to come up out of them jeans and that nasty looking T-shirt and get yourself cutified—if that's a word. I'm sure everybody who's anybody is going to be there. I've been hearing about this new spot for a while now. I even heard that Robert DeNiro is a secret partner. I'm talking upscale all the way. There won't be any broke-assed wannabes trying to get up in our face all night," Yanté said as she pulled a silver compact out of her purse and surveyed her face.

With a critical eye she searched for any imperfections, finding, of course, none. Even though it was cloudy and gray outside, she was in a sunny mood, which meant she'd have to break out something sexy, bright and minimal. She examined her eyes more closely and realized that she'd have to skip out of work a little early in order to have time to get the arch of her eyebrows touched up for tonight.

"Look at you…talking like you know the brother. You just met him and you're all psyched up over his little party," Azure responded.

Yanté glanced over the top of her mirror, eyeing Azure suspiciously. She pursed her lips and studied her cousin closely.

"What are you going to wear?" she asked pointedly.

"I'm not going," Azure said matter-of-factly.

Yanté snapped the compact shut, considering her cousin's solemn face and waiting for the punch line. When none was forthcoming, she hopped off the edge of the desk and began pacing the floor. She searched for the right way to put what was in her mind into words.

"Azure, I love you…you know I do. And that's why I've always stood by you—even when I didn't agree with the things you were doing. You are talented. You certainly paint just as well as, if not better than any of these artists you've got hanging on these walls," Yanté said in a level tone, sweeping her hand around the gallery. "Yet for some reason, you don't want anyone to know about it. You stay holed up in this place, creating masterpieces that no one will ever see and I ask you, time and time again, what's the point of art if only the artist gets to enjoy it?"

"Yanté—"

"No, let me finish, Ashes. Now, I respect your need for privacy and whatever else it is that stops you from letting your light shine. And I know I may tease you about dating and guys and all of that stuff, but it's just because I worry about you. You live like a seventy-year-old widow. All that's missing are the cats. It's not…not…"

"Not normal, Yanté? Are you trying to say that I'm not normal?" Azure asked.

"Well, if the straitjacket fits… What do you have against going out on the town from time to time? Getting your swerve on is not going to kill you, you know. I mean, closing yourself off from the world like this is not going to change things, Azure."

"I know that," Azure said, shooting an unmistakable don't-go-there look at Yanté.

Yanté heeded the warning and backed off. The last thing she wanted to do was upset Azure by rehashing the past. Yet it seemed as though Azure was still so entrenched in a time that was long-ago lost that it didn't need to be dug up at all. She shook her head and sighed.

"I just don't get you," Yanté said softly, her concern for her cousin running deeper than her worry about whether she was having sex.

Azure held her head down, eyes fixed on the numbers in her inventory book. As she continued staring, not trusting herself to look at Yanté, she chewed her bottom lip. The figures began to blur in front of her as her eyes grew moist. She couldn't answer Yanté's questions because she couldn't bring herself to reveal that painful place in her spirit that she kept locked away. No one knew how deeply what she had gone through had affected her and as far as she was concerned, no one, not even Yanté, needed to know. It was enough that the scars she wore on her heart and soul kept her from having the courage to open up to anyone ever again. Everywhere you went, people were always talking about falling in love and living your life, but no one ever talked about what to do when love left you beaten down, lost and virtually lifeless. There were no quick-fix answers that she could use to help her heart heal.

Yanté eventually threw her hands up in frustration at Azure. She realized that trying to get her to talk about her feelings was like trying to fit her own size-eight feet into the cute size-six shoes that were always on display in stores. Wishing just wouldn't make it happen.

Azure handed the guest passes over, adamant about not attending the opening, citing her disdain for clubs as the main reason. She was definitely not going to admit to Yanté that the thought of being around Amir again was more than she could handle. While his physical attractiveness was disquieting in itself, there was something so compelling resting in those smoky eyes that it was almost frightening. She couldn't trust herself with a man like that. Besides, since Yanté had set her sights on him—and it was a safe bet that if Yanté wanted him, she would have him—Azure sent Yanté off to the party with her blessings, determined to exorcise Mr. Amir Swift, in all his fineness, from her mind.

Chapter 3

The telephone rang, its shrill tone jolting Azure out of her slumber. She looked at the iridescent digits of her alarm clock and saw that it was just after two o'clock in the morning. Instinctively, she knew who was on the other end of the line. She sighed heavily, as she toyed with the idea of not answering it at all. However, she knew that would be a pointless attempt at avoiding the inevitable. Reluctantly, she snatched up the receiver on the fourth ring.

"Hello," she said flatly.

"Baby sis, it's me. Did I wake you?"

"No, Patrick. I'm always up in the middle of the night. I was just sitting here, waiting for you to call."

"Come on, Azure, don't be like that. I'm sorry. You know I wouldn't bother you if it weren't an emergency," Patrick said.

Patrick was Azure's only brother. He was actually her

half brother, from her father's first marriage. He was seven years older than Azure and had grown up with his mother in Maryland. He'd spent school holidays and sporadic summer vacations with them until he was about seventeen. By then he had been in and out of all kinds of trouble, including several expulsions from schools, vandalism charges and misdemeanor convictions for disturbing the peace and rioting. Patrick was a pothead by the time he was in middle school, having gotten in with the wrong crowd down in Maryland. His mother passed him off to anybody who would have him, yet refused to let him live with his father on a full-time basis. When he did come to visit, he was more and more distant and hostile toward their father as the years went by.

Patrick ran away from his mother's home on more than one occasion. Every time, their father would get the call from Patrick's mother and jump in his car and go searching. He usually found him staying with a friend either in Maryland or in D.C. He graduated to experimenting with all types of drugs and alcohol, often lying and stealing to get what he wanted.

Growing up, he never paid very much attention to Azure. He treated her like an annoying little sibling when he acknowledged her at all. No matter what he did, Azure continued to look up to him. She felt as if he understood her, since neither one of them got along with their mothers. Unfortunately for him, however, he did not have their father with him every day to keep the peace.

Now that they were older, Patrick in his early thirties, his life still had not found balance. He moved around frequently, never staying in one place very long. He was battling a serious cocaine addiction and could not hold down a job. His mother had washed her hands of him completely and even their father had grown tired of bailing him out of trouble. When he had gotten arrested in Virginia on drug charges a few years back, it was Azure who had visited him every couple of weeks and sent him clothes and money for cigarettes and toiletries. Every time Patrick got into trouble, she prayed it would be the last time and for a while he would seem to be doing better. Before she could get too comfortable, however, the phone would ring, often in the middle of the night, and her peace would be disturbed by his latest drama.

"What's wrong, Patrick?" she asked.

"See, right away you assume it's something bad. Why can't I be calling with some good news?" he asked.

"That's because good news doesn't usually happen when it's pitch black outside," Azure replied.

"There's where you're wrong. I was actually calling to tell you that I got a job offer—a good job, too. The only problem is that it's in Atlanta. They need me down there to start by next week, and I was all set to stay with this woman I know, but her old man got out of jail earlier than he was supposed to so…"

"So now you have nowhere to stay," Azure finished his thought for him.

"Now you see my dilemma. I really think Atlanta would be a good place for me to go, you know…to get a fresh start. And this job, Azure, it's a good job. Not like those dead-end gigs I've been getting. I've really been trying to get my act together, you know? Now this."

"Patrick, what exactly do you need me to do?" Azure asked, knowing that whatever it was, she was going to do it.

"I just need a little loan. You know, some money for a motel or something. Nothing fancy. Just someplace to lay my head until I can find an apartment. Of course, I'd pay you back as soon as I get on my feet."

Azure rolled her eyes in the air, knowing that that was an empty promise. She got the particulars of when Patrick was planning to arrive in Atlanta and promised that she would make arrangements for him to have a place to stay when he got there. She told him to call her when his bus got in and she'd give him the name of the hotel. She had no intentions of sending him any cash directly, having learned a long time ago that having money in hand was the surest way to send him straight to the nearest street corner.

Azure hung up feeling depressed, as she usually did whenever she spoke to Patrick. She couldn't understand how he'd turned out the way he had. Even though he'd had a mother who couldn't have cared less about him, he'd also had a father with a heart of gold, who had tried to give him the love and nurturing that his own mother hadn't, but he'd fought it all the way. It was almost as if he'd believed that he didn't deserve his family's love and so he did everything in his power to abuse it.

She fell asleep with thoughts of Patrick invading her dreams. Later, as she drifted into a deeper state of slumber, visions of another man swam through her subconscious. This man brought a smile to her lips and by morning, she awoke embarrassed by the torrid dreams of passion she'd had about Mr. Amir Swift.

Chapter 4

Days passed in their normal fashion and the gallery had a particularly busy week. Yet no matter how many customers she served or how many new faces she saw, Azure remained haunted by the image of Amir. The sheer beauty of the man was indelibly imprinted on her brain and made her wish she knew more about the man behind the facade.

Settled comfortably on a stool in the studio at the back of the gallery a week later during her favorite time of evening, Azure was lost in her life's passion. The gallery was closed for the day and the sun had set, leaving behind a purple, starless sky that provided a breathtaking backdrop to the canvas she'd positioned in front of the window. She'd been working on a painting of a brown-skinned toddler crawling through a field of burnished yellow hay, but somewhere she had taken a wrong turn. The eyes she'd drawn were those of the alluring man who had invaded her dreams since the day she'd discovered he existed. Those eyes were all wrong for the face of the chocolate doll-like baby, but she could not seem to stop herself from painting them, nor did she want to.

Yanté had reported that she'd attended the party Amir had invited them to and she boasted that she'd had a blast. What she didn't reveal was the fact that Amir seemed disappointed by Azure's absence. Yanté had not missed the crestfallen look on his face when he'd asked after Azure and been told that she had had other plans.

Amir had gone on to give Yanté VIP treatment, setting her up with a table in the exclusive section of the club and instructing the waitstaff to put her drinks on his tab. He was a generous, engaging host and spent the evening shaking hands and personally greeting all of the guests. He visited Yanté's table often and introduced her to a number of people during the course of the night. While he was a perfect gentleman, it became apparent to her that he did not return her obvious interest in him. Undaunted, Yanté spent the bulk of the night searching for other potential connections, fully intending to get to know the elusive Amir Swift a little bit better at another time. To Azure, she simply stated that it had been the party of the year.

Azure acted as nonchalantly as she could during Yanté's report of the evening, not daring to let on that Amir had been plaguing her thoughts since she'd laid eyes on him. Indeed, she had made valiant efforts to push him from her mind, thinking it better if Amir remained a pleasant memory. A man that fine could bring nothing but heartache and misery, she told herself. And those were two cups from which she'd drunk more than her fair share in the past.

Still, he was magnificent. There was no denying that.

He was mesmerizing, in fact. His voice, deep and rich, still rang in her ears. His slow, deliberate manner of speaking, as though he had all the time in the world to get his point across, made her think of lazy winter days and lovers holed up in a private Shangri-la. The way he had looked intently at her as she'd described the work of the artists on the gallery's walls, as if she were explaining the secret of life, had made her feel like the most important person in the world at that moment.

A fluttering heart and quivering gut cautioned her that she was in way over her head for a man she didn't even know and would probably never see again. Once more, she attempted to forget about him and get back to the toddler on the canvas. That lasted all of three minutes before she was imagining herself running a finger across his full, tawny lips.

The sound of the gallery's doorbell pulled her from her revelry. Annoyed by the intrusion, Azure carefully placed her paintbrush in its cup. She wiped her hands on her T-shirt and made her way to the front of the gallery, leaving the studio door open behind her. She reached the door just as the bell sounded again, her annoyance growing by the second. Pulling back the shade, she peered out into the darkness and astonishment seized her delicate face.

She hesitated for a moment before opening the door. One deep breath, then two. Finally, she disengaged the lock and pulled the door open.

"Mr. Swift?" she queried.

"Ms. Monroe," he replied, his mellow voice sending a shiver down her spine. "I saw a light coming from the back and took a chance that you were in."

A soft drizzle had begun to fall and there was a noticeable chill in the air. Amir pulled the collar of his rust-colored leather jacket closer to his ears.

"Forgive me," Azure said, as the cold air released her from paralysis. Stepping aside, she said, "Come in."

Amir entered the gallery and Azure closed the door behind him, switching on the lights. For a moment, neither of them said anything. Azure believed that somehow she had willed him there, her incessant day-dreaming transporting him to her doorstep. She waited without asking for him to tell her exactly what had brought him to her. He, however, seemed to be at a loss for words.

He smiled at her and she would swear the temperature in the room had reached one hundred and fifty. His lips were inviting, the kind that would make a woman ache to kiss them every time she saw him.

Finally, when so much time had passed that they were both beginning to feel ridiculous as they stood staring at one another, Amir apologized for the intrusion. He informed Azure that his sister had loved the painting so much, he'd come to purchase the second piece in the series.

"Oh, I see," Azure replied, clearly disappointed that he did, in fact, have a reason for being there.

There was polite chatter between the two, filled with an electricity that was both static and frantic, as Azure showed him the painting again. She described it in depth, getting swept away both by her love of the artist and her awe of his creation. A conversation steeped in historical context ensued in which Azure was pleasantly surprised to find out that Amir was a very well-versed man.

Satisfied with his purchase, Amir stepped aside to allow Azure to remove the painting from its place on the wall.

As she busied herself preparing the painting for Amir, she prayed that he didn't notice her shaking hands. He was standing very close to her as she wrapped the painting in bubble wrap. When she reached for the brown wrapping paper she normally used, he backed out of her way and then proceeded to wander the length of the gallery. When he reached the open studio door, Amir peered inside. The half-finished painting of the toddler caught his eye, drawing him farther into the room. Moving from the polished, orderly gallery into this room was the equivalent of stepping into a different world. It was artistically chaotic; half a dozen easels were situated around the room, each bearing a different-sized canvas. Dozens of completed paintings of landscapes, people, animals and other subjects leaned against the walls. The floor was stained with a mingling of paints in an array of colors. There was a small cot with rumpled sheets in the far corner of the room, a table supporting a coffeemaker, condiments and a box of tea biscuits. The room itself was dark, with the exception of the bright branching floor lamp, whose four bulbs had to be at least one hundred watts each. This lamp was situated behind the canvas of the toddler, illuminating it as if it were the sole performer on a Broadway stage of a sold-out show.

By the time Azure realized that Amir was in her private studio, he had already gotten an eyeful of her work. Inexplicably, she offered no protest as her deepest secrets were exposed to this stranger. Silently, she stood in the doorway and watched him survey her creations. It was as if all of her life she had been holding her cards pressed firmly against her chest, hiding them from the world at large. Now, this man, a virtual stranger who had, in two brief meetings, drawn her to him like a mosquito to warm, supple flesh, had gently loosened her tight grip on those cards and she didn't mind at all.

The passion of the pieces in that room confirmed for Amir what he had really come back to the gallery to find out—Azure Monroe was definitely as beautiful and alluring on the inside as she was on the outside. The day he'd first walked into the gallery he had been feeling lost. The problems in his life were eating him up with particular anguish that afternoon and he had sought temporary escape by shopping for a present for his sister. Bridgette had always been his raison d'être, so to speak, and he was extremely proud of her accomplishments, beaming whenever he thought of her. She had been an excellent student, and he had never had to worry about her getting caught up in the self-destructive behavior of her peers in high school. Buying her a housewarming present to celebrate the completion of her degree, securing a promising job and finding a fabulous new apartment was precisely the distraction he had thought would help get him through that trying day. Little did he know at the time that entering that gallery would affect his heart, as well.

Dressed that day in blue jeans, sneakers and a black T-shirt with the outline of a mother holding her baby drawn in white on it, Azure was the epitome of what he imagined the word *peace* would look like in human form. His fingertips seemed to tingle with the urge to touch her brown skin, dark and smooth like double-dipped chocolate. Her face with its petite features, slanted eyes and pouting lips was made more beautiful when she smiled at her friend's flirtatiousness, exposing strikingly white teeth. Long eyelashes curled over those beautiful eyes and to him, she looked as if she could soothe even the most savage beast with a soft word or a stroke of her hand. The image of her had done more to lift his spirits that day than anything else could have. He'd thought about her nonstop in the days that followed, trying to convince himself that she could not possibly have been all that he'd thought she was.

Amir was a man who had known a lot of women, both intimately and superficially. He had no real preference in terms of looks or body types, always more attracted to a woman's essence than to her physical beauty. Tall, short, thick or thin, blackberry molasses to butter pecan, he loved black women with the ferociousness of an ancient Zulu warrior. While he respected all women, for him, no other woman could hold a candle to the mother of civilization. Sometimes people joked that this was because he was so "light, bright and damned near white" himself. But whatever the reason, as he matured he realized that as a black man, his place was by the side of a black woman, and his duty was to protect and to cherish. Unfortunately, he had yet to find a woman who did not allow the legacy of the black holocaust in this country to prevent her from trusting and loving a black man. He had yet to find a soul mate who would not blame him for all the wrong that had been done by brothers before him. He was prepared to treat his woman as the queen that she was, yet he needed someone who would keep the drama at a minimum and bring serenity to his soul. Something about Ms. Azure Monroe spoke to him, to the very core of his being. Finally, unable to get her out of his mind, he had worked up the courage to come back tonight to see if she was only a dream.

Amir questioned Azure about various pieces, and although

he noticed her slight hesitation, he pushed forward. He wanted to know the person who could paint with such passion and sensitivity. He felt as though the shapes, the colors, the souls laid out before him were images of his own emotions and desires pulled from his very heart. How could she have painted what he had been feeling when they did not know one another—had never known the other existed before a week earlier? This question raced through his mind, now feverish with the intensity of the moment, and threatened to spill from his lips. *How could you know me?* he thought.

With the exception of Azure explaining the context of some of her work, and Amir praising her talent, few additional words were exchanged between them that night. It quickly became apparent to both of them that there existed a magnetic pull, quite like gravity's hold on all of Earth's objects, working diligently to bring them together. Two hours passed in virtual slow motion as Azure surprised herself by allowing Amir the out-of-the-ordinary privilege of viewing her work. She had not realized how much the human psyche needed to be stroked until he reached out a strong masculine hand and did so. Each emphatic word of praise delivered softly from Amir's lips stirred her soul, and she grew more and more at ease in sharing herself with him.

By the time Amir prepared to leave, both of them were overwhelmed by the sensations they felt for one another. She felt out of breath, as if she had been in a ten-kilometer race across hilly and rocky terrain while wearing a twenty-pound backpack. For him, it was more a feeling of having come home after a long, arduous trip. They were still foreign to one another, yet oddly they felt as if their meeting had happened a long time ago, perhaps in another lifetime. He thanked fate, destiny, luck or whatever it was that had directed his path to her doorstep, knowing instinctively that his life was now changed forever. He let his imagination run free, creating scenarios and possibilities for what future time spent with her could be like.

At the door, Amir held both of Azure's hands in his for a long while, gazing into her angelic face as if to convince himself that she was real. He had realized how pretty she was the moment he'd first laid eyes on her. The tiny heart-shaped face, button nose slightly turned up at the tip like that of a pixie and the liquid brown eyes of a new-born fawn were themselves an image to behold. But the true attraction was the serenity which emanated from her features, giving her a glow that, for him, was like a light at the end of a long dark tunnel.

"May I see you again?" he asked shyly.

He felt like a pimply-faced teenager asking a girl out to the junior prom. He almost crossed his fingers as he waited for an answer.

"Sure, but I don't think your sister's going to need any more paintings anytime soon," she joked.

"No, you're right," he agreed. "How about dinner tomorrow night?" he asked.

"Sounds like a date," she answered.

In spite of all the barriers Azure had placed around herself for the past few years, her heart seemed to leap right out of her chest and into Amir's hands that night. It was a simple start to a love affair such as neither had ever known. Neither one would be prepared for all that it promised to bring into their lives, and only time would tell if they were strong enough to handle it.

Chapter 5

The sun began its snail-like ascent over the horizon, bringing with it the start of a brand-new day. It was already muggy, even at this early hour, guaranteeing an oppressively hot day to come. Amir sat facing the window, sipping his breakfast— a shake made from fresh kiwis, mangoes, bananas and strawberries, with a teaspoon of wheat germ thrown in for good measure. Clad in snug black boxer briefs, which defined his sculptured rear and thighs, he had already completed two hundred arm curls with the fifty-pound dumbbells he kept in one corner of his apartment, as well as two hundred and fifty push-ups. He worked out as much for the physical benefits it provided as for the mental release it provoked.

The ceiling fan blew cool air across the nest of soft hair covering his bare chest. He lazily combed a hand through his locks as he watched the sun meet the world. Its warm rays caressed his face, and he once again thought of Azure.

He had thought of nothing else all night long as he lay awake, his body motionless, but his mind tossing and turning. Finally, when sleep had eluded him for hours, he rose and showered. Now, as he greeted a new day without the aid of a night's restful slumber, he contemplated how a step in a different direction or the opening of a door could change a person's life forever. In his wildest dreams he would not have imagined that stepping into Monroe Galleries, Inc., would have had the effect that it had had on him.

The ringing telephone pulled him away from his fevered thoughts, reminding him that he had harsher realities to contend with. He let the machine pick up and immediately tensed at the sound of his brother's voice.

"Amir, what's up, man? Listen, Sean told me that he left word for you to meet him about that thing and you never got back to him. What's going on, man? Give me a call… let me know you're all right. Peace."

Amir let out the breath he had been holding. This was the third such phone call his brother, Tavares, had made in the past month. Amir knew he was wrong for not being completely up-front with Tavares. At first it was just that Amir wasn't handling business the way he was expected to. Tavares gave him space to work on his party promotions business, letting him know that he'd cover for him for a time. Tavares had taken up the slack for him, handling his areas of responsibility. The crew continuously gave Tavares heat, of that Amir was certain. For years they had only tolerated Amir because he was Tavares's brother, and they knew that the two were inseparable. However, they had made their feelings known from the first moment when Tavares had begun to school Amir on the business and had given him responsibilities that had once belonged to each of them. Tavares had made it clear that he wanted his baby brother to follow in his footsteps and even though the fellows didn't think Amir was cut out for their lifestyle, they'd gone along with it. Now Amir was proving them right.

He hadn't simply walked away—it had not been that cut-and-dry. It had been an incredibly difficult process. He knew that he couldn't go on the way he had been. He had been slipping up, missing appointments and shirking his responsibilities. It was only a matter of time before the fellows would have gotten really pissed off, if they hadn't already. He knew that Tavares would be able to run inter-ference only for so long, and then they'd be all up in his face and all over his case. Now, with weeks having passed since the last time Amir had been in touch with any of the crew, with the exception of Tavares, they were asking ques-tions. Amir didn't believe for one second that they cared so much about his welfare or wanted so desperately for him to come back to work with them. Their biggest concern was themselves. For them, there was no such thing as walking away. In their mind, if you weren't on the team, then you couldn't be trusted. They had too much to lose to allow Amir to leave with their secrets unless they were con-vinced that his lips were sealed. Amir knew of no way he could make them believe that he meant their operations no harm, but he had to figure out something sooner, rather than later. It didn't help that Tavares was telling them that Amir had not, in fact, left. He'd have to find a way to make them, Tavares included, understand that he wasn't just on sabbatical—he was out for good.

Amir thought about all he had gone through in his twenty-six years. As a little boy, he had believed that life was as simple as a game of stickball in the street or bas-

ketball at the recreation center. His biggest concern was
getting the wax to melt properly in the bottle tops in order
to play a decent game of skellies. Then one night, a drunk
driver changed all of that for him. He was twelve years
old and he lost both of his parents in the blink of an eye.
The carefree little boy that he was also died that night and
nothing would ever be the same. It was Tavares, his big
brother and best friend, who had held it all together. He'd
kept what was left of the family together and even though
nothing was ever normal again, he made sure that they had
food, shelter and all the necessities of life. He also insisted
that Amir finish high school, which he did. Together,
Tavares and Amir made sure that their sister, Bridgette,
went on to college. She graduated from high school with
honors and received a partial scholarship to Princeton
University; the boys paid the rest of her tuition in cash.

There had never really been time for dreams after that
tragic night. Amir used to tell himself that he had no regrets
and that nothing mattered but keeping the family together.
He thought he had accepted the cards that had been dealt to
him and believed that as long as Bridgette succeeded and had
a good life, then all was fine. But that had been a lie. Every
day he found it more and more difficult to rationalize who
and what he had become. With Bridgette having just completed her master's in psychology and landing a position at
the Washington Hospital Center in northwest D.C., she was
capable of taking care of herself. Big brothers Tavares and
Amir were free to do whatever they wanted to do. Yet Tavares
continued living as a two-bit hustler and wanted Amir to
remain by his side. *Why?* There was no answer, and he knew
that no matter how many times or how many ways he posed
the question to himself, he would not find a suitable response.

Amir picked up the framed photograph of himself, Bridgette and Tavares as kids with their parents. While both Bridgette and Tavares favored their mother more, with skin the color of burnished copper, hair black and wavy, Amir was the spitting image of their father. With his fair complexion, thick, sandy-brown hair and eyes the color of steel, he was his father reincarnated. Growing up, people often called Amir Junior.

Amir's heart still ached when he thought about what they'd had to endure. The little boy in him still missed his parents immensely, and the man he had become felt short-changed. He felt as though, despite his best intentions about keeping what was left of the family together and helping to raise Bridgette, he had let his parents down. He didn't blame Tavares because he knew that his brother had done the best he could. Still, he knew that their parents had expected more from them, and this knowledge made him feel like a complete and utter failure.

He returned the photograph to its perch. He had to find a way to honor his parents and himself. If he didn't, it would be only a matter of time before he could no longer stomach his own reflection in the mirror. In a haze of fast cash, flashy cars and nameless women, he had lost himself. Now that he had turned his back on it all, his hope was that maybe it was not too late to get back what he'd lost. If it was too late, there was no way he could completely step to a woman like Azure. Intuitively, he knew that she was someone he'd like to get to know, someone he could grow with. But first, he'd need to become the man he was destined to be.

Chapter 6

"Just a minute, just a minute," Yanté grumbled as she staggered toward the front door of her Cape Cod–styled home. She glanced at the grandfather clock in the corner of the foyer before pulling back the curtain on the window next to the door.

"What the…" she began as she turned the locks. "Azure, what are you doing here this time of morning?" Concern coated her question as she looked her cousin up and down for any sign of trouble. "Are you all right? Is somebody hurt? What's going on?" Yanté fired breathlessly.

"I brought breakfast." Azure smiled, offering the bags of doughnuts she held in her hands. "Mocha lattes with double whipped cream, just like you like it."

She slid past the stunned Yanté and proceeded into the kitchen.

"Azure, did I forget to set my clock ahead for daylight

savings or something?" Yanté said as she stumbled behind her, scratching her head.

"No, it's really a little after six o'clock." Azure began emptying the contents of the bags onto the counter.

Yanté sat down on a stool at the breakfast nook and held her head in her hands. She tried to wake herself from the nightmare she had to be in. Azure turned on the television mounted on the back wall of the kitchen and the voices of *Good Morning, Washington* leapt into the room. She took a seat next to Yanté and began sipping her cup of joe.

Yanté stared at her cousin for a moment, noticing the bright, energetic light which bounced off her. She wrinkled her brow as she struggled to figure out what was different about Azure, choosing her next words with care.

"Azure, sweetie, uh…I'm not sure what particular brand of crack you're smoking, but honey, I promise I will help you. Rehab, detox…whatever it takes."

"You're so silly." Azure giggled, nudging Yanté with her shoulder. "Drink your coffee before it gets cold."

"I don't want to drink coffee. It's six o'clock in the damned morning. I don't want to eat doughnuts or watch *Good Morning, America* or *The Early Show* for that matter, either. What the hell is wrong with you?" Yanté snapped.

"There's nothing wrong with me. I was up early and just wanted to have breakfast with you. Shouldn't you be getting ready for work anyway?"

"It's Memorial Day, Azure. It's a national holiday."

"Oh, that's right. My bad, girl."

"*Your bad?* You can't be serious," Yanté spat.

She scratched the top of her messy head of curly brown

hair and stared at Azure with an incredulous look. Azure took another long sip of coffee, smiling sweetly at her.

"Oh, by the way, that guy who works at the bakery said to tell you to have a good morning."

"What guy?" Yanté asked, screwing up her face.

"The guy who cleans the windows and mops the floors. The last time I went in there with you, you told me that he asked you out once a few months ago."

"The guy with the bad breath? Yuck! I don't know why that man won't leave me alone. A couple of times a week I stop in there, and he's always grinning at me."

"Don't tell me you're a snob! Don't like men in the service industry, huh?" Azure scolded.

"No, it's not even about that. I just don't like men who are missing teeth, smell bad and look old enough to be my father. Anyway, why are we even talking about him? It's too damn early to be talking, period," Yanté snapped.

"What? Okay, so you don't have to go to work today, I woke you up early and now you're cranky. But look…it's a beautiful day outside. You're not planning to sleep it away, are you? I've got the perfect idea. What do you say we go out and ride our bikes? We can go to Rock Creek Park and look at the horses. You know you love the horses. Come on, Yanté, please. We haven't done that in a long time."

"Ashes, I'm not going anywhere with you until you tell me what's got you glowing like high beams on a pickup truck this morning. You act almost as if you…you…no, uh-uh. No way!"

Yanté looked at her cousin with wide-eyed suspicion. In her head she knew it was far from the realm of possibilities, but she couldn't help but hope. It killed her to have to stand by and watch Azure cut herself off from the world, living like a nun. She understood the pain Azure had suffered: wasn't it she who had stood by Azure's side, day after day, night after night? But really, enough was more than enough. Unfortunately, it seemed as though Azure had taken some sort of vow to never love again. No matter what Yanté said, no matter how much she pushed and prodded, Azure was rigid. What was worse, she also refused to talk about it. Yanté knew that keeping her emotions bottled up inside could not be good for her cousin. Maybe something she said had finally gotten through and Azure had decided to venture out into the world.

"What are you talking about?" Azure smiled sweetly.

"You're acting like somebody put something on you that was so real last night, it had you speaking in tongues. That's not possible…is it?" Yanté asked, fingers on both hands crossed.

"I swear, your mind is permanently entrenched in the gutter. Really, Yanté, everything that happens in the world is not about sex."

"Hmmph, I never said everything was about sex. Now good sex, on the other hand, that's something else entirely." Yanté giggled.

Despite Yanté's prying, Azure repeatedly insisted that she was just in a good mood, having woken up with the desire to celebrate life. She convinced her cousin to get dressed and they headed out on their mountain bikes, laughing like schoolgirls. After nearly two hours of riding through the park's almost two thousand acres of winding bike and nature trails, stopping to chat with a couple who were riding as part of their training for an upcoming marathon, they went their separate ways. Yanté was planning to return home to her slumber and Azure headed to the gallery to get in some painting before opening up for the day.

Yanté bit her tongue as she bade farewell to Azure. She figured it was just a matter of time before she got to the bottom of this innocent "good mood" which had suddenly descended on her otherwise reasonable cousin. She'd just patiently wait it out. She hoped that it did turn out to be a man because, despite what Azure thought, love really was a cure for what ailed the body, and Azure could certainly use a little medicine in her life.

Chapter 7

"Hey, baby brother, what's popping?" Tavares asked, giving Amir a hearty pound, their two palms smacking loudly, followed by a brotherly embrace. Tavares was slightly taller than Amir, with a more solid build. He wore an expensive velour jogging suit and Nike Air Force sneakers which looked as though they'd just come out of the box.

"I can't call it," Amir replied.

"What were you into last night, or should I say who? She must've been Gabrielle Union fine to keep you out of touch like that! I thought we were going to get together for dinner."

"Nah, man, it was nothing like that. I, uh, listen, can we talk?"

"Sure man, what's up?"

Amir glanced around. A couple of the guys, Marques and Sean, were shooting pool at Tavares's sixteenth-century Bensinger game table. Big Rick was sitting nearby on a stool with his back turned to them, reading the news-paper. The only member of the crew who wasn't present was Clifton, and he was most assuredly out spending money. Clifton was apt to tell people how poor his family had been when he was growing up, and now that he had money, he planned on spending every dime of it. He spent money as fast as he made it—on clothes, jewelry and season tickets to almost every sport.

"Not here," Amir said softly.

He felt so self-conscious even being around the fellows now that things had changed so much. Tavares glanced around the room and then looked at his brother. Worry immediately settled onto his expressive face as it always did when one of his siblings had a problem. He had been taking care of both Amir and their little sister, Bridgette, since before his first facial hair had grown in fully. He'd made sure they'd always had enough to eat, had gone to school every day and had stayed out of trouble. Now, although they were all adults and able to take care of themselves, he couldn't stop worrying about them. Their problems had been his problems for so long, it was difficult for him to not want to jump in and fix things for them.

"Let's take a walk," Tavares said to Amir. "Hey, Rick, hit me on my cell if anything comes up. I'll be back."

Rick nodded without looking up from his reading. Amir followed Tavares out of the brownstone. Tavares had purchased the building a little over a year ago. It had three separate apartments, each one containing two bedrooms, one and a half baths, a spacious living room and formal dining room. Tavares had spent a lot of money restoring the place, putting in everything from new floors and plumbing to modern windows and antique light fixtures. It was now easily worth twice the amount he had paid for it.

With the exception of Sean, who lived across town with the mother of his young son, and Amir, who had moved out six months ago in search of something that resembled peace, the rest of the crew lived there. They were all single men who ranged in age from twenty-three to thirty-five, Sean being the baby of the bunch. Each of the men who lived there paid a reasonable amount of rent each month to Tavares and they each had their own space to occupy. The basement served as a recreation room, complete with a bar, pool table, a fifty-six-inch-screen HDTV system equipped with a satellite dish and several video game systems. Everything was top-notch and the room was more comfortable than most people's entire homes.

Amir's apartment paled in comparison. It was a nondescript studio located a few blocks from Howard University, with a nice view of the school's Founders Library Tower and illustrious clock. He often spent time walking around Howard's campus, secretly wishing he had been a student among the throngs of young scholars who occupied the grounds. McMillan Reservoir was especially attractive to him. He had spent numerous lazy afternoons this past fall sitting on a knoll, contemplating his life and the choices he had made.

While he had not been an especially good student, he had managed to graduate from high school with a grade point average of about 2.8. He'd excelled in math and history, but had had a difficult time with other subjects, including science and literature. As an adult, he had recently become a prolific reader in an attempt to improve his reading abilities. Some of the stumbling blocks he had faced as a child were largely related to interest. Now that he was able to read things of his own choosing, he found that he put more effort into it, took his time and thoroughly enjoyed what he read. He had also discovered that since strong reading skills were the key to many other areas of life, he was becoming a rather learned man, even if self-taught. This was one reason why he had come to realize that life had so much more to offer him than what he and Tavares were currently doing.

Tavares hadn't understood when Amir had first decided to move out and had taken the apartment near the school. Unlike Tavares, Amir didn't care about flashy clothes, cars and jewelry. At first those things did attract him, but eventually they lost their shine in his eyes and became merely the trappings of an inconsequential existence. As he matured, he began to prefer simplicity and moderation. He didn't mind one bit if his residence reflected that. But for all his apartment lacked in ambiance, it provided him with a haven in which to think and to plan. He loved coming home to his solitude. So much so, that it had been almost a month since he'd even stepped foot into the brownstone. Unfortunately, all of that thinking and planning had yet to produce any solutions to his dilemma. He still felt trapped in someone else's nightmare.

"So what's going on, man?" Tavares asked after they'd walked a quarter of a block in silence. "Are you in some sort of trouble?"

"Nah, Tavares, it's nothing like that. I know you and I had plans last night but—"

"Yeah, we did. I haven't seen much of you in weeks and when I do you see you, you're always busy or can't stick around long. I guess stuff happens sometimes, right?"

"Yes…and no. I mean, stuff happens, true, but that's not what was up last night. See, Tavares, I've been trying to find a way to tell you this for a minute now and I…I just don't know how you're gonna take it."

The men stopped walking.

"Just spit it out, baby brother. All we've been through—there's nothing you can't tell me," Tavares said as he placed a hand on Amir's shoulder.

Amir took a deep breath, realizing the moment of truth had come and prepared or not, he'd have to tell his brother exactly how he was feeling.

"You know I've been trying to start my own business and things are actually picking up for me."

"I'm happy for you. Didn't I support you when you said you wanted to promote parties?" Tavares asked.

"You did and I appreciate the support," Amir responded.

"So what's the problem?"

Amir hesitated. He needed to put this in the right words, so that there would be no more ambiguity between them.

"I'm out, man. For good, and I can't do what I need to do for myself if I'm around…this anymore, Tavares," Amir said.

"This? What *this*?" Tavares asked, confusion peppering his words.

"*This*, man. The game. The women, the setups…the hustling. I…I just can't be around it anymore," Amir spat, more hotly than he had intended but unable to control the emotion in his voice. He had wanted to say those words for so long that he had been choking on them. To finally be able to expel them from his throat was liberating. At the same time, the moment his confession hit the air, he was filled with a renewed sense of dread.

Tavares was quiet for a long while as he searched his

brother's face, a face that was so much like their father's
and similar to his own, yet devoid of the jagged edges that
time's harsh caress had carved into Tavares's countenance.
The gray eyes at times appeared haunted, but there still
possessed a light within them that was life and hope all in
one—those eyes now contained a fiery look of determination. Tavares could not remember when a fire like that had
burned in his own eyes.

"A., man, what is all this? Where is this coming from?"
Tavares asked.

"I've been telling you this for a minute now, but you just
haven't been trying to hear me. Or maybe I haven't said it
in the right way. Either way, there it is," Amir said.

When Tavares just stared blankly at him, Amir continued. He believed that it was now more vital than ever that
he got Tavares to understand what he was feeling.

"Look, Tavares, for as long as I can remember, you've been
there for me. You took care of us after Mom and Dad died,
and you've been taking care of us ever since. I know it
couldn't have been easy for you…you did what you had to
do to put food on the table for us. I appreciate that, man. Don't
ever think for one moment that I don't appreciate it. But that's
you, man, not me. I never wanted any of this. I don't care
about the money, the cars and all that. That stuff is temporary
and in the end, it all adds up to a bunch of nothing."

"So what do you care about? Huh, Amir, what?"

Amir hung his head for a moment, trying to gather the
words that would make his brother understand where he
was coming from and that would erase the disappointment
he could hear in Tavares's tone.

"I want something different, man—for me and you. I've
found a business—a legitimate one, where I'm providing

a service and people are actually paying me for it. I'm building a different life for myself, Tavares, and…we could both have a different life. You could work with me—"

"Work with you?" Tavares asked incredulously.

"Yeah, or, if that's not what you want to do, you could open a business or something yourself. You've got enough money to do anything you want to do…something respectable," Amir pleaded.

"Respectable? Like what?" Tavares asked, his laugh sardonic.

"I don't know, Tavares, just *something* else. All I'm saying is that once I came to the realization that I couldn't live the rest of my life scamming people and hustling for a dollar, I also realized that I can't be around you if this is what you're going to keep doing. I won't be able to move forward if I do."

"So what, man, you've found religion now?"

"Come on, Tavares, that's not what this is about," Amir snapped.

"Well, what is it about, then? What has got you tripping like this? Did somebody threaten you? Is somebody trying to step to you, 'cause you know I'll take care of it," Tavares said, his protective instinct surging through him.

"Nah, man. It's not that, either."

They stood silently, searching one another's faces for answers that weren't there.

"Well, talk to me, man," Tavares pleaded, wanting desperately to find a way to help his brother through whatever it was that had him so upset. "We've come too far from nothing to turn back. I mean, like you said, I did what I had to do to take care of us. I wasn't even out of high school yet when Mom and Dad had that accident. I tried to find work, but what kind of job was there for a black kid with no diploma? Nothing that would pay enough to take care of all three of us."

"I know that, man—"

"No, hold on a minute, Amir. I'm not saying you don't know what was up. But do you *understand?* There were things I dreamt about…things I wanted for myself. But hey, those things just weren't in the cards." Tavares sighed, his voice drifting off.

A horn sounded loudly, drawing both men's attention toward the street. A black Lincoln Navigator cruised past them slowly. The driver, with his seat almost in a horizontal position and his left arm draped outside the window, exposing a solid platinum bracelet with diamond studs, nodded his head in their direction. It was Clifton. *No surprise there,* Amir thought with disgust. Tavares nodded back at Clifton while Amir turned his head in another direction.

Amir looked at his brother, who was only six years his senior but who looked more like he was ten or better. The burden of caring for two children when you were just barely crossing the threshold into adulthood yourself had worn him down. Amir was immediately filled with a sense of guilt. He felt like he was betraying his brother by even speaking these words, but he could not deny what was in his heart.

"And now, Tavares? What about now?"

"Now?" Tavares asked as if he had never heard the word before. "Now…this is it, man. This is all there is for me. I don't know how to do anything else."

"That's bullshit, man."

"Nah, Amir, it's not bullshit. It's reality. I'm not the one here who's talking about change. I'm okay with who

I am and what I do. This is about *your* newly found self-righteousness. All of a sudden you give a damn about where the money is coming from? What we do is not any worse than what big business or those jokers on Wall Street do. We provide something people want and we get paid for it. Plain and simple."

Amir sighed, taking a step back from his brother. He looked down the block in the direction from which they had come. The tree-lined street with its symmetrical brownstones on either side and cars of varying degrees of luxury and affordability punctuating the scene seemed to be the wrong place to be having this conversation. He felt out of place, his words not coming out right. But then he looked in the other direction and suddenly the desire to head that way, away from where he'd come, became urgent.

"Amir, look, man. Why don't you maybe get away for a while. Get your head cleared. When you come back, we'll talk."

"The conversation will be the same." Amir sighed absently.

It was obvious that Tavares and he were not going to see eye to eye about this, not today and possibly not ever. They were brothers, true, but they thought nothing alike.

"Maybe. Maybe not. Let's just wait and see. I want you to think about what you're saying. Before you sit back and judge me or anybody else, think about the fact that we built this operation from nothing and we're good at it. Me, the fellas…and you. Not everyone could do what we do for this long and have nothing go wrong. You're good at this, man, whether you *feel* good about it or not."

"Damn, Tavares. Haven't you heard a word I've said?" Amir shouted.

He turned his back to Tavares, anger and frustration

making his blood boil. He ran his fingers through his hair, trying to calm himself down. This had gone about as poorly as he had expected it would. He had to find a way to turn things around and take the edge off of the situation.

"Tavares, I don't want to fight with you. I just need you to hear me out, man. Try to understand where I'm coming from," Amir said softly.

"I hear you, Amir. Believe me, I'm hearing you. Now, hear me. Just take some time. That's all I'm asking you to do. We're brothers, man. That's deeper than anything else. What you're asking me to do…look, just take some time and then we'll get together and talk. If you still feel this way…"

"I will," Amir answered quietly, not looking at his brother.

"Well, let's see about that then. Just give it some time, okay?"

Amir thought that his brother sounded as old as he was beginning to look at that moment, even more so. Like an aged, tired man who had scratched and clawed his way through a long, long life.

"Yeah, Tavares," Amir acquiesced, "whatever you say, man."

Tavares smiled then, the same dazzling smile that both men had inherited from their father. He pulled Amir toward him and hugged him openly in that masculine yet loving way that black men reserve for one another.

"Come on back to the house for a minute. I'm about to stew some red snapper, just the way you like it."

"I've got some stuff to do. I'll give you a call later," Amir said as he turned to walk away from his brother. The last thing he thought he could bring himself to do right now was to return to the brownstone and sit around with Sean, Rick and the rest of them. For the most part, he didn't really dig them, especially Sean and Clifton. Knowing that they felt the same way and merely tolerated him because of Tavares didn't help to ease his discomfort.

"All right, man. And I meant what I said—get away for a few days. Find one of them fine freaks that be sweatin' you to hook up with and take your mind off of things for a few days…a week, whatever. Take as long as you need," Tavares said, playfully slapping his brother on the back.

"Yeah."

To Amir's retreating figure, Tavares yelled, "It's gonna be all right, baby boy."

Amir kept walking and pretended not to hear his brother's parting words because in his heart of hearts he knew that things were not going to be all right for a long time to come.

Chapter 8

"So, go ahead," Amir said.

"Go ahead and what?" asked Azure, confused.

"Go ahead and ask me those five questions that have been swimming around in your head all day long."

"What five questions?"

"Come on now. You know what I'm talking about. The five questions that every woman wants to ask from the moment she starts to spend time with a man—Are you married? Have you ever been incarcerated? Do you have any kids? How much money do you make? And—"

"Are you gay?" Azure laughed as she completed Amir's statement.

"No, no, no, enough and no, I'm definitely into women," Amir responded quickly.

Azure laughed. "Honestly, I wasn't going to ask you any of those questions."

"Yeah, right," Amir said skeptically. He had yet to meet the woman who didn't have at least three of those five questions poised on her lips from the second she met a man she was interested in.

"Seriously. I mean, I didn't need to ask you those questions because I already knew the answers."

"Oh yeah?" Amir asked, surprised. "How could you?"

"Have you ever heard the expression that the eyes are the windows to the soul?"

Amir nodded.

"Well, there you go. Your eyes, Mr. Swift, tell a million stories."

Azure stopped walking and turned to face Amir. At just under five feet five, she had to tilt her head back to look him squarely in the face. She looked up into the eyes that had been haunting her for weeks now, eyes that she could see clearly even when she closed her own.

"What tales are they telling right now?" he asked softly, a smile playing at his lips.

Azure considered whether or not to tell Amir the truth about what she had already surmised about him. She hadn't been joking when she'd said that his eyes were the entrance into his soul. From the moment she'd looked past their unusual color and sexiness, she'd seen much more than a great-looking guy. She also knew that she had yet to meet the man who would willingly share the troubles of his soul. Unlike women, men kept their true selves tucked securely in a pocket and if you were lucky, they occasionally let you take a quick peek.

"They're telling the story of a man whose heart is heavy. A man who's carrying loads that he's not quite sure what to do with," she said at last.

Amir glanced away, made uncomfortable by the raw words which Azure had just spoken. When he looked back into her eyes, he saw that truth reflected there and this time he could not pull his gaze away. She squeezed his hands.

"That man," she continued, "is kind, sensitive, caring and…"

"And?"

"And powerful."

"Powerful? How so?" Amir asked, his curiosity outweighing his discomfort.

"Powerful, because he has the strength to create his own fate. Whether he knows it or not, he possesses the courage to go after what he wants—as soon as he figures out what that is. He will create his own destiny. I'm jealous of him," she admitted.

"What do you have to be jealous of?" Amir asked, as he raised a hand and ran two fingers along the side of her face, still marveling at the velvety softness of her skin.

"Sometimes I feel as though Yanté is right about me. Am I living or am I just existing? Am I going to look back one day and realize that all I ever did was sit on the sidelines and watch the parade go by? There are times when I want to jump in and wave the flag, carry the banner, scream, shout…act a fool."

"So why don't you?"

It was her turn to hesitate. She felt so comfortable with Amir, yet there was still a part of her that held back. How could she tell a man whom she was just beginning to get to know that there was a part of her heart that still belonged to another? That would scare away the most confident of men. Instead, she told him only part of her truth.

"Because unlike you, I have yet to figure out what I'm

supposed to be doing in this life. I can't plan my future because I have yet to uncover my destiny. I just don't know what to do with myself," she replied.

"You'd know if you listened to your heart," Amir said.

Azure was quiet as his words rang in her ears. Right now, she wasn't really thinking about destiny or future plans. At this moment, her heart was filling her chest, threatening to burst through her skin and bones because it was so full of him. He seemed to have all the answers, even to the questions she hadn't yet asked. She wanted to believe what he said, but she had long ago stopped listening to her heart. That was because if she listened to it, she'd have to allow herself to do what it told her and the thought of that was still too scary a prospect.

Amir drew his face closer to hers, and when their lips met, her heart seemed to swell even more. She returned his kiss, matched his fervor and passion. His arms encircled her slim waist, pulling her closer to him. Her hands found their way into his mane of locks, and he sighed because it felt like she was massaging all of his worries away.

When their lips parted, a comfortable silence settled between them. They walked for hours, holding hands, stopping for frozen yogurt at a local treat shop. They rested for a while, joining a circle of people who stood in front of a group of young street performers doing the latest hip-hop dances, which were just a recycling of the dances made popular in the seventies and eighties. The contagious bass thumped from their boom box and they found themselves moving to the beat, clapping their hands. Amir watched the subtle sway of Azure's hips and was mesmerized. With each passing minute Amir became more certain that he had found the woman with whom he could spend the rest of his life. It didn't matter that he hadn't known her for that long. Something had just clicked between them, and he didn't care about what the conventional rules of dating said—she was perfect for him. He also knew that he had to put into place all of the changes he had been planning, fast and in a hurry. Being with a woman who was uncomplicated and unassuming made him realize even more that the life he had been leading up until a few months ago was tearing his conscience apart. He could not let his sense of obligation to his brother lure him back in or distract him from his goals. He definitely would not let his burdens weigh down a love that was just sprouting its wings, even if it changed things between him and Tavares forever.

Chapter 9

Clad in a silk kimono, Yanté stood in the middle of her kitchen in slippered feet. With her arms wrapped around her, she absently watched the coffee brewing in the pot. Normally, she wouldn't be caught dead awake at this hour in the morning, especially after having worked all week long. However, there were times when she made an exception.

She heard the shower water begin running in the bathroom and smiled to herself. Jeffrey Montague had slept over last night, but they had done everything but sleep. She felt invigorated by their night of passion and was certain that the karma sutra type of loving she'd put on the man would send him off with a smile on his face this morning. But send him off was what she planned to do.

What she had with Jeff was fun and very pleasurable indeed, but there was nothing remotely permanent about it. Yanté needed a man who could match her ambition as much as her libido and Jeff wasn't that man. He was content with his low-management-level position with a small investment company. He was not interested in furthering his education, did not attend trade conferences and didn't even look for advancement with his own employer.

One of the first questions Yanté asked a man when she began dating him was where he saw himself in five years. She liked to know up front if a man had a master plan or at least a penciled blueprint. Jeff's answer had been a resounding, *I don't know.* Beep—wrong answer!

Some people might misconstrue Yanté's attitude as that of a gold digger, which couldn't have been further from the truth. She made her own living, a very good one at that. She had never sought financial security from a man. What she craved was a man who was about progression and advancement. She needed to be with someone who was a lifelong learner, just as she was herself. She had just decided to begin working toward a second master's degree this fall. While she was fulfilled working at Dartmouth Hotel for the time being, she also knew that there were even greater opportunities awaiting her. If a person was truly committed to self-improvement, job advancement was a part of the package. If there was one thing she also knew, it was that that type of motivation was not something a person could learn in his or her thirties or forties—that level of drive and thirst had to develop at least by puberty in order for it to truly take root.

Yanté poured herself a cup of coffee, added two teaspoons of sugar and sipped it, dark and sweet. Jeff entered the kitchen, dressed in his dark slacks from the previous night, his shirt unbuttoned, exposing a solid chest. Even though he was not marriage potential in her book, he sure was a good-looking man to spend the right-now with.

"Save some for me?" he asked.

She loved the tenor of his voice. It was one of the things that had first attracted her to him when he'd asked to borrow her pen as they waited in line at the bank. When she'd turned around to see the man attached to such an arresting voice, she had been pleasantly surprised to find a tall, clean-shaven face, skin the color of dark chocolate and a hundred-watt smile. She'd boldly used her pen to scratch out her phone number on his deposit ticket before handing it to him.

"Mmm-hmm," Yanté said as she reached inside his shirt and rubbed her hand across his pectoral muscles.

Jeff responded, pulling her to him and giving her a deep kiss. Jeff had wanted to spend the entire day with her, but she'd made it clear that even after a night of passion as riveting as theirs had been, it ended with the sunrise. She didn't want him to confuse a good time with an ongoing, indefinite relationship. Jeff was now tonguing her ear, his hands roaming freely across her behind. His movements sent tiny ripples of pleasure throughout her body. She moved against him, the silk kimono opening to expose her naked body. She was glad that the sun was not fully on the horizon yet.

From outside, through the slightly parted curtains, a pair of eyes aflame with envy watched this early-morning coffee break.

Chapter 10

"Look, partner, the only reason I let you sit down next to me is because you said you had something important to tell me about my brother. This," Amir said angrily, sliding the tan envelope which Giovanni Vesnas had placed in front of him back toward the man, "you're going to need to take up with Tavares."

He pushed the untouched Corona beer bottle away from him and leaned back on the bar stool. He was seated at the far end of the bar, in his usual spot. He had come to the Peach Tavern to have a couple of beers and to think. He was tired of sitting in his tiny apartment and feeling the walls closing in on him. He hadn't been able to pull in any new business in the past couple of weeks and he was getting nervous. Admittedly, he had been spending more time with Azure and less on developing and marketing his business, but he couldn't help it. The last party he'd thrown had been for the launch of a new television series and it had gone well. He'd expected to receive more business from that particular network, but things were not moving as quickly as he'd hoped they would.

Tonight, with nothing but time on his hands, he'd come into the bar hoping to mellow out and ease some of the anxieties that were causing every muscle in his body to be tight with tension. When he was working with Tavares, he'd come to the Peach frequently. He liked to be discreet when discussing business and found that the only other people who entered a bar and walked as far back as they could go before taking a seat were people who wanted to be discreet. Whether they be cheating spouses, undercover cops or, like him, brothers getting their hustle on, the back of the bar was where they settled. The last thing those folks wanted was conversation with anyone besides the person they came to meet. Eye contact was not made nor was anyone back there interested in anyone else's business.

One of his former duties that he had hated most was collection. That was the part of the business that had made him feel the dirtiest, and it was the part that had convinced him, even when he had tried to tell himself that what he was doing was not so bad, that he had to walk away. He knew that every aspect of what they were doing was wrong on one level or another, but he still felt most ill at ease when he had to collect money for those wrongs.

The way the operation worked was that the crew did all of the research and the legwork. They scoured the financial papers and corporate magazines. A prime target might be a woman who had recently been widowed and whose late husband had been a high-ranking business executive. It didn't matter what type of business it was, as long as he wasn't too high profile. Said woman usually did not work herself, or, if she did, it was a small, nonprofit type of organization. Timing was everything. The setup depended on it. Too close to the death and she was respectfully unavailable. Too long afterward and she was already banging the tennis instructor or the pool boy. But if you hit them at the right moment, they'd be so starved for affection that they'd be an easy target.

Once the subject was located and properly researched, she was matched with the perfect man from their list of candidates. The men they used had to fit a certain profile. Uneducated, inarticulate street dudes didn't qualify. The men they worked with had to be well-read and well-versed on a variety of subjects. They had to be attractive, well-groomed and respectful because, for the most part, these women were grieving, not desperate. They also needed to have clean records; not even a misdemeanor was acceptable. That's not to say that these guys were law-abiding citizens—they just hadn't been caught at anything criminal yet.

Amir had learned very quickly how to match the right man with the right target. Pretty soon, he became such an expert at it that Tavares took this particular duty away from Sean and assigned it almost exclusively to Amir. In addition, Amir's other duties included monitoring the setups, which he did by observing the couples in public places, and making periodic contact with the men. Collecting money was something Amir only did when no one else was available for one reason or another. He remembered the last collection he'd made, months ago. He had vowed that day that it would be his last and here he was seated at a bar with a guy trying to make him break that vow.

"Come on, man, you gotta tell Tavares to cut me some

slack. She's not as easy with the cash as she was in the beginning, but you guys still want me to pay the same amount every month. That's leaving me with nickels and dimes in my pocket, chump change," Giovanni said.

He'd spotted Amir when he walked in and had invited himself to the stool next to him right after Amir had received his second beer.

Amir studied the man as he spoke. Giovanni Vesnas was an attractive man, of Hispanic and German descent. Although he was only twenty-five years old, he was already on his second marriage. He had been paired with Victoria Roman, the thirty-seven-year-old widow of the CEO of a major communications conglomeration who had died of a massive heart attack while golfing. At nearly sixty years old, Mr. Roman had had the world on a string, with a beautiful young woman by his side to boot. Unfortunately, he had not secured his enterprise or his finances well, leaving everything to the little woman. She didn't know the first thing about protecting her assets and was, therefore, a prime target. Giovanni wooed the former Mrs. Roman in a matter of weeks and married her one year after her husband had died. They had been married for only a couple of months and Giovanni was already beginning to get the itch. Amir could tell. Men like Giovanni couldn't be faithful to one woman for all the tea in China. He had varied appetites and didn't hesitate to whet them. If Amir could see that Giovanni's mind and eyes were wandering, surely so could the missus. That would probably explain why she was beginning to tighten the purse strings.

The problem with men like Giovanni was that they sometimes forgot that this was a business transaction, pure and simple. Sometimes they fell for the woman, getting feelings and developing a conscience. All that did was muddy the waters and mess up the money, which was something Tavares and the crew did not stand for. That was where Big Rick factored into the picture. At six feet, five inches tall and almost three hundred pounds of mostly muscle, he wouldn't hesitate to put a beat down on someone who messed up the money. While the need for Rick's services had only arisen on a small number of occasions, he was always there, ready and waiting.

Other times, the man got greedy. That was what seemed to be happening in this case. Giovanni wanted more of the pie, and the fact that if it weren't for the crew he wouldn't be sipping Moët & Chandon and dining on caviar had slipped his mind. Once again, Big Rick would be on hand to remind him.

"Look, Giovanni, you know the game. As long as you keep the little woman happy and satisfied, it's all gravy. Now, if the well is starting to dry up, then maybe you'll need to call this one quits a little bit sooner than planned," Amir said without emotion.

"At this point, I can't even do that. I don't have enough money to get me through the time it would take to get the divorce and hook up with the next one," Giovanni complained.

Amir considered him for a minute, hating his slick, pretty-boy looks. He was surprised that women could not see through his exterior and uncover the snake that he was. Everything about him looked dishonest and fabricated, from head to toe. If it were solely up to Amir, he would not have used Giovanni again after the first time. But Tavares had insisted that Giovanni had a charm that the women could not resist. Indeed, his first marriage had been sweet.

By the time he'd gotten out of that one, he'd made a pretty penny for himself and the fellows. Amir, however, did not trust him. No one could be trusted in a business built on lies and deceptions. That was another thing he found difficult to swallow every day. He didn't want to have to question everyone he came into contact with, always believing that people were out to harm him in some way. Right now, he considered for one second that Giovanni was being honest about being broke, but he didn't care.

"Whatever you do, man," he said stiffly, "has nothing to do with me. Now, do you have something to tell me about Tavares…something I care to hear about or not?"

"I just thought that you could talk to him," Giovanni said.

"Nah, can't help you with that," Amir said as he rose, wanting to get as far away from Giovanni as he possibly could. As an afterthought he said, "Listen, you might want to consider finding another line of work. I mean, how long do you think you can continue like this before your luck runs out?"

Amir took one final swig from the bottle of beer, turned and walked away from Giovanni without looking back. He almost felt sympathy for the man, knowing that Tavares would be pissed off by Giovanni's reluctance to pay. As he made his way out of the bar, he grew further disgusted, but only with himself. Realizing that in order to completely rebuild his life he had to stay far away from areas where he had formerly conducted business, he knew that this would be his last visit to this particular watering hole.

Night had fallen. Amir stepped out onto the street and took a deep breath. He wanted to cleanse himself of the seediness of his barroom conversation. But no matter how many breaths he took, the sickening sensation rose from

the pit of his stomach into his throat, threatening to as-
phyxiate him. This was no use, and he knew it. He had to
get out.

He started walking, feeling like a mere shell of the man
that as a child he'd thought he'd grow up to be. For the
umpteenth time he thought about how different his life
would be if his parents had lived. He knew he had no right
to make excuses. He had followed Tavares into this business with his eyes wide open and his mouth sealed shut.
Yet, in his heart and soul he believed that both he and
Tavares would be different people if their parents had been
there to see them through. The little boy in him still ached
for the days when his father would yell for him to take out
the trash and his mother would scold him for leaving his
dirty socks lying around. As a boy, he didn't understand
the lessons they had been trying to teach him about responsibility and self-respect through everyday chores. Before
he could comprehend and truly appreciate the values
which they were trying to instill in him, they were gone.
Try as he might, Tavares had been a poor substitute and
now, here they were. Two men whose lives meant nothing
to anyone. Two men who preyed on other people's misery
to make a buck. Amir was certain that his parents were rolling over in their graves at what had become of them. His
only hope was that they were proud that they had managed
to keep Bridgette on the straight and narrow and raised her
to be the wonderful, educated young woman that she had
become.

Except that was not his only hope. The other was that he
could find the courage to walk away from all this and build
a new life for himself. A life in which he could hold his head
up and respect himself again. A life, he hoped, in which a

woman who could read his soul like an open book stood by his side and kept him strong. He smiled when he thought of her, and for a moment, his future did not seem as bleak.

Chapter 11

The days took on a new meaning for Azure as they sped by, each one unearthing different reasons to smile. The initial hesitation she'd felt on the night that Amir had returned to the gallery to see her had all but vanished. In its place was an eagerness to see him and an overwhelming desire to converse with him. They had more things in common than either had suspected. He was only about sixteen months her senior. Both of them had grown up in D.C., he in the Carrolsburg housing projects in the southeast section of the city, and she in a small tenement about a fifteen-minute drive away. They'd both attended public schools, both played musical instruments throughout school. He told her that his parents were originally from Barbados and had moved to the United States when his mother was pregnant with Tavares. She shared that her parents were both born in St. Croix and had relocated to

America several years before she was born. Her parents had known one another as children but did not connect until they were reunited in America. As second-generation immigrants, they discussed their love/hate relationship with the land of the free, home of the brave.

He understood the anguish she felt over her brother Patrick's tortured soul. He couldn't imagine what he'd do if Tavares or Bridgette for that matter were in trouble, but he knew that, like Azure, he'd be there to bail them out. He didn't think there was anything either of them could ever do that would make him turn his back on them. Azure talked freely about Patrick with Amir, something she hadn't been able to do with anyone else, including Yanté. It was sometimes difficult for families to talk to one another about situations going on within the family, so everyone usually just avoided the conversation altogether. Amir counseled her to just keep being there for her brother and to keep praying that one day he'd want as much for himself as she wanted for him. He did find it hard to believe that having a sister as positive as Azure had not rubbed off on Patrick.

They also shared a love of books, classic movies and most musical genres, especially jazz. Azure quickly realized that Amir was as much of an arts-and-culture buff as she. At his suggestion, they spent an entire afternoon at the Black Fashion Museum. Since visitors were only admitted with an appointment, she was pleasantly surprised to find that Amir had not only taken care of that, but had also made dinner reservations for them at a trendy new Indian restaurant nearby. Together they rediscovered D.C., seeing things through each other's eyes, which brought a fresh perspective on things previously experienced as well as those which were new to both of them. Afternoons were spent lunching right outside her store, in the circle. The urban part at the center was frequented by an eclectic mix of folks, from the newly defined metrosexual to gay and lesbian couples, musicians to mimes, businessmen and women to unemployed street artists.

Interestingly enough it was Amir who pointed out to her that the Dupont Memorial Fountain had been designed by Daniel Chester French, the artist who had sculpted the Lincoln Memorial. They strolled the neighborhood, viewing from the outside the mansions lining Massachusetts Avenue that were at one time grand homes designed to show off the nation's new wealth after the Civil War, but which were now occupied by embassies and other institutions.

They spent one Saturday morning at the Frederick Douglas Museum and Hall of Fame for Caring Americans, captivated by the stunning antiques and artifacts as well as the rich historical transcripts and artwork. They talked incessantly, the conversation never growing dull or stagnant. They argued their opposing views good-naturedly and before they knew it the museum had closed and they had to find a security guard to let them out.

On more than one occasion Azure expressed an interest in Amir's party promotions. He grew excited as he talked to her about all of the details involved in putting together an event, including finding appropriate locations, assisting clients with the creation of guest lists and the selection of caterers and entertainment. He told her that his secret dream was to launch a full-scale party-planning service, and she encouraged him to look into it seriously. During their outings, she noticed that he was quite a people person. Everyone they encountered seemed to be attracted to him and sometimes went out of their way to accommodate him.

It was somewhat alluring to find that other people found him as attractive as she did on more than just a physical level.

Amir loved to listen to Azure talk and often prodded her with probing questions. It did not slip past him that she grew hesitant, even evasive, when he asked her about past boyfriends. It was obvious that she had been in love once upon a time, and without her confiding anything substantial to him, he could tell that she had been hurt.

Over a late lunch at the gallery one afternoon, Azure had been giving a vivid description of the bicycle she used to ride around Atlanta College of Art's campus when she was a student. He pictured her with a heavy knapsack filled with books on her back, every bit the coed. She recalled the day her bike hit a deep crack in the ground and sent her flying through the air. Suddenly, her face clouded over and her voice trailed off. He knew then that she was thinking about the person who had picked her up and driven her to the hospital, where she had received the stitches that had left the tiny scar on her left knee.

Amir didn't push, certain that when the time was right, she would tell him more about her past relationships. He was not the type of man who needed to believe that his woman was some innocent virgin until the day he came along. So to him, her past was just that. There was no need to dissect it or rehash it, as long as it was truly in the past. Besides, he was in no position to ask any more of her than she was willing to share, since there were so many skeletons in his own closet.

Marathon conversations, long walks and spontaneous visits to her at the gallery brought Amir closer to Azure than he had been to any other person in a very long time.

It also took him further away from his old life. During his alleged hiatus from the business, he scarcely allowed himself to think about Tavares, the brownstone or any of that. He filled his thoughts and his senses with Azure. Outside of periodically checking on Bridgette and trying to secure more parties and promotions, he spent the remainder of his days and nights with Azure or else he was planning things for them to do together. He also read up on art and artists, wanting to develop a more critical eye and ear than he'd had before. She was eager to talk about painting, and he learned a great deal just by listening to her. Not wanting to sound like a complete airhead, he tried his best to learn some of the terms she used as well as expressions from different periods and the various styles which artists used.

As they peeled back layer after layer of themselves for each other, it was equally apparent that they complemented one another in many ways. Whether this fact would be enough to conquer the obstacles that were as yet unknown to either remained to be seen. For now they were enjoying a romance that moved quickly, carrying their hearts as if riding on a meteor across the heavens.

Chapter 12

"Yes, Mom, I called Grandma to wish her a happy birthday," Azure said.

She held the cordless phone tucked between her cheek and shoulder. She was in the process of varnishing an oil painting which she had finished creating several months ago. It was a portrait of her parents and she planned to surprise them with it for their thirtieth wedding anniversary. She had secretly removed one of their wedding pictures from an album on one of her rare visits to their house in Columbia Heights, on the other side of town, and painstakingly recreated the black-and-white photograph on canvas.

It was a beautiful picture of them together. Her mother, Vetta, was sitting down. Her wedding gown was off the shoulders, with a fitted bodice and the upper chest area covered in a sheer organza fabric. Her father, Nicholas, stood behind her, his hands resting lightly on her shoulders.

They looked so young and happy, as if this weren't just the start of their lives together but a continuation of some blissful time before. Her mother's smile was apparent in every feature of her face, and Azure realized that she could not recall ever seeing her mother wear in person so pleasant a countenance. Maybe that was because Vetta Monroe seemed always to be so critical and displeased with her. Azure had never noticed that the woman possessed any other expression.

She had had to wait until the canvas was completely dry before finishing it. Yesterday, she had carefully cleaned the now-dry painting with a damp piece of cotton wool and water which she had previously boiled and kept in a special container in the refrigerator. She then wiped the excess moisture from the painting with another bit of wool, and left it to dry overnight.

Now it was time to apply the varnish and the last thing she needed was to listen her mother harping on at her about something she had or hadn't done while she worked. She didn't understand why their relationship was the way it was and had grown tired of trying to figure it out.

"Listen, Mom, I've got a ton of work to do, so I'm going to have to cut this short," Azure said, begging off.

"What work? What are you working on at this hour? Isn't the gallery closed?" Vetta asked.

"Yes, Mom, the gallery is closed, but that doesn't mean I don't have work to do. This is a business, you know," Azure said, annoyed by her mother's prying.

"I know it's a business. Why do you always have to be so sarcastic?" Vetta asked.

"I'm not being sarcastic, Mom," Azure said, rolling her eyes up into her head.

On cue, Vetta launched into a litany of complaints about why she was not able to ask Azure a simple question without receiving a nasty response and why Azure kept everything to herself all the time. She threw in a good dose of guilt about the fact that Azure would not always have a mother around to be mean to. There was nothing new about this conversation and Azure listened quietly, inserting an occasional grunt by way of response in all the right places. She had learned a long time ago that once Vetta was on a roll, there was no stopping her. The best course of action was just to sit back and wait until she was finished.

It was several more agonizing minutes before she was able to get her mother to hang up. By the time she did, a dull headache had begun to creep up into her temples. She reached into the mini fridge she kept in the studio to retrieve a can of soda. Popping the top, she took a hasty swig, enjoying the cold carbonated taste as it slid down her throat. By the time she had drained the can, she was able to smile, say a heartfelt *Thank you, Lord* for having a mother to get angry with, and return to work.

With a flat bristle brush, she slowly applied a matte varnish to the painting. She worked from top to bottom, using parallel strokes from one edge to the other. It was a slow, painstaking job that, if rushed, could be disastrous to the painting. Azure did not mind the process at all. In fact, there was no aspect of painting that she didn't love. Each step was met with relish and she derived pleasure from every part, even the most difficult tasks. The second coat of varnish was applied at right angles to the first, with the same deliberate strokes.

Her parents' anniversary was in two weeks and the painting would have long since dried by then. She couldn't wait to see the looks on their faces when they saw it, especially her dad's. Unlike her mother, he appreciated her art, having dabbled in stencils and decorative arts himself. He was the one who had convinced her mother that they should loan Azure some of the money she'd needed to open the gallery in the first place early last year. He had helped her do the work on the empty storefront and move in. Nicholas Monroe was the best father a girl could hope for and together they united to deal with Vetta's sometimes difficult persona.

She knew that it hurt her father a great deal to have his only son remain so out of reach to him. He had loved Patrick with the same generous hand that he'd loved her with, yet Patrick seemed unable to accept that love while she had blossomed under it. From time to time her father would ask her if she'd heard from Patrick, and she always tried to make it sound more positive that it actually was. He could tell she was lying, but was grateful still that she was in touch with her brother.

The Monroes were having a small anniversary celebration at Grandma Ida's house. It would be attended mostly by family and close friends and Yanté was pressuring Azure to find a date to accompany her. She'd even offered to fix her up with someone, a suggestion Azure vehemently rejected. She and Amir had been spending a lot of time together, yet she had not told anyone about him, not even Yanté. She was, simply put, just not ready to share him with the world. So while she did not feel comfortable enough to bring him to the anniversary party, she had no desire to be fixed up on a blind date, either. Her parents, especially her mother, always had to make a comment about why she still wasn't seeing anyone. It didn't matter how many times she explained, it didn't stop the questions or the insinuations.

Azure stared at the painting of her parents, pleased with her work. As she considered their happy faces, she wondered if she would ever have that kind of happiness in her own life. She'd thought she had it once upon a time, but that felt like a fleeting moment from a long-ago life. It made her sad to think about it, so she blocked it out as best she could. Some days, it was easy to do, especially now that there was Amir. Her head told her that she should be guarded with him, protect her heart at all costs. However, that was something she found absolutely impossible to do. He made her feel like talking all the time, laughing and playing, too. She felt herself slipping from the ledge she had placed herself on—that space above the fireplace reserved for fragile things. She had sat up there, dust collecting on her body and spirit, for too long, she knew. For the first time, all of the prodding from well-meaning family and friends notwithstanding, she had the motivation to get down and jump back into living.

Chapter 13

Sitting at her desk for the first time all day, Yanté smiled as she sniffed the fragrant flowers in the tall glass vase. The receptionist had accepted them early that morning and placed them on her desk, yet Yanté had been running around since she'd arrived that day putting out fire after fire. She'd gone out to lunch with a potential beverage supplier who was trying to land the hotel's business. The martini she'd had to drink with her meal had taken the edge off what was a hectic morning, and she was much more relaxed coming into the afternoon.

She plucked the card from the center of the gorgeous bouquet and opened it.

"That's strange," she said aloud. The small card with the signature logo of the floral shop located down the block from the hotel was not signed. In block handwritten letters it read simply, Enjoy.

She searched her brain, trying to think of who would send her flowers and be so clandestine about it. Although there was a couple of guys she'd been spending time with, she wasn't dating anyone seriously at the moment. Carl, the cardiac specialist she had gone out with a few times, was in Geneva, Switzerland, at some medical conference. There was Jeffrey, with whom she had spent last Saturday night and the Saturday night before that, but she doubted that the flowers came from him. He didn't seem the secretive type. Besides, he would have wanted her to know they were from him.

She pulled out her cell phone and scrolled through the phone book. Methodically, she considered and then disregarded every man on the list. While there were a couple of prospects, men whom she had dumped for various reasons who may have been trying to get back in her good graces, no one really jumped out at her. She did have a date scheduled for later that evening with a doctor who she had met working out at the gym. Although he did seem like the type who would send flowers without signing the card, he didn't yet know where she worked.

Stumped, Yanté sniffed the flowers again, plucked an orchid from the center of the bunch and shrugged her shoulders. It was a nice gesture, and whoever it was had certainly scored a few points with her. She just hoped it wasn't someone she'd vowed never to give the time of day to again. Not that a simple bouquet of flowers would change that, but she would feel a little bit bad about rejecting them a second time. She dated a lot, often giving men to whom many women would not give a second glance to a chance. She firmly believed that sometimes a man could be a diamond in the rough. She was not opposed to applying a little polish where need be; however, she wasn't into doing complete overhauls.

"Oh, well," she said aloud, as she returned to the paper-work on her desk. She figured whoever the secret Romeo was would make himself known sooner or later.

She had no idea how right she was.

Chapter 14

"You look nice," Amir said as he stepped into Azure's foyer. He extended his arm, offering her a bouquet of a dozen long-stemmed red roses. A white satin ribbon tied in a huge, elaborate bow held the flowers together.

"Thank you for the compliment," she said. She accepted and inhaled the fragrant flowers and smiled. "And thank you for these," she repeated.

Amir followed Azure through the entryway and took a seat in the living room. Azure continued into the kitchen, where she retrieved a vase from a cabinet beneath the sink. She filled it halfway with water from the tap. With a pair of scissors found in a drawer reserved for tools and miscellaneous items, she carefully snipped the stems one by one. After placing the flowers in the vase and arranging them for a moment or two, she offered Amir a tour of her home.

The house was a two-bedroom, ranch-style home. It was no surprise to Amir that it was decorated with a colorful, artsy flavor. There were numerous plants of all sizes and types scattered around the living room. The walls were painted a bright sunset orange and the peach-colored futon and chairs blended perfectly. There was no way anyone could be depressed in a room as vibrant as that. The moment Amir entered it, he felt as if he had just taken a breath of fresh air.

Azure's bedroom was done in various shades of blue, from the lightest hue of sky blue to the deepest navy. The bed was a wooden platform with a high mattress and was covered with a half a dozen pillows of different sizes. The bathroom was large and spacious, because she'd had a wall from an adjoining walk-in closet knocked out. She hated tiny bathrooms, feeling confined and restricted in them.

The kitchen was classic, with white walls and stainless-steel appliances. The cabinet doors were made of blown glass with pewter handles. Sparkling white ceramic tiles covered the floors. One could easily have eaten off the floor in that room, which did not surprise Amir. In fact, the entire house was a perfect reflection of Azure's personality and Amir felt as though being there gave him an even stronger insight to her. It was a warm, inviting haven, quite the way he had come to see her. He held her hand as she led him from room to room, the warmth of her palm touching his, heating his entire body.

From the small dining area, they exited through sliding-glass doors onto a redwood deck. The patio table was set with candles, wine and glasses. A fresh garden salad, a cool pasta medley and baked dinner rolls were laid before the two place settings. The grill was set to warm, the steaks Azure had just finished cooking waiting beneath the cover.

"You have a beautiful house, Azure. I may never leave." Amir laughed.

"Well, make sure you put half of the bill money on the table and remember to let the toilet seat down," Azure quipped back.

They laughed together and Amir kept to himself the fact that he was only partially joking. Azure kept a warm, cozy home. It was definitely the kind of place he could get used to coming home to every night.

Before being seated, Amir leaned on the deck's railing and took in the garden. An in-ground pool shimmered beneath him, surrounded by terra-cotta tiles. The pool took up most of the property, leaving a small rectangular area of grass, which was surrounded by a bed of colorful impatiens and begonias. On all sides the yard was embraced by trees that appeared to have been assigned the job of assuring privacy. It was the kind of place he would love coming home to. He immediately struck the thought from his mind, knowing that he was getting way ahead of himself. He was grateful for the distraction when Azure called to him that dinner was ready.

"This is good," Amir remarked as he chewed a mouthful of the tender filet mignon.

Azure had marinated the meat in a mesquite sauce from the minute Amir had accepted her dinner invitation the day before. She had slow-cooked the steak on the grill and it had paid off. The tricolored pasta was boiled to perfection and, using a recipe she had watched Aunt Janet work from for years, she'd blended just the right amount of olives, peppers, onions, spices and seasoning to make a pasta salad which would shock his taste buds alive. She wanted everything to be just right and was thankful that things had cooperated with her.

An hour later, they were still seated on the deck across from one another, Amir working on his second helping and enjoying every ounce of it. Azure delighted in watching him eat as though he had truly never enjoyed a meal more. As much as she hated to admit it, there was something innately satisfying about being in the presence of a man and, even more to the point, having one in your home. Especially one who was so sensuous and, at the same time, humble. Amir was a man who did not use his good looks as a stepping stone to conquering women. He was a man whose personality outshone his physical attractiveness. To her, he was miles above many of the other boys and men she had known in her lifetime in that he was not into game-playing and slick talking.

Conversation flowed so easily for both of them. She could feel herself sliding into a comfort zone with him, and, while she was alarmed by this, she was also excited to see where it would lead. There was no denying the physical attraction she felt for him. Being around him reminded her of just how long it had been since she had been intimate with a man. However, it was much more than lust. She could actually feel her soul pulling closer to his. She could feel the beginning of a bonding of sorts happening between them and it felt sticky-sweet, like sugar-coated candy melting in your mouth—so good that you couldn't imagine anything in the world tasting better.

"It's so humid tonight," Azure complained, wiping her moist forehead with a napkin. The mugginess of the atmosphere paled in comparison to the heat that was rising within.

"Yeah, I guess summer is finally here," Amir agreed. "Your pool looks inviting."

"I use a service. They get it ready every year for me, like

clockwork. I could never balance all of the chemicals correctly. Do you swim?"

"Yep."

Amir laughed as a sudden memory took shape in his mind.

"When we were kids, we used to go swimming at the recreation center. One time this neighborhood jerk dared my brother, Tavares, to go into the deep end of the pool. Now, Tavares knew he couldn't swim, but he also knew that if he didn't at least try, this kid would taunt him for the rest of the summer. He was about thirteen and was embarrassed by the fact that he was afraid of the water. I think that's why we hung out down there so much—he was trying to overcompensate, I guess. You know, throw people off by being around the water all the time. It worked for a while, too, because no one ever noticed that he never went past the three-foot mark. He spent more time running around than he did in the water. That is, until this big bully, Leonard Wiley, dared him that day."

"So what happened?" Azure asked.

"Well, Tavares goes down the steps at the three-foot marker and starts walking toward the deep end. The other kids are egging him on, the bully is talking junk. Me? I'm walking along the side of the pool, keeping up with Tavares. When the water began to reach his chin, he looked up at me and even though he didn't say anything, I knew what he was thinking. I nodded my head and he turned forward and continued walking. When the water touched his lips, he took a deep breath, closed his eyes and went under. He kept moving forward, beneath the water until he was smack in the middle of eight feet of water."

"Why didn't the lifeguard do anything?" Azure asked.

"Please…we're talking about the city pool. That old

dude was probably busy hitting on one of the young girls somewhere. Anyway, everybody started clapping, and then I yelled to Tavares that he could come back now. Just at that moment, he ran out of air and tried to lift his head above water for more. He started flailing about, trying to fight his way to the top of the pool. I had never been so scared in my life."

"So what did you do?"

Amir shrugged his shoulders.

"I did what I'd silently promised him I would do. I jumped in and pulled him to the side of the pool. He was choking and sputtering, spitting up water for the next five minutes, his face beet red. Man, if he wasn't my brother I would have laughed so hard at him. But he was and, believe it or not, I was proud of him. He had stood up for himself, no matter what the risk. That's one thing I will always admire about my brother."

"What about you? You saved his life!" Azure said emphatically.

"Yeah, but I think about it like this—would I have jumped into that pool if I couldn't swim? Sometimes, I don't think I would have."

"I think you would have still saved him. Even if you had to swallow a gallon of water while you were doing it." Azure laughed. "You guys sound like you're pretty close."

"Yeah, that's my man. I don't know what I would have done growing up without him," Amir said.

For a moment he stared into space and Azure noticed that his eyes got a faraway look. He took a sip from his glass, and while still looking at some distant place in his memory, he spoke.

"My parents died when I was twelve," he said plainly.

Azure was silent for a moment, studying his face. She didn't know what to say, so she leaned across the table and took his hand in hers, waiting patiently for him to continue saying whatever it was he needed to say.

"My grandmother had just come out of the hospital after having hip surgery, and she lived alone. She was the type of woman who was always independent and even when she could have used some help, she refused. She wouldn't let my parents hire a home attendant or nurse. Fought them tooth and nail when they forced her to let someone come in and take care of the laundry and housecleaning.

"Anyway, my mother wanted to go over to her house and move some of the furniture around and fix a few things for her. She had been after my father all week about it and finally, on that Friday evening, he got tired of her nagging him. So they left after dinner, around seven o'clock, and headed over there. Grandma only lived about five or ten minutes away from us."

Amir paused and then a slight smile appeared on his lips.

"I remember bugging my mother because I wanted to go with them. But my dad said no, telling her that I'd only get in their way. He wanted to get over there, do what he had to do and get back home. It was playoff time and he wanted to get back to see the San Antonio and Los Angeles game. He had money on the Spurs."

"My dad was always a big Lakers fan, too." Azure laughed. "Still is."

"That night, Tavares was in the living room, hanging out with his girlfriend of the time. My mom told me to watch a movie with Bridgette. She was only seven and her favorite movie was *The Lion King*. She'd watched that movie so much, I was surprised the tape still worked."

"Uh, I've got a confession." Azure smirked. "I think that's my all-time favorite movie, too," she admitted shyly.

Amir shook his head and smiled at her.

"I should've known," he said.

Then his face grew serious again, his brow wrinkled and a pained look accompanied the memory that had just come to him.

"We were up to the part when Mufasa died. Bridgette was getting teary-eyed and I was rubbing her back, amazed that even though she'd seen the movie at least a thousand times, she still got upset on that part. The phone rang and Tavares answered it. All of a sudden, I heard him shouting at someone. I ran into the living room and the look on his face…I just knew something had happened, something so terrible that nothing would ever be the same.

"It was my grandmother's next-door neighbor. My grandmother lived right off a main boulevard. My parents had been driving across the intersection, onto her block when an oil truck slammed into them. People said it came out of nowhere, barreling down the street. There was no time for them to stop. My grandmother had heard the crash from her living room…everyone on the block heard it. Her neighbor recognized my parents' car."

"I'm so sorry, Amir," Azure said, tightening the grip she had on his hands.

"My dad died instantly. Never made it out of the car. But my mom…she hung on for a couple of days. She never woke up, but it seemed like she was refusing to let go. They let us see her and I remember sitting there, watching the ventilator breathing for her. I kept thinking about how bad she looked. Every part of her was bandaged up, broken and bruised. After a while, it looked like every breath she took was hurting her. I started feeling like every breath was hurting me, too. And then I told God to take her. I begged him. I just couldn't bear to see her like that, and I told him that he needed to take all her pain away and just take her. And he did."

"It must have been hard for you to let go," Azure said.

"Yeah, it was. But I kept telling myself that my dad needed her. I mean, she did everything for him. I don't think that man would have been able to get dressed in the morning if it weren't for my mother. No matter how much he complained about her nagging and fussing, you could tell that he'd be lost without her, and he knew it. So I figured that since he was gone, she needed to follow him. Take care of him."

"What about you, your brother and your sister?"

"We had each other. We stayed with my grandmother for a little while, but she wasn't in the best of health and she took my mother's death hard. A few months later, she ended up going to live in a nursing home."

"So what happened to you guys after that? Did you have other relatives?"

"Not really. No one who was capable of taking care of us. My mom was an only child and so was my grandmother. My grandfather died before I was even born. We have a couple of cousins on my grandfather's side who live somewhere on the West Coast, I believe, but we didn't even know them. My father has a brother, Uncle Joshua, but he was all messed up from the Vietnam War. Last I heard, he was in a veterans' hospital somewhere in Virginia. His wife had left him years before, and I think he had a son, but no one was in touch with him.

"Anyway, we spent some time in foster care after our

grandmother went into the home and then Tavares turned eighteen, so he became our legal guardian. Believe me, the child welfare system was more than glad to appoint him because that was three less kids they had to worry about finding room for in an already crowded system."

"Wow. At eighteen? That's a big responsibility. How'd he support you guys?"

Amir shifted his eyes away from her. Here was his chance to come clean. The perfect opportunity to explain to her how his life had turned out the way it had and why he was just now finding his own way when most men his age were already established. Maybe she would understand that they had had almost no choice. He looked at her face, saw the concern in her eyes and he froze. He tried to make his mouth move and make the words come out, but he couldn't do it. The thought that that beautiful face which held so much promise for the future, their future, could turn cold with disgust for him stopped him in his tracks. He looked away again, afraid that his own eyes would betray him as he spoke a half truth.

"We got some benefits from my parents' life insurance and savings plans. We were all right."

The truth was that the insurance policies were minimal. By the end of the first year, they'd used up a good portion of the money on rent, food and clothing. Tavares was working at a clothing store in the mall, but he wasn't making enough to pay the rent each month. That was when he and Sean, who had been best friends since elementary school, hooked up with Marques and started running scams on people. By the time all of the insurance money ran out, the trio had a nice little business going, but they were still making chump change. Marques had an uncle, Pete

Farmer, who had been married three or four times and whose pockets stayed fat with women's money. Spending time with him gave Tavares the idea that they could use Uncle Pete's experiences as a lucrative lesson. By the time Amir was beginning his junior year in high school, Tavares and the others had a thriving business and were making more money than any of them had ever seen.

Amir couldn't admit to her that at first he was in awe of his brother's success. While he didn't know all the ins and outs of what they did, he knew that they weren't sticking people up in alleyways or anything criminally insane like that. Therefore, whatever they were doing to get paid couldn't have been that bad. Tavares assured him that they weren't doing anything that could be construed as illegal and that was enough for Amir.

How could he now tell Azure that once he understood exactly what type of business his brother was involved with, instead of running in the opposite direction, he'd ended up joining him? She would never understand the position he was in. He owed Tavares everything and he also wanted to make sure that Bridgette had everything she needed. So he told himself that it was all good, and the rest was history. How could he make her understand all that when he couldn't truly rationalize it himself?

Amir stood and walked to the edge of the in-ground pool. He knelt down on the mosaic tiles, leaned over and dipped two fingers into the crystal-clear water.

"Ooh, it feels nice. I should jump in here," he said laughing.

"Go ahead."

"I didn't bring a suit."

"So?" Azure said, a mischievous smirk playing at her lips.

Amir looked at her for a moment, trying to determine if she was serious or just teasing him. The sight of her, her face illuminated by the soft deck lighting, was truly a vision to behold. She made him feel almost as if nothing in his past mattered because when he was with her, there was no yesterday, no tomorrow. There was only today. This moment. Right now all he could think about, all he wanted, was to be close to her and to extinguish the fire that she had ignited in his loins from the moment he met her.

Finally, Amir decided to call her bluff, if that was what it was. He stood and looked around the sprawling backyard. The dense trees separating Azure from her neighbors provided seclusion and privacy. He kicked off his flip-flops and pulled his T-shirt over his head, exposing a taut chest. Azure watched over the rim of her glass as she took a long sip of the red wine. She was not entirely surprised at his actions because Amir had already proven that he was a man who was willing to step outside the box and be impulsive. However, at the same time she found his move extremely daring and undeniably titillating.

Amir smiled as he watched Azure. Her effort to appear unfazed failed, and it was clear to him at once that she was moved by him as much as he had been by her from the moment he'd laid eyes on her. Slowly, he unzipped the denim shorts he wore, allowing them to drop to his feet. With deliberate motions, he stepped out of them. He stood with parted legs in pale-blue boxer shorts that stopped in the middle of his muscular thighs, his buttery skin illuminated by the soft lights surrounding the pool.

Azure felt her insides stir to the core. His was an image

of near perfection, as if he had been painted with an artist's brush rather than born. She gave in to the uncontrollable urge to lick her lips as her eyes traveled from his dread-locked head to his muscular body and down to his feet.

Amir tossed his locks back over his shoulder and shot Azure one last glance before diving into the pool. He cut the water expertly with his hands and quickly submersed himself into the cool water. He swam toward where he'd left Azure seated. When he finally came up for air, she was kneeling at the edge of the pool. She reached down and smoothed his wet hair back from his face.

"You're crazy," she said.

"Yep," he responded. He grabbed both of Azure's arms and made a threatening motion as if he would pull her into the pool with him.

"Uh-uh, Amir. Don't you dare," she screamed.

"Everybody into the water!" he teased.

Azure wrestled away from Amir's strong grip and stood, backing away from him. She smiled at him, feeling in-fected by his bold behavior. Quickly, before she lost the nerve, Azure slipped the straps of her dress from her shoul-ders and slid it down her curvaceous body. Amir could tell through her clothing that she had a nice shape, but nothing had prepared him for how awesome it actually was. Looking at her took his breath away and he felt his man-hood rise to attention, his loins tight with wanting.

Clad in a black lace bra and panties, she walked down the pool steps slowly. She felt as though she were having an out-of-body experience, the excitement of this clandes-tine interlude driving her forward. Her hot body met the cool water, but the temperature only seemed to rise as slowly she drew closer to Amir.

"I guess crazy's got company." He smiled when she waded next to him.

Beneath the water, his hands found her waist and he pulled her against his body. Their lips began a fevered dance, egged on by the racing drumbeat of their hearts. It was as if they had shared this level of intimacy before, perhaps in their subconscious minds while submersed in dream-filled slumber. They seemed to know each other's bodies well, knowing what touch would bring the other pleasure, causing titillating gasps or moans to escape. With each passing moment the passion intensified until neither of them thought they could hold back any longer.

"I didn't think this was going to happen…I mean, I don't have any protection," Amir whispered against the soft hollow of her neck.

"I do…in the house," Azure moaned softly.

They had both been honest with one another early on about past sexual encounters and the fact that they had both undergone testing for sexually transmitted diseases within a year of those relations. Yet another thing they had in common was their consciousness about the importance of good health and safe habits.

Azure buried her face in his hair and breathed in deeply the scent of almond oil. Everything about him drove her wild, and she knew that part of what she had been feeling since the day she'd met him was the desire to have him inside her. She arched her body against his, letting him know that she was ready to get closer to him, as close as two people could physically be.

Amir looked at her, stroked the side of her face, and, for a fleeting moment, felt that he should stop this thing before it went a step further. He felt it was wrong to take this delicate gift she was offering him, knowing that he was not the man she believed him to be. Yet it also felt like the most *right* thing he had ever done in his life.

He led her up the pool's steps, across the deck and into the house. They made it as far as the kitchen. His mouth dined on every part of her supple skin that he could reach, tasting her neck and ears, traveling down until it met the peaks of her breasts. He alternated between strong, hard sucks and soft kisses, which drove her mad. Her head was thrown backwards, her eyes closed, as she marveled at the sensations he was driving through her body.

For his part, he could not get enough of her. Her skin was smooth and warm and he loved its velvety feel against his own. He strove to take her to heights she had never been before, wanting to express to her in physical terms what she had come to mean to him emotionally. She left him momentarily and while she was gone, he once again wrestled with the knowledge that he should have been completely honest with her before things had advanced this far. Yet when she returned to the kitchen, her nude body still glistening from water and perspiration, all coherent thoughts left his mind.

Both of his hands held tightly on to his locks as she tore open the condom package and, with trembling hands, rolled the barrier onto his shaft. Against the striking, classic white walls, her legs straddling his muscular thighs, he took her. Her body closed itself around him, enveloping him like a glove as she sought a physical pleasure which would match the spiritual one she had found the day he returned to the gallery to see her.

When Amir's strong legs threatened to give out, Azure leaned across the kitchen table, where he took her from behind. With both arms wrapped around her upper body, he held her tightly as their joined bodies gave and received in a slow, delicate dance. They rode the waves of passion in that room, let it carry them through the house into the bedroom, where they climbed again and again, never tiring of one another. The food left outside was forgotten, as was everything else beyond those walls. For the time being, it was all about them. Nothing and no one else mattered. Tears slid down Azure's cheeks as for the first time in over two years she felt that she was not alone. The loving that Amir put on her that night warmed her from the inside out, and she knew that she did not ever want to live without that feeling again.

Chapter 15

"Huh…what? Did you say something to me, Aunt Melissa?" Azure stammered.

"Girl, I've been talking to you for a full minute and you didn't hear a word I said." Melissa laughed. "What on earth are you thinking about?"

"Nothing," she lied.

She couldn't admit that she had been distracted all night. From the moment she'd arrived at her parents' anniversary party, she'd regretted not having invited Amir. Almost everyone in the house was part of a couple. With the exception of herself and a few cousins under the age of eighteen, there were nothing but married or seriously dating folks in attendance. Despite her earlier rebellious attitude, she now felt as though she stood out.

She thought about Amir and immediately felt bad. As much as he denied it, she realized that she had hurt his feelings. He had wanted her to ask him to attend her parents' anniversary party with him, but she'd made excuses. Those excuses now seemed weak and transparent to her, and she shuddered to think how they'd sounded to Amir. She'd told him that it was a small party, only immediate family was expected. She'd also told him that she didn't plan to stay long and that he would be bored. He'd said that it was fine with him, but for the remainder of their evening together he'd seemed distant.

Barely an hour had passed since she'd arrived at the party and she had alternated between glancing at her watch and halfheartedly talking to relatives whom she hadn't seen in months or years. The house reflected the festive mood of its guests. Her father had updated the old house in which she had grown up by having new windows installed and new light fixtures hung in the kitchen, dining and living rooms, and the kitchen cabinets had been replaced. He'd pulled up the old brown tweed carpet in the living room and now the hardwood floors sparkled and gleamed, bringing new life into the place.

Everyone was complimenting the Monroes on how well they'd kept the house up. It was a great evening of celebration and of reunion as family members who hadn't been around in years hugged and kissed and caught up on each other's lives. Azure felt as though she was on the outside looking in, however, unable to relax completely and enjoy herself.

"I'm sorry, Aunt Melissa. I'm just a little tired. My allergies have been tormenting me, and I guess I haven't been getting enough sleep," Azure offered to excuse her inattentiveness.

"Well I certainly can relate to that. I've got this acid

reflux thing going on and, I tell you, most nights I'm walking the floor. It hurts to lay down…hurts to sit up. That doctor, humph, he ain't worth his salt. I'm just about through with him. He's given me three different medications already and each one of them makes something else go wrong and my chest still feels like it's on fire," Melissa complained.

"I'm sorry to hear that, Aunt Melissa," Azure said.

Looking at her aunt, she realized for the first time how much Yanté looked and sounded like her. The Lourdes had both been in their forties when Yanté was born. They had tried unsuccessfully to conceive for the first ten years of their marriage and had all but given up hope when Yanté came along. Now they were both past sixty, both retired and, although she hated to admit it, Yanté was right—they were definitely becoming victim to many of the troubles that came along with aging.

"Ahh, don't worry about it. This old body of mine is tough. We'll get through this. Now what about you? How have you been, honey? You used to come by and see us all the time. Now, I have to get updates on you from my daughter, when I can catch up with *her!*"

"I'm doing good, Aunt Melissa. In fact, better than good. Things couldn't be better." Azure smiled, meaning every word she said.

Aunt Melissa studied Azure for a moment, a slow smile spreading across her face.

"Uh-oh. Sounds like somebody's been bit by the love bug," she said.

"Aunt Melissa! Where'd you get that ridiculous idea from?" Azure asked, looking around nervously to see if anyone else had heard her.

"Child, please. I may be a little older, but I know new love when I see it. Your tail is beaming like the moon, not to mention the fact that your mind is a million miles away from here. Now if that don't mean that somebody is loving you right, I'm gonna go get my eyeglass prescription changed."

Azure momentarily began to protest. But after thinking about who she was talking to, she realized that it was pointless.

"Well, there is somebody—" she began.

"I knew it!" Aunt Melissa shouted, prompting looks from those people who were seated near them.

"Hold on now, Aunt Melissa," Azure whispered. "Before you blab to the whole free world, I'm not ready to broadcast."

"Why not?" Melissa whispered back. "What's wrong with him?"

"Nothing's wrong with him." Azure laughed. If she hadn't believed before that Yanté and her mother were just alike, she certainly did now. "I just want to keep it on the down low for a while. Can you do that?"

"I guess so…I mean, are you sure there's nothing wrong with this young man?" Melissa asked.

"I promise you, he's wonderful. I just want to keep him to myself for a little while. I need to see where this is going first. Do you know what I mean?"

"Mmm-hmm. I know just what you mean. You don't want that iron-drawers-wearing mama of yours all up in your business. Don't worry, baby, I got you covered," Melissa said conspiratorially.

Azure stifled a laughed.

"Thank you, Aunt Melissa," Azure said, kissing her on the cheek. "Now remember, mum's the word. *Nobody* means absolutely nobody."

Aunt Melissa patted her hand and smiled by way of confirmation.

"Just tell me one thing…is he a cutie?"

"Yes, Aunt Melissa, he's definitely a cutie."

"Well, all right now," Melissa said, looking around the room. "'Cause there's certainly enough damned ugly people that done snuck up in this family!"

Azure cracked up at that one. Aunt Melissa would never change and that was one thing Azure was glad of.

Chapter 16

"Mrs. Dartmouth will see you now," the receptionist said, her Southern accent swaying across the waiting area.

"Thank you," Yanté replied.

She uncrossed her velvet legs and rose from the hard-back chair in which she had been sitting for the past fifteen minutes. Her appointment with Mrs. Dartmouth had been set for noon and it was now about twelve minutes past that time. Yanté smoothed the ice blue jacket of her suit and picked up the wrapped sixteen-by-twenty canvas which she had propped against the legs of the chair. She walked around the secretary's desk, the three-inch heels of her Miu Mius clicking against the parquet floor.

Taking a deep breath, she turned the brass doorknob leading to the inner office and stepped inside. She had only been in the boss lady's office one other time and that was during the second phase of the interview process, four years ago. The office hadn't changed much and was still as breathtaking as she remembered. All of her other encounters with Joan Dartmouth had taken place either down in the sales and catering department of the hotel, where Yanté's office was located, or during one of the frequent banquets or other hotel functions.

"Yanté, come in. Please, have a seat."

"Thank you, Mrs. Dartmouth."

"Joan…call me Joan," Joan Dartmouth said, rising from her chair to shake Yanté's hand. "I'm sorry to have kept you waiting. I was stuck on a call with two of the hotel's board members, one of whom is in Europe, calling the other who is on vacation in Uruguay. The first called the latter to report that our stock dropped an eighth of a percent on the overseas market. So, in a panic, they both jumped on the phone and called me, and I just spent the better part of the past hour trying to persuade them that the company is doing better than ever and that we're not about to go belly-up."

"Wow, I thought I had a rough morning trying to get my goldfish to stop chasing each other around the shrubbery in their tank." Yanté laughed.

Joan Dartmouth laughed with her.

"So, what can I do for you?" she asked once Yanté was seated in one of the two plush chairs in front of her expansive mahogany desk.

"Well, Joan, I'll get straight to the point. I understand that in connection with the redecorating project going on here at the hotel, you are considering changing some of the artwork," Yanté said.

"Yes, that's true. I've wanted to modernize this place for quite some time. Maybe take away some of the staunchness…the drab colors and the conservative style. My husband was an astute businessman, but not much of a risk taker when it came to certain areas. I think this place could use a breath of new life."

"I couldn't agree with you more. The other day I went up to the honeymoon suites and the work is coming along quite nicely," Yanté acknowledged.

"That's good to hear. When I started this project, those were the rooms I was most concerned with," Joan said.

Yanté decided that this was the precise moment that she had been waiting for. She began tearing the wrapping from the package on her lap, revealing a painting.

"However, there is one thing wrong," Yanté added.

"Oh?" Joan asked, her curiosity peaked.

Yanté turned the painting around so that it faced Joan.

"You're missing pieces like this," Yanté said.

Joan studied the canvas intently for several seconds without speaking and finally, a broad smile spread across her narrow face.

"Fascinating," Joan breathed at length. She stood up and reached across the desk, taking the painting from Yanté's hands. She held it up inches from her face and surveyed it some more. Still smiling, she walked across the room toward the fireplace on the other side. After moving a few items from their positions, she sat the painting on the mantel and took a step back.

"This is so different…refreshing. I don't think I've ever seen work with this much quiet intensity. The colors…the detail. I love it. I absolutely love this. It truly is like nothing I've ever seen. Do you know who the artist is?"

"Better than that…she's my cousin. Her name is Azure Monroe."

"I don't believe I've ever heard of her. Has she had any showings in the area?"

"No, not exactly. Well, here's the thing. She owns a small gallery over in Dupont Circle, and she's doing quite well. Unfortunately, she doesn't show any of her own work. She's sort of a closet artist."

"That's a shame," Joan said. "She's really quite talented."

"Believe me, I've been trying to tell her that for years, but I don't think she believes that she is as good as she actually is," Yanté lamented.

"And you intend to show her differently," Joan said, turning away from the painting to face Yanté.

Though the women were of equal height, Joan Dartmouth's slimness gave her the appearance of being slightly taller. Only a few years separated them—Joan was a little older—but both women possessed a refined beauty. Yanté remembered the first time she'd met Joan Dartmouth and how impressed she was by the impeccable taste and style the woman displayed. Having always taken pride in her own appearance, Yanté had learned by watching Joan Dartmouth over the years the fine art of subtlety. She infused her own vibrant style with what she observed as Joan's classic refinement and found that she began to receive even more compliments from admirers than she had previously. Additionally, she began to notice a change in the way she was dealt with professionally.

Yanté had begun her career at Dartmouth Hotel as a catering manager, after earning a bachelor's degree in hospitality and business at Georgetown University. Within three years she had moved up to the position of Assistant Hotel Applications Project Manager, a title which increased her responsibilities from overseeing banquet scheduling and services to coordinating contracts with vendors, implementing support systems throughout the hotel and on-site management and supervision of over a dozen employees spread across three departments. She was proud of her transition and was eager to learn as much as she could so that she could progress even further in her career.

The growth in Yanté had not gone unnoticed by Joan Dartmouth. She made a point of monitoring her employees, always keeping a special eye on those she felt had potential for advancement. Yanté was developing into a remarkable young woman. Joan had hired her personally, handpicked her from a sea of applicants. There was a zest for life, a hunger that Yanté possessed that most of the other applicants lacked. She was sharp, confident, and what she lacked in experience, she more than made up for in the areas that counted most with Joan—first and foremost, eagerness. Yanté had risen in the ranks as a result of her strong personality, drive and desire to learn. Yanté Lourde was a young woman who was ambitious and willing to work hard to succeed. Joan admired that quality when she saw it because it was precisely what had gotten her to where she herself was today.

Joan Dartmouth had been born in the 1960s to dairy farmers in Idaho. By the time she had reached middle school, Joan Smallwood had felt she had milked one cow too many. She decided that she wanted a lifestyle as different and far removed from the farm as she could get. Her parents never understood their daughter's ambitions, hoping that she would settle down in Idaho and live a simple life like their own. But Joan had mapped out a different plan for herself.

An exceptional math student, Joan received a scholarship to Yale where she earned a dual degree in applied mathematics and economics. She met William Dartmouth during her senior year, and while it was not love at first sight, there was a strong attraction built on intellectual compatibility. William Dartmouth was ten years older than she, but youthful in every way that counted. At the time, the Dartmouth Hotel was still in its infancy. He had bought the establishment from a man who hadn't the vision to move it past being just another hotel, an ordinary one at that.

The romance between William and Joan was born not out of a raging fire but from a slow-burning flame. Joan graduated and took a job with a small hotel chain. Four years later she and William were married and side by side they worked diligently to transform his hotel into what was now the renowned Dartmouth. William had readily admitted that Joan was a major part of his success, and she was proud to be able to show her parents that she had, in fact, fulfilled her dreams.

Their marriage was a good one with deep commitment instead of overwhelming passion, which was okay with both of them. In business, they were a dynamic pair and the future seemed to promise prosperity and happiness. But their time together was shorter than anticipated. Five years after they'd said I do, William was gone. Joan had scarcely had a moment to grieve, since all the responsibilities of running the hotel and attending to their other holdings and business dealings rested squarely on her shoulders now. She refused to let William down, and worked tirelessly to see that his dream of making the Dartmouth a landmark hotel came to fruition. She protected their assets ferociously and surrounded herself with people who would work to keep the Dartmouth name respected and cherished.

To say the least, it had been a lonely road for her. She'd had to make decisions affecting the lives of all the people who worked for her as well as her own on a daily basis.

Since the terrorist attacks of September 11, 2001, travel and hotel stays had been dramatically reduced. While Joan had managed to keep the hotel operating with its full staff, changes desperately needed to be made. This redecoration project was an attempt to breathe new life into the hotel and, she hoped, attract new customers. Joan had hoped to find artwork representing the diversity of the world as well as the warmth of the hotel. Looking at this piece by an obviously talented, yet unknown artist, Joan was finally able to put a finger on the look she had been trying to create.

"I can't sit back and watch her waste her talents in the back of some dusty gallery," Yanté was saying. "She's an excellent salesperson and knows everything about every artist who has ever picked up a paintbrush. She's great at explaining theme and motif of other people's works, making even the most inexperienced purchaser feel like he or she has just had a crash course in Art History 101 and can now distinguish a Rembrandt from a Picasso. However, her work is just as good, if not better than most of what she sells every day and nobody knows about it."

Joan considered what Yanté had said for a moment. She returned her gaze to the painting on the mantel.

"I'd like to see some of her other work. Do you think you can get her to show it?"

"I'm not sure," Yanté said, suddenly nervous at the thought of Azure's response when she discovered that the painting she had given to Yanté as a birthday gift last year was now sitting above the fireplace of the owner and CEO of the Dartmouth Hotel. "But I'll damn sure give it a try," she concluded.

"Good. Check with my secretary and schedule a time for me to come to the gallery. This is precisely the type of art that I've been looking for to liven this place up a bit," Joan said.

"Thank you, Joan, for your time. I think we will definitely be able to work something out."

"I hope so," Joan said. "But remember, time is definitely of the essence. The hotel is losing money every day that those rooms are unoccupied."

"I understand. I'll get right on it."

Yanté left Joan Dartmouth's office with a spring in her step. She could not have been more excited if it were her own artwork being considered. She returned to her office with the intention of phoning Azure immediately, but was bombarded by a list of phone messages and other business to attend to. Although the buck stopped with her manager, it was her job to see that problems with dozens of vendors were dealt with before they reached that level. Her engaging personality was the perfect secret weapon, and she used it to her advantage. For the most part, she was an enchanting keeper of the peace, able to soothe the most irate vendor, patron or employee. Today was no exception. She worked her magic and was able to secure a ten-percent discount on the hotel's next meat order, get a guaranteed on-time delivery from the linen service and increase the volume of food for a prominent high-society couple's wedding reception by three times the original amount ordered.

It was after five o'clock by the time she was able to pick up the telephone to call Azure. To her dismay, she received no answer either at the gallery or Azure's home. She continued working, shuffling through the tasks on her desk, and by the time she left the hotel for the evening, the time that had passed had done little to diminish her excitement over Azure's art.

* * *

Yanté paced around the gallery, alternating between glancing at her wristwatch, the clock on the wall and through the window onto the street. She sighed repeatedly, wondering where on earth Azure could be at this hour. She had called her at the gallery and at the house for hours. Finally, she'd taken a chance and come to the gallery, hoping to find Azure tucked away in her studio ignoring the outside world. Using her spare key, she'd let herself in when Azure did not answer the door, only to find the gallery empty. Puzzled, she called Azure's parents, who had no idea where their daughter was. Yanté teetered between worry and annoyance as she waited for her cousin. She called the house again and was contemplating calling the police when a key turned in the door.

Yanté opened her mouth, poised to give Azure the what for, but froze. Her eyes enlarged as wide as they could as she watched Azure back into the door, arms entangled with and lips glued to none other than Amir Swift!

"What the—" she stammered, surprising the couple.

"Yanté," Azure screeched. "What are you doing here?"

A stunned Yanté stood speechless and slack-jawed, her eyes as wide as saucers. Amir cleared his throat and offered her a weak wave of his hand.

"Uh…well, Yanté, you remember Amir, don't you?" Azure sputtered.

"Yes, I most certainly do. Well, I guess you could blow me over with a feather right about now, huh?" Yanté said.

She backed up and plopped down on the edge of Azure's desk to steady herself.

"Listen, Yanté, I've been meaning to tell…well, I mean, I was planning to…I—"

"Hey, hey, really. You don't owe me any explanations," Yanté said, wounded feelings coating her every word.

"Listen, babe, I'm going to get on the road and, uh, let you two talk," Amir said.

He wanted to get away not just for the reason he'd stated, but because he was once again caught off guard by the reminder that Azure had not yet told anyone about their relationship. First there'd been the anniversary party he hadn't been invited to, and now this. He'd tried to understand her reasons for keeping their relationship a secret, but he couldn't help being worried all the same. He wanted to shout from the rooftops that he was falling in love with this magnificent woman. He had told Bridgette about her and would have told Tavares if it were not for the strain between them. Only time would tell how far this love affair would go. He was making every effort to steer things in the right direction, knowing deep in his heart that she was the best thing that had ever happened to him. However, he had to admit that Azure keeping him a secret was not a good sign.

Azure placed her palms on his chest and kissed him lightly on the lips.

"Thank you," she whispered.

Amir kissed her forehead, turned and walked back to the door.

"It was nice seeing you again, Yanté."

He turned back to Azure and mouthed, "Call me."

Azure closed the gallery door behind Amir and locked it. Through the glass, she watched him walk down the street and kept watching until he was out of sight. Reluctantly, she turned to face the waiting Yanté.

Chapter 17

"Before you say anything, let me explain," she began.

"I'm all ears," Yanté said snidely.

The look in Yanté's eyes told Azure that she had exercised poor judgment by not confiding in her. Yes, she felt that she was right to want the relationship between Amir and herself to remain only theirs for as long as possible. She didn't want anyone trying to define or classify it, and she certainly did not want people pushing them to a wedding chapel. With the exception of Aunt Melissa, no one knew that she had met and was falling head over heels for Amir, and she had honestly thought she could keep it that way for just a little while longer.

Additionally, there were Yanté's feelings to consider. She had told herself that it was because Yanté was attracted to Amir and she might think that Azure had purposely played her in some way by hooking up with him behind her back. But even as she had concocted this line of reasoning, she knew it was weak. The truth of the matter was she was afraid to put a name or a title on what she and Amir had. As long as it remained between the two of them, then it was special and, more importantly, it was safe. She wanted to believe in happily ever after, even if only for a little while, and by keeping her relationship with Amir private, she could do just that. She had fallen so hard and so fast for the man, and she believed that Yanté would be sure to cast doubt on things by telling her that she was rushing it or that Amir was out of her league and would only end up hurting her. Azure didn't want to be talked out of something that felt so right. For the first time in as long as she could remember, she was happy. She could hear crackling in her cereal bowl in the morning and it sounded like music from a concert orchestra to her ears.

Despite all of this, she had unintentionally hurt her cousin. Yanté had been both best friend and cousin since Azure had been born when Yanté was a toddler. They'd gone through so much together and, notwithstanding the fact that they were like night and day, had been more like sisters than cousins. Azure had never had a close relationship with her mother. Vetta Monroe was an aloof woman who was not comfortable with displays of affection. She was a mother who believed that a stern hand and strict rules were the best way to raise a child. In grade school, if Azure received a score in the nineties on an exam, her mother would tell her that next time she should study harder and receive a hundred. Vetta made sure that Azure had all of the necessities of life and was a supportive parent, attending PTO meetings and participating in bake sales. Yet she was very critical and highly demanding. As a result, they didn't talk much about things other than school, chores and curfew.

Nicholas Monroe had always been a quiet man. His love for his daughter was unquestionable, yet he tended to defer to his wife over most decisions involving Azure. Hers was a family that never sat around playing family games or watching television together. The nurturing and camaraderie Azure had received in her young life had come from Yanté. Azure spent as much time as she could with Yanté and her parents, Melissa and Marvin Lourde. It was at times difficult to believe that Vetta and Marvin were brother and sister. He was extremely humorous and light-hearted, almost a class clown. It was hard for anyone to feel down in his presence because he had a way of making people feel good without trying. Aunt Melissa was outspoken and zany, and together they made a perfect match. Azure had spent most weekends at Yanté's house and that was the closest she'd come to having a relaxed, carefree upbringing. The bond that grew between the girls was one that had withstood puberty and college and seemed impenetrable. Azure could only hope that her present deception had not driven a wedge between them.

"Yanté, I didn't plan on this. It just happened. A few days after you and I met him, he came back to the gallery to buy another painting and, it was…it was like…" Azure sighed. "I still don't understand it. We talked and we just clicked."

Even now Azure had difficulty explaining the soul-stirring passion she'd felt for Amir from the moment she laid eyes on him. It went beyond his arresting looks and his charm. There was something about him that touched a part of her that no one else had ever reached. As she shared herself with him, it was as if she was getting to know herself at the same time—through his eyes. Together they peeled back the layers that life had added to each of them and the newness beneath was like ripe fruit, juicy and nourishing.

"Azure, are you happy?" Yanté asked finally, regarding her cousin with ever-present concern.

"Very."

"Well then, I guess that's all that matters," Yanté said.

Azure realized that it was difficult for Yanté to disguise the hurt she felt. She walked over to her cousin and put her arms around her, hugging her tightly.

"Thank you," she whispered.

"Yeah, yeah, yeah."

Yanté was trying her best not to be critical. She needed to digest the whole thing before she voiced her concerns, and she knew that anything she said now would only be coming from the place within that was hurt by Azure's deceit. The last thing she wanted to do was to seem jealous, even if she was—slightly.

"What were you doing sitting here in the dark, anyway?" Azure asked, pulling away.

"Oh, yes, all this undercover secret-rendezvous mess made me forget why I'm here in the first place. I came by to make you an offer you can't refuse," Yanté said in her best *Godfather* character voice.

"Really now?" a skeptical Azure retorted.

This wouldn't be the first time that Yanté had approached her with a scheme that had ended up turning out badly. Azure began preparing herself to say no and to run away, kicking and screaming, if need be.

"Have you had dinner yet? I'm starved. Let's go eat and talk. My treat," Yanté said.

Half an hour later the speechless Azure sat across from Yanté at the M Street Bar and Grill. Azure pushed her half-eaten plate of grilled salmon, red bliss potatoes and steamed carrots away from her, folded her arms across her breasts and stared at her cousin. Of all the outlandish things Yanté had said or done over the years, this had to be the most ballsy.

"Say something," Yanté commanded, absently chewing her lips as she nervously waited for Azure to respond.

"You are unbelievable," Azure finally said at length. "Here I am feeling like crap for having kept you in the dark about Amir, yet all the while you knew that what you had done was ten times as conniving and deceitful. How could you?"

"Azure, I really wish you didn't see it that way. I did this for you," Yanté said.

"For me? No, Yanté, you didn't do this for me, because if you had even thought about me for one second, you wouldn't have taken something that I had created especially for you and practically sold it."

"I didn't sell it, Azure. I wouldn't do that," Yanté said, sounding genuinely hurt by the accusation.

"Look," she continued, "Mrs. Dartmouth is interested in seeing more of your work. She loved that piece and I guaranteed her that she would love your other paintings just as much. However, there was no discussion of money or any other business details. I told her that you are not really seeking to go public with your work just yet. She understands that if you are not interested, then there will be nothing further to talk about."

The skeptical look on Azure's face was not lost on Yanté. She continued talking, making every effort to keep Azure from saying no.

"Seriously, cousin, this is strictly preliminary—an opportunity for you and Joan to feel each other out and see what's what. But, Azure, come on, this is the opportunity of a lifetime, and if you weren't so busy being selfish, you could see that."

"Selfish? How on earth did you come to the conclusion that I'm being selfish?"

Yanté felt as if the wind had been let out of her sail. When she'd learned that the artwork was being changed at the hotel, she'd jumped on it. She had been so jubilant about the idea of Azure's work being hung in a prestigious hotel for all the world to see, she had all but forgotten Azure's reclusiveness. She was certain that faced with a once-in-a-lifetime deal like this, Azure would not be able to say no. Listening to her now made Yanté feel as though she really didn't know her cousin at all. It also made her angry and she didn't hesitate to show it.

"You have God-given talent. The kind of ability that some people would give their right arm to possess. Your work brings smiles to people's faces, makes hearts feel a little lighter. Yet all you can think about is yourself. *Your* art, *your* talent. Your way or no way. What gives you the right to keep something that you've been blessed with all to yourself? Isn't it every person's duty—your responsibility—to do what you can to make this world a better place?" Yanté spewed.

Azure's eyes grew wide as Frisbees as she took in Yanté's expression. She was dead serious.

"If you start singing 'We Are the World,' I swear I will reach across this table and slap you silly," Azure said through gritted teeth.

"Well then, get to slapping 'cause I'm not joking. What the hell are you so afraid of, Azure?"

Azure glared at Yanté for a moment longer and then

turned her head away. She leaned back against the chair, unfolding her arms and dropping her hands to the table in front of her. *What am I so afraid of?* The question sat on her chest like a boulder, weighing her down and seeming to restrict her very breathing.

"I don't know," she whispered aloud.

Yanté leaned over and took her hands. For a moment, neither woman spoke.

"Sweetie," Yanté finally said, "I would never do anything to hurt you. I only want the good things in life for you, you know that. This is a good thing, Azure, I promise you it is. Just meet her. Do that for me, and if you still feel the same way, then fine, just walk away. No harm, no foul. But start out by doing this one little thing for me…until you can do it for yourself," Yanté pleaded softly.

Azure nodded her head slowly, still uncertain. Tears clouded her brown eyes, but did not fall. The unanswered question held them, and her, in check.

Chapter 18

Yanté walked to her car, aggravated as she approached because there rested under the windshield wiper what appeared to be a parking ticket. She couldn't understand why a traffic cop would mess with her car. She was several feet away from the fire hydrant. She plucked the paper from the car irritably and opened it. To her surprise it wasn't a ticket. It was a handwritten note, the lettering bold and black. It read, I'm watching you always and enjoying the view.

Little hairs stood up on the back of Yanté's neck as she read the words a second time. She flipped the paper over but the other side was blank. She looked up and down the quiet street, but there was no one in sight. Quickly, she clicked the locks on the car using her remote keypad and hopped inside. She started the car and, with another push of a button, locked the doors. Again, she looked up and down the street, searching for what, she didn't know.

Finding nothing amiss, she released the breath she had been holding.

"Knock it off, Yanté," she said, laughing and chiding herself for being nervous.

She told herself that the note, like the flowers, was probably from some guy she had dated and dumped who thought the way to get back into her good graces would be to hit her with a little mystery or intrigue. Whoever it was would soon realize that she wasn't moved and knock it off. She crumpled up the note, rolled the window down and threw the paper outside into the street.

Yanté slowly pulled out of the parking space. She turned the corner onto a main boulevard and was immediately sucked into downtown D.C.'s never-decreasing stream of traffic. Had she glanced in her rearview mirror as she made that turn, she would have noticed the headlights on the brown Chevrolet which had been parked a half a block behind her as it crept out of its space and followed her into the night.

Chapter 19

"Things cool between you and your cousin?" Amir asked later that night when Azure called him.

He was lying on his back across his bed, clad in striped drawstring pajama pants. He was glad that Azure had finally called him. Yanté's appearance had interrupted his plan to spend the night with Azure, and he couldn't help but feel disappointed. In the month that they had been together, he'd grown more and more dependent on their time together, needing her companionship as much as he needed food and water. Making love to her was like making love for the very first time every time. She was like an open vessel waiting to receive him, mind, body and soul and, like a fiend, he craved her welcoming embrace. He loved lying on the cot in her studio and watching her paint, loved the way she cocked her head first to one side, then to the other, completely immersed in the most minute detail of whatever she was working on. Periodically, she would glance over at him and smile and his heart rate would speed up. He could watch her work for hours, honored to be in the presence of the making of another masterpiece. When she was done, she would join him on the cot and as they spooned on the tiny mattress, little speckles of paint dotting her face, he would stare in amazement at the simple beauty that was hers, grateful just to be beside her.

He'd wanted to hold her tonight. Just wrap his arms around her, press his body close to hers and hold on to her. He loved the way the vanilla of his skin looked against the chocolate of hers, the contrast arousing him in unimaginable ways.

When he was with her, it was the only time that his troubled soul seemed to rest. She had been so right when she'd said that he was carrying a load that was way too heavy for one man to bear. He'd wanted to tell her everything at that moment, but was afraid of what she'd think of him. How could he expect her to understand and not to judge when he didn't understand the life he led himself? And even if she chose to continue seeing him, he knew that things between them would change and that was the last thing that he wanted. His time with her was the best part of each day and even though he knew he was being selfish, he refused to mar the peacefulness that she brought into a room by telling her the truth.

It was when he was away from her that reality smacked him upside the head. He could not pretend then that he was living a different life. He went back to being Amir Swift, con artist and manipulator. That other life. Tavares thought that he was away on vacation somewhere, getting his head screwed on right so that he could get back to business. In fact, he'd never left town. He spent many of his days and nights with Azure, either at the gallery or at her house. She'd only been to his apartment a couple of times. He knew this hiatus could not go on forever. Just yesterday Tavares had left him a voice-mail message prodding him, with gentle firmness, to get in touch sooner rather than later. He knew that his brother was expecting him to return with a clear head and with no further talk of changing his life. He also knew how impossible that was, now more than ever. The truth was, he had long ago stopped being able to look himself in the face. He felt like the lives he and Tavares were living had dishonored their parents and themselves and he just couldn't do it anymore. The only thing that kept him there was Tavares and even that was not enough anymore. With Azure in his life now, there was no turning back. He had to make a change, even if that meant hurting his brother. He hoped and prayed that Tavares would stick with him and that together, they could take the money they'd saved and start over, legitimately. But whatever Tavares's decision, Amir steeled himself to do what he needed to do. His eternal soul, as well as his future with Azure, depended on it.

"We worked it out," Azure said absently. She was still shaken by what Yanté was asking of her.

"Why do you sound so preoccupied then?" Amir asked.

"No reason," Azure lied.

"Do you want me to come back over?" Amir asked, concerned.

"No, it's late. Not that I don't want to see you…"

"I can be there in twenty minutes," he pressed.

"No…really, it's late. I'm okay."

"Azure, will you please talk to me? If you don't tell me

what's wrong, I'm coming over there. Did Yanté say something? Are you sure you two worked everything out?"

"Things are cool between us." Azure sighed, deciding to tell Amir about Yanté's proposal. "Yanté showed one of my paintings to her boss at the hotel where she works. They're doing some redecorating or something and they're looking for artwork. Long story short, the woman wants to see more of my work—maybe commission me."

"And that's a bad thing?" Amir asked.

"No, yes…I don't know. It's both, I guess. At first I was angry with Yanté for doing that. She knows how I feel about my painting. But then she asked me what I was so afraid of and I couldn't answer her. I still can't."

"I know I'm no critic, and feel free to tell me to shut up, but I think Yanté's right. Your paintings are more than just chemicals on paper, or a mixture of colors thrown together. They're stories, they're dreams. They make you want to climb inside them and experience the scenery in a physical way. You are too talented to stay holed up in that little room of yours."

"So now you're dissing my studio?" Azure teased.

"Not at all, baby. I just think that you deserve a little light, some shine, that's all," Amir replied.

Azure considered what he was saying momentarily, soothed by his words even though they also invoked nervousness. She just wasn't sure what was right anymore. She thought that she knew. Was convinced that she had everything figured out, but now she wasn't so sure. Amir had been a surprise—sort of a sneak attack. She realized now that she would not have been able to resist him even if she had wanted to. His allure was just too strong for that. Or maybe it was that she had been resisting for too long.

Despite her protests to Yanté to the contrary, she had been very lonely over the past couple of years. The thing that Yanté had lost sight of, however, was that she wasn't interested in hooking up with someone just to ease that loneliness. She didn't believe in casual liaisons, no matter how lonely a person was. When Amir came into her life, the connection they'd made was too deep and too kinetic to be considered casual. It took a man like Amir to make her want to open up to the dangerous and uncertain playing field that defines an intimate relationship. She was glad that she had, yet now she was being asked to open herself up even more.

Amir stirred her from her thoughts.

"I have a surprise for you," he said.

"Really? I love surprises. Now tell me what it is," Azure responded.

"Nope, nosy, my lips are sealed. You'll have to wait until tomorrow, birthday girl." He laughed.

"No fair. Why'd you bring it up if you weren't going to tell me?"

"Just to make you squirm. Anyway, I've got big plans for you tomorrow so you should get some rest. I'll pick you up, bright and early."

"How early?" she asked, uneasy.

"Stop it. Don't you know that by now I know how much you love your birthday? You'll be up before the sun, like a frenzied adolescent."

"True. I guess you're right, though, I am very sleepy," she said, yawning.

They bade each other goodnight and Azure fell asleep as soon as her head hit the pillow. Her sleep was fitful, due primarily to the decisions that loomed before her. As predicted, however, she was up with the crows and by the time Amir arrived, she was dressed and ready to go.

"Okay, so where's my surprise?" she said, greeting him at the door with a kiss.

"Woman, would you please just get in the car and be patient? This is going to be one birthday you won't ever forget," Amir said.

The special day which Amir had planned began with a three-and-a-half-hour train ride into New York City. They arrived at New York Penn Station during the morning rush hour. Azure was immediately bubbling with the ill-contained excitement of a young child. She had only been to New York on two occasions that she could remember and both of those visits were a long time ago. She felt what she perceived as a change in the atmosphere as soon as they disembarked from the train, and while walking through the crowded terminal she commented on it to Amir.

"It's amazing how a short train ride can transport you into a totally different climate. Can you feel the difference between here and D.C.?"

"Yeah, New Yorkers have got a whole different vibe going on," he agreed.

"Exactly. It's like a different world. Look how everybody's rushing about. Not that people don't do the same in D.C., but here it seems like they're going at warp speed," she marveled. "Oooh, sorry," she said.

She had accidentally bumped into an older, refined-looking woman dressed in business suit.

"That's all right, dear," she said.

They continued on their way, Amir steering the delighted Azure along lest she do serious damage to herself or someone else.

"See, people are always saying that New Yorkers are rude. I don't think they're any more rude than people are anywhere else."

"Yeah, but the right New Yorker will knock you out faster than you can blink if you do something they don't like," Amir stated.

"Oh, stop it. I still think New Yorkers get a bad rap. Anyway, what are we going to do all day?"

Amir silenced her with a kiss, promising her that the day would be full of fun. First they had bagels and coffee at a café near the train station. They walked up to 42nd Street and Times Square. Blending in with the hundreds of other tourists who teemed through the city's streets, they took photos in front of some of the theater houses such as the Hirschfeld and the Barrymore. They visited Madame Tussaud's Wax Museum, both of them amazed by the lifelike replicas of famous people.

By afternoon, they had made their way uptown. They paid a visit to Harlem's Schomburgh Center for Research in Black Culture and the Studio Museum of Harlem, Azure never tiring of viewing sculptures, paintings and photographs by African-American artists. Lunch was catfish at Amy Ruth's Home-Style Southern Cuisine. They strolled through the streets of Harlem, the various vendors at the outdoor markets calling to Azure. She responded eagerly as she purchased crafts, T-shirts and other items, until Amir told her that he couldn't carry another thing.

They capped off the day with a visit to the legendary Apollo Theater, where they watched a live taping of Amateur Night. Afterwards, exhausted, yet reluctant for the day to end, Azure leaned on Amir. She was completely fulfilled, having just had the best birthday that she could remember. Amir took her hand as they exited the theater.

"Had fun?" he asked.

"Can we do it again tomorrow?" Azure beamed.

"Woman, please! You've completely worn me out today," Amir joked. "But seriously, we've got one more stop to make before we head back to the train," he said.

"Where?"

"I've got a friend who lives down near Central Park. Isaiah and I went to high school together."

Amir hailed a yellow taxi and they rode downtown to 60th Street and Fifth Avenue. The sun had set and the city was lit up like Christmas. Azure, who couldn't get enough of sightseeing, had her faced pressed to the taxi window all the way downtown.

"You guys have a lovely home," Azure said, smiling, after Amir had made the introductions to Isaiah and his wife, Nona.

"Thank you," Nona replied.

"She's in the bedroom," Isaiah said to Amir.

Azure looked at Amir quizzically as he pulled her toward the back room.

"Who's in the bedroom?" she asked.

"Come see for yourself."

They entered the bedroom to find a rust-colored Pomeranian lying on a fluffy dog pillow. Next to her were two puppies, and all three were sound asleep.

"Oh, my goodness. Look at them," Azure exclaimed.

The mother opened her eyes and looked up at them. Disinterested, she closed her eyes again.

"That's Mollie. She's three years old and we've had her ever since she was a puppy," Nona said.

"The vet thought it was a good idea to breed her early, and then consider having her fixed. So we took her to a breeder and she got pregnant on the first try. We had six buyers lined up for the puppies. Who would have thought she'd have eight babies, all of them perfectly healthy? Anyway, I've been making calls for a week now, trying to find someone to take the last two. Before I heard back from Amir, I was beginning to get a little worried because the condo association only allows for one pet per household," Isaiah explained.

He picked up one of the puppies and carried it over to Azure. She took the puppy from him and cradled it in her arms.

"Oooh, he's so cute. What's his name?"

"I don't know. Why don't you tell me?" Isaiah said.

Azure looked up from the puppy licking her fingers to Isaiah and then to Amir, confusion knitting her brow.

"Surprise…he's yours." Amir beamed.

Azure looked into the sleepy face of the puppy and felt her heart melt like chocolate. He was the cutest thing she had ever seen in her entire life. She held him close to her face, rubbing his snout with two fingers. He nuzzled against her body, closed his eyes and fell asleep again. There was no way she could put him down.

Nona and Isaiah gave them a small cardboard box lined with newspaper to carry the puppy home on the train. He had already had his first shots and all she would need to do was find a vet in her area to follow up with. They headed home with Amir carrying their bags and Azure carrying the box. On the train, Amir dozed while Azure stroked the dog's soft fur, smiling like a new mother.

"This is too much, Amir. These dogs are very expensive.

At least let me give you back a little of what you paid for him," Azure said.

"Nah, baby. It's your birthday. If I want to spoil my girl on her birthday, I can," Amir answered.

"Are you sure?"

She was not surprised by Amir's generosity. In the short time that she'd known him, he had shown that he was a giving spirit. However, she also knew that he was struggling as a freelance party promoter, and she didn't want him to think that he had to spend gobs of money on her every time they went out.

"Relax. My man Isaiah gave me a good deal. So what are you going to name him?"

"Bud," she said.

"What kind of name is that for a ferocious beast?"

As if in agreement, Bud let out a yelp. Unfortunately, it was a tiny little sound, not at all like that of a ferocious beast.

"Bud it is, I guess." Amir laughed.

The perfect day they'd shared couldn't have been any better. Azure nestled against Amir and closed her eyes. Little Bud, tired out already from his momentary burst of activity, curled up and returned to his nap.

Chapter 20

A loud knock on Azure's front door ruined the climax that Amir was approaching. They both froze and listened until the knocking commenced again. Amir rolled off Azure reluctantly, and she immediately jumped out of bed. He watched as she slipped her bathrobe on, her delicious body causing him to wince with desire. Tying the belt around her nude body, she left the room, turning a light on in the hallway. Amir slid into his boxers and followed her out, stopping just outside the foyer.

Azure peered through the peephole and shook her head in disbelief.

"Who is it?" Amir asked, poised to attack if it were some sort of threat.

"My brother," Azure replied.

Azure turned the locks and opened the door to find a disheveled Patrick standing before her. His eyes were bloodshot and the tattered jeans and thin T-shirt he wore were filthy.

"Hey, sis, how're you doing?" he said, his words slurred.

"Patrick, what are you doing here? I thought you were in Atlanta," Azure said.

"Well, you know me…never stick around too long… makes it harder to get caught, you know?" He laughed as he staggered past her into the house.

His smell was a nauseating mixture of booze and funk. She frowned in disgust as she closed the door behind him. Amir stood where he was, his arms folded across his bare chest.

"Hey now, sis, who's this?" Patrick almost stumbled into Amir's solid frame.

"Patrick, this is my boyfriend, Amir. Amir, this is my brother, Patrick," she said.

"What's up, man? Uh-oh, did I interrupt something? What, are you living here in my sister's house, man?" Patrick said, puffing out his chest and trying his best to sound imposing, but the liquor he'd consumed made it quite difficult.

Amir didn't bother to respond.

"Patrick, do you have any idea what time it is? What are you doing here?" Azure asked.

Patrick staggered into the living room and plopped down on the sofa.

"Uh…I just need to lie down for a little while, sis. I've been on the road for a long time…and I'm tired."

Patrick dropped his head back against the sofa and closed his eyes. Little Bud had been awakened from his slumber. He climbed off his fluffy bed in the corner of the living room, and approached Patrick, his gait still lopsided like a toddler's. Bud sniffed at Patrick's pants legs before letting out a disturbed yelp as Azure scooped the puppy up into her arms.

"Uh-uh, buddy, not so fast. First things first. You smell like you just escaped from the zoo. Go take a shower. Amir, could you put on some coffee, please?"

Amir took Bud from Azure's arms and headed to the kitchen, all the while listening to Patrick protest.

"Come on, Azure, I can't take no shower now. I just need some shut-eye, and I'll be good as new."

"You are not funking up my house with your foul-smelling self. Get up now," she commanded.

Azure pulled Patrick up from the sofa and ushered him into the bathroom. She turned on the water and handed him a towel, closing the door behind her. She stood outside while he bathed, her heart torn by the sight of him. When he finally emerged, he smelled a whole lot better, but looked just as bad. She threw a pair of sweatpants and a T-shirt at him and headed to the kitchen while he dressed. She was seated at the table with Amir when Patrick emerged.

"Sit down and drink," she ordered, pointing to the mug of steaming coffee on the table.

Patrick did as ordered. He took a few sips of coffee, closed his eyes and laid his head down onto the cool tabletop.

"What's going on, Patrick?" Azure pressed.

Realizing that she was not going to let him get some rest until he told her why he was there, with great difficulty he found the words to explain his current predicament.

By the time he'd finished, they'd pieced together his disjointed story. He'd had to leave Atlanta in a hurry, something about some woman and her boyfriend, a stolen car and forged checks. He'd hitchhiked all the way up to D.C.

and had spent the last three days with an old buddy of his who was living on disability payments in his mother's basement. He'd obviously not had a sober moment in quite some time and pretty soon, he'd be coming down off whatever high he'd been on.

Disgusted, Azure and Amir carried Patrick's bony frame into her spare bedroom. By the time his head hit the pillow, he was snoring heavily. Azure set the house alarm, motion detectors and all, so that she would be alerted if Patrick got up in the middle of the night and tried to depart with any of her belongings. She felt bad that Amir had to be there to witness this incident.

"You should go on home, Amir. I'll deal with my brother," she said halfheartedly. As much as she wished he hadn't had to meet her brother under these circumstances, there was a big part of her that was grateful that Amir was there.

"Nah, I'm not going anywhere. Who knows whether trouble followed him here or not. Besides, you shouldn't have to deal with this alone," he said.

Back in bed, he pulled her to him and held her in his arms. Her body was stiff at first, tension having its way with her. However, in his arms, against the warmth and stability of his chest, she relaxed. She was aware that she was becoming more and more dependent on Amir. His mere presence was enough to bring a smile to her face and a lightness to her heart. She'd thought that she would be frightened by this dependency, but ironically, it felt as normal as the ritual of night turning into day.

Silently, they dozed, neither one of them fully sleeping as they listened for sounds of Patrick stirring. Strangely, Azure did not feel embarrassed by her brother's behavior. She was certain that without them having to exchange a word, Amir understood her need to help her brother, even when he didn't want her help. Amir was prepared to do anything she asked him to in that regard, as well.

It was late in the afternoon when Patrick finally woke up. He was ashamed by his behavior and sheepishly introduced himself to Amir. Once Amir could see that things were under control, he excused himself and headed home. He wanted to give Azure the space she needed to deal with her brother, but implored her to call him if she needed anything.

Azure made more coffee and toasted a bagel for her brother. He said he wasn't hungry, but she knew that was due to the latest binge he'd been on. She sat down with him at the kitchen table and forced him to eat. She watched as he chewed slowly, his face gaunt and drawn-looking. His skin was ashen and his hair in need of cutting. Otherwise, he still looked a lot like their father. He had the same wide nose and full lips. His smile, whenever he chose to smile, was equally as handsome. Now, however, he looked older than their father did and nowhere near as attractive. Patrick caught her staring at him and grew self-conscious.

"I'm sorry, sis. I shouldn't have come here," he said.

"Patrick, you know my door is always open to you. I just wish you could find the strength to get your life together. It hurts me to see you like this," she said.

Patrick sat back in his seat and ran his hands through his hair.

"I'm tired of living like this. I really thought this time was going to be different. I hadn't done any drugs in almost six months. Hadn't had a drop to drink, either."

"So what happened?" Azure asked, trying desperately to understand.

"Man, seems like even when you're doing your thing and not looking for trouble…when you're doing everything in your power to stay away from it, it finds you. That shit is like a bloodhound looking for a runaway slave. I just can't get away from it…not for long," Patrick said, defeat making his words thick like syrup.

"That's such a cop-out, Patrick, and you know it. Temptations are a part of life—not just for you, but for everyone. We've all got issues, Patrick, but you just let yours run your life. Don't sit here and act like some sort of helpless victim."

"That's all fine and easy for you to say, Azure. Look at you. You've got the perfect life, always have had!" Patrick shouted.

"Perfect life? Are you crazy? I had a regular life and upbringing, no better and no worse than anyone else. Oh, so you think that because you had a witch for a mother that excuses the things you did?" Azure fired back.

She was sick and tired of playing the poor-Patrick game. How long was she going to be expected to make up for what his mother did or didn't do for him? She thought about Amir and what he'd had to endure as a child—losing both of his parents—and could not bring herself to feel sorry for Patrick. Amir had managed to grow up drug-free, without fifty babies running around and without a prison record. As far as she knew, the only thing Patrick could boast about was that he didn't have any children who he wasn't claiming—unless the mothers just hadn't caught up with him yet.

"At least you were wanted, Azure. Nobody wanted me…not her and not Dad. He bolted before I took my first steps. Came up here to D.C. and started the perfect little family."

"You think Dad left Maryland because of you? How

self-centered can you be? He left because he couldn't get along with your crazy mother. That had nothing to do with you. And he tried to get you up here with him every chance he could get. He and my mother reached out to you, but you refused their helping hands every single time."

"Are you really that blind, Azure? Did you ever stop to think about what went wrong between Dad and my mother?" Patrick questioned, his mouth screwed into a grimace.

Azure studied him, confused by what he was getting at and very sure she didn't want to know, whatever it was. Unfortunately, the motor was already running on the freight train headed at her, and she knew that there was nothing she could do to stop it.

"It was your mother. *Your* mother is what made *my* mother act crazy. Dad had been having an affair with Vetta for years behind my mother's back and when she found out, she kicked him out. Dear old Dad is the main reason why my mother was so damned bitter and angry."

Azure stood up from the table, fire in her eyes, aching to reach over and slap Patrick. There was no way what he was saying could be true. She wouldn't accept it.

"You're lying, Patrick. You are…Dad wouldn't…"

Azure turned her back to Patrick, unable to face him. Facing the windows behind the sink, she leaned her palms on the countertop. Patrick's words were pounding inside her head, reverberating in her ears. Memories of her childhood came back to her suddenly. Hushed conversations had usually surrounded Patrick's visits, and there were heated voices whenever Patrick's mother called. She never really knew how her parents had met, nor what their courtship was like. It wasn't something that they talked about around her, and she never questioned it.

All she could think about now was the old adage that hindsight is twenty-twenty. Some part of her had always known that there was something going on that she didn't know about. Finally, Azure turned around to face her brother. Patrick sat in the same place at the table, staring down at his hands. He felt her watching him, turned his eyes toward her and saw that she was looking for confirmation. She started to speak again, to demand that he take back what he had just said, but looked into his eyes and stopped herself, the truth smacking her in her own face. He wasn't lying…not about this. She could see it in his eyes, along with all the pain he'd been carrying for years. Slowly, she sank back into her seat, reeling from his shocking words. She shook her head from side to side.

"I'm sorry," she said at last.

"No, Azure, I'm sorry. I shouldn't have told you all of this…not in this way. Sometimes, I just hate what happened and what it did to my mother…to our lives."

"Patrick, people mess up sometimes. Even parents aren't above screwing up. They don't always do the right thing because sometimes they don't even know right from wrong themselves. But, Patrick, that's their mess. Nothing they've done has anything to do with what you're doing to yourself," Azure said softly.

Patrick shook his head slowly from side to side. Azure reached out and grasped Patrick's chin in her hand.

"Do you hear me, Patrick? That was their dirt to sort out, not yours. As messed up as the situation was, you shouldn't have allowed it to direct the entire path of your life. At some point you're going to have to take responsibility for yourself," she said, releasing Patrick's face at the end of her statement.

"I just feel so messed up all the time. Every time I try to do something right, I end up going all wrong. I know that probably doesn't make any sense to you. You're doing your thing…you've got the gallery, a nice house, everything."

"Patrick, those things didn't just get handed to me. I mean sure, Daddy helped me get the gallery, but he would have done the same thing for you. He's always wanted to help you. You don't even call him and all he does is worry about you."

"He does?"

Azure leaned back in her chair and threw her hands up into the air.

"What do you think, Patrick? He asks me all the time if I've heard from you and if you're okay. Sometimes he even gives me money and tells me to hold on to it in case you call needing something. Whatever faults he has, Daddy is a good man and he loves his children—both of us," Azure cried emphatically.

They both sat silently for a time, each lost in their own disturbed thoughts. Azure stood up and stretched. She went into her bedroom and changed into her swimsuit. At this point she realized that Patrick needed some time alone to think about things and so did she. She went outside for a swim, allowing the cool water to work the tension out of her body. She hated what Patrick had revealed to her, despised what it all meant in her own life. She now had to figure out a way to reconcile herself to the information in the same way that she had just advised Patrick to do. She needed to talk to someone about all of this and for the first time in a very long time, she realized that Yanté was not the best person. The fact that she was family would make revealing such personal information about her parents' past awkward, at best. A few laps later she grew even more honest with herself and admitted that Amir was the person she wanted to talk to. More and more he had become the ear she relied on, the confidant she sought out.

An hour later, while Azure lay on her back, floating and staring up at the sky, Patrick came out to join her. He sat on the deck and looked down at the pool, watching the minor ripples Azure created in the water.

"Listen, sis. I'm going to need to get up out of here. I've disturbed you enough. I'm sorry if I ran that dude out of here," Patrick said.

Azure climbed out of the pool and wrapped a beach towel around her body. She joined Patrick on the deck.

"You didn't run him out of here. He left on his own, figured we needed some time to talk. He'll be back."

"He seems like a cool brother. Is he treating you good?" Patrick asked, unable to resist being the overprotective brother.

"Very. I'd like you to spend some time around him, get to know him. He's had a pretty tough life, too, but he's making it somehow."

"Yeah, all right. Maybe next time. I'm not really in the mood for socializing."

"All right, Patrick," Azure said, knowing that pushing him into doing something he didn't want to do was pointless.

Patrick stayed with her for three more days. He slept most of the time and his appetite seemed to come back. By the end of the second day, he was even joking a bit, appearing more like his old self.

"I'm going to head down to Maryland. Maybe I'll see my mother for a minute. I've got to get my head together and, like they say, there's no place like home," he announced over breakfast on day three.

"Are you sure about that?" Azure asked, concerned that going back to his old stomping grounds was probably the last thing that Patrick needed to do right now.

"Yeah, I'm sure. Do you think you could buy me a ticket for the bus?"

"Yes, Patrick, of course."

They were eating the breakfast that Patrick had made. Since Patrick said that he wanted to get an early start, Azure showered and dressed as soon as they were done eating. She didn't hold out much hope that going back to Maryland would be good for him, but at least he was making an effort. She wondered how much longer her brother could last living the way he was living. She also wondered how much more she could take from him. Once again, she knew that for as long as he needed help, she'd continue to give it. While recognizing that she was what therapists called an enabler, she still could not imagine not doing everything in her power to help her brother. Maybe one day that would change, but for right now, he was her brother and she had it to give.

On the way to the bus station, they stopped at the mall. At her insistence, he picked out a couple of pairs of pants, a few shirts, some undergarments, toiletries and a pair of comfortable sneakers. She bought him a small travel bag to put his belongings in and waited with him for the next bus. From the terminal she bought him a couple of sandwiches, a few sodas and some snacks for the ride. She silenced his promises to pay her back, telling him that the only payback she wanted was for him to get himself together.

When the bus pulled into the gate, she hugged her

brother. It was a long, clinging hug in which she tried to make him understand how much she loved him and was pulling for him. She slipped a fifty-dollar bill into his pocket, kissed his cheek and watched him board the bus. She stood there waving until the bus pulled out of the terminal and disappeared into traffic.

Chapter 21

For the fourth week in a row, a large bouquet of assorted flowers was delivered to Yanté at the hotel. She had already contacted each of the florists from which they had been sent, but the clerks had been unable to tell her anything more than that the orders came in over the telephone and were paid for by postal money orders which came in the mail the next day. There was no return address on the envelopes and the money orders had already been submitted to the banks.

The name used by the purchaser was John Doe. When she commented to the fourth clerk how stupid it was for him to accept an order from a person with an obviously fake name, he had no comment. She had slammed down the phone, irritated beyond description. She didn't know exactly who she was angry with, but hoped that people steered clear of her for the remainder of the day because she was in an incredibly foul mood.

Today, looking at the expensive bouquet, she felt nauseous. This game had moved past anything resembling exciting, and she was growing anxious. She did not have the faintest idea who was doing this, but it was obviously someone who did not know her at all, for if he did, he would know that it was time to cut it out and make himself known. She thought briefly about calling the police, but realized how ridiculous and hysterical she would sound.

"Yes, officer, someone has been sending me flowers and leaving me notes on my car, telling me how attractive I am and that they're watching me." She could hear herself now and could imagine the officer's reaction. She dismissed the idea as quickly as it came.

Instead, she picked up the flowers and took them to the outer office, where she shoved aside a stack of magazines and placed them on an end table. She couldn't stand to look at them. Next she went out to the concierge's desk and instructed the staff to refuse any future flower deliveries with her name on them. Whoever was sending them would certainly get the point. She was not interested.

Chapter 22

Azure paced back and forth across the studio, intermittently exchanging one painting for another, adjusting the lighting in the room and wringing her hands. Yanté and her boss would be there at any moment, and as the hands on the clock crept forward, Azure grew more and more nervous. *What am I so afraid of?* The question stole its way into her consciousness, having never strayed far from it for long since Yanté posed it.

She heard the chime above the gallery door and instinctively sucked in a lungful of air. She straightened the collar of the crisp white cotton shirt she wore as she walked out front.

"Hey girl, what's doing?" Yanté's singsong voice preceded her through the door.

For some reason Azure was surprised when she laid eyes on Joan Dartmouth. She had expected a much older, far less attractive woman than the one who stood before her. This woman was tall and youthful looking, her slim frame clad in an off-white Prada pantsuit.

"Mrs. Dartmouth?" Azure queried as she extended a hand.

"Joan, please…just call me Joan," she said, shaking Azure's hand.

"Joan. Welcome to Monroe Galleries. Come on in and take a look around," Azure said nervously.

Azure kissed Yanté on the cheek and Yanté in turn gave Azure's sweaty hand a quick, reassuring squeeze.

"How long have you been in business?" Joan asked as she walked around the gallery, admiring the paintings and sculptures of artists whose work she knew and many whose work she didn't.

"I opened about a year or so ago. This place used to be a dry cleaners, believe it or not," Azure said. "My dad helped me with the financing, and with a little elbow grease, we turned this place around."

Several minutes passed in which Joan admired the works on the walls. Azure followed her, explaining some of the works when Joan lingered in front of them. Yanté remained at the front of the gallery, talking softly into her cell phone. From her body language and occasional giggle, Azure could tell she was talking to a man. Briefly, Azure allowed her thoughts to shift to Amir, and she silently wished he were there to hold her hand.

"So, I'm sure Yanté has told you how much I absolutely loved the painting she showed me," Joan said.

"Yes, she did, and I appreciate the compliment. But Mrs.…I mean, Joan, let me be honest with you. I wasn't entirely thrilled when Yanté told me that she'd shown you my painting. As you can see," Azure said, waving her hand to indicate the artwork around them, "I don't show my work."

"Yes, she did mention that. Frankly, I don't get it. If I had your talent…but be that as it may, Azure, while I may not understand your reasons for wanting to remain anonymous, I do respect your position. If you consider what I'm asking and then tell me that you don't want to pursue this, then I'll walk away. No hard feelings."

Azure weighed Joan's words, momentarily unsure of what to do. She had never thought of her art as a product, something to be critiqued, assessed or sold. She had not even opened the gallery with a desire to be in the business of art per se. For her, the satisfaction derived from sharing the beauty of an artist's interpretation of the world around him or her was what it was all about. The aesthetic nature of the images depicted on a particular medium was in and of itself the value, not how much someone was willing to pay for it. She had had to take courses in business, marketing and sales in order to balance her views with the realities of owning and operating a business. But now that she was being asked to view her own work as a business, she was uncertain whether she was capable of doing so. Even more, she wasn't sure if she wanted to.

She looked at Yanté's anxious face and then at Joan's interested one.

"Follow me, Joan," she said at last.

She led the way to the studio and stepped aside as Joan entered. There was a charged silence in the room as Joan walked slowly around the circumference. She inspected each piece with an interested eye.

"Azure, I am blown away. Words cannot even express

what I'm feeling right now. You are an amazing talent," Joan said finally.

"Thank you, Joan. That's kind of you." Azure smiled.

"No, I'm not being kind. You could make a lot of money on what you have here alone, not to mention having your name on the lips of people for years to come. I have to tell you…in a world where fame and fortune are as sought after as oxygen, it's amazing to meet someone as humble as you."

Joan's compliment made Azure feel good for several reasons. The first was that Joan was an art connoisseur in her own right. As owner of a major hotel, it was her job to create an attractive atmosphere for people. Secondly, the woman had gone out of her way to come to see Azure's work and was now praising it highly, something she wouldn't do unless she meant it. In the short time Azure had known her she had gotten the distinct sense that Joan Dartmouth was a very authentic person—one who could be taken at her word.

"I don't know what to say." Azure smiled. "You're making me blush. But honestly, Joan, I look at it this way— if a tree falls in the forest, it definitely makes a sound, whether or not there is someone there to hear it. I appreciate the effect that my paintings have on people, but they are really not designed for that purpose. I don't paint to get a reaction."

"So tell me, why do you paint?" Joan asked.

"Because as long as I am painting the things that I want to paint, in the way that I see them, I'm in control," Azure said firmly.

She realized now what her fears had been all about. Control. She did not want to lose control over the one thing in her life that had been constant, dependable and all hers.

No one could take her painting away from her in the way that so many other things had been snatched from her grasp. If she began to paint for other people, she was afraid that all of that would change.

She felt silly now and recognized that she needed to move forward. It was not that her fear was not valid, but, like a light being switched on, she realized that she had to face that fear and erase it.

"Where do we go from here?" she asked Joan.

Yanté let out a little squeal of delight, clapping her hands excitedly.

"First, I'd like to negotiate with you for a few pieces for the honeymoon suites at the hotel. I am willing to make you a considerable offer for your work. After that, you should consider having a show."

"A show? I don't know about that." Azure was skeptical about the soundness of that idea. "Where would I have it? No, I couldn't do that. I wouldn't even know who to invite to something like that."

"Slow down, dear. We can work out the details at a later time. If you'd let me, I'd like to help you out with this. You know, serve as sort of a sponsor or adviser. And, if you agree to pick up the tab for the expenses, I'll do my part gratis."

"Joan, I really don't know how to thank you," Azure said.

"No need to. It would be my pleasure." Joan smiled.

Joan and Azure made arrangements to meet in her office later in the week to begin planning for this exhibition. Yanté was excited beyond all reasoning, believing that she'd finally managed to draw her cousin out of the closet. Maybe Amir was due some of the credit, but still, she rejoiced. All in one short afternoon Azure had gone from closet artist to another realm of thinking and planning. When Joan and Yanté left the gallery to return to the hotel, Azure excitedly picked up the telephone to call Amir's cell. She was anxious to tell him her good news. She giggled as the line rang, acknowledging that lately she had been anxious to share a lot of things with him.

Chapter 23

"Have you told him yet?" Yanté asked.

She couldn't see Azure's face, but she knew that that familiar pained expression had probably descended upon it. She had held off asking this question for as long as she could, but it was apparent that things were progressing rather rapidly with Amir. It had only been a couple of months since he'd walked into Azure's life, but Yanté could see that already she had changed. She seemed to have blossomed, and, while Yanté was happy to see her cousin smiling and enjoying life, she also knew that she had yet to completely let go of her past.

"No, I haven't," Azure replied at length.

Her eyes were closed, and she tried to allow her mind to sink back into the relaxed state she'd been in before Yanté had posed her question. The women were both lying face up on cushioned tables, clad only in thin cloth gowns. They had just received full body massages from expert technicians at their favorite place in D.C., the Soul Day Spa located on Florida Avenue in the metro area. Yanté had discovered the spa while reading *Essence* magazine a while back, and they had been loyal customers ever since. The Vichy shower was a particularly fabulous treat for Azure, and if she could afford it, she'd undoubtedly come there every week.

During the past two hours they had both been kneaded, plucked and pinched until every nerve in their bodies had come alive. They had been scrubbed, rubbed and exfoliated until their skin shone like new pennies. Now conditioning cream covered their tension-free bodies and cucumber masks cooled the skin on their faces and necks.

For the first time in the past couple of weeks, Azure had allowed herself to forget the predicament she was in— leave it to Yanté to remind her.

"You do have to tell him, you know," Yanté scolded.

Yanté had decided that Amir was good for Azure. She had been glowing for the past few weeks, and that was a definite improvement on her overall attitude for the past couple of years. She would hate to see Azure ruin things with Amir over something that was an impossible dream.

"Don't you think I know that?" Azure snapped.

Precisely as Yanté had suspected, Azure had not truly moved on, but was instead stuck like gears on a stick shift between moving forward and going in Reverse.

"Are you still visiting?" Yanté asked cautiously.

"I haven't in the past couple of weeks. I feel guilty for staying away, but I'm sure I'd feel just as bad going." Azure sighed.

"I don't know why you live in this constant state of guilt.

You feel guilty over things which are totally out of your control. Why do you put yourself through that?" Yanté asked.

Azure closed her eyes, her mind traveling back to the last time she had visited Jevar, her former fiancé. She hated going to see him, but still felt it was her obligation to do so. For the past two and a half years, once a week she had driven forty-five minutes to Virginia to sit with Jevar for a few hours at his family's home. Every time, her heart ached to see the man she had once loved so dearly so changed in every way imaginable. Even Jevar's parents kept telling her that she shouldn't come so often, but she couldn't stop herself. It had been two years and five months since the accident that had propelled Jevar into a coma. For her, it seemed like an eternity.

All the medical evidence stated that Jevar would never recover. All the praying in the world had not made one bit of a difference. Azure had long since accepted all of this. Yet she could not move on. At first, she did not have the desire to move on—that is, until she'd met Amir. For the first time since the day she'd lost Jevar, she felt alive. Amir made her feel special, attractive and desirable. What was developing between them was different than what she had shared with Jevar. After all, she and Jevar had been high-school sweethearts and their love had matured along with them during their first three years in college. Had it not been for the accident, they would have graduated and married, as planned.

The feelings she had developed for Amir were mature and robust—full with the passion that comes with that maturity. They both bore scars from their pasts, and to her it felt as though Amir had everything it would take to help her heal. However, before that could happen, she would have to do two things: one, be honest with him; and two, bury the past, once and for all.

"Yanté, do you believe in soul mates?" Azure asked at length.

Yanté had been dozing, not expecting Azure to respond to her. If there was one thing her cousin was good at, it was dropping a subject like a hot potato when it grew too uncomfortable for her.

"Hmm, soul mates…that's a notion that people toss around a lot, but I'm not sure if it is something as simple as it is made out to be. I think there are truly people who are destined to be together, but I don't necessarily believe that there is just one person for every person. Maybe God created four or five…maybe even ten people who should be together. He makes sure those people are born in or around the same decade, in the same geographic region and then…the rest is up to us. If we are careful and patient, eventually we bump into one or two of our predestined mates. Voilà! There you have it—soul mates. On the other hand, if we are impatient and reckless, we jump in and out of relationships with the wrong people and block the way for the right ones to come into our lives."

"That's actually not a bad philosophy, except for one major thing. How can you be sure that you've bumped into one or more of the right people for you?" Azure asked.

"That's easy. Like my mama always says—listen to your heart because that's the one thing that never lies."

Aunt Melissa strikes again.

Chapter 24

"You're so tense," Azure said. She was straddling the backs of Amir's thighs, slowly massaging his back and neck, which felt like impenetrable stone beneath her fingers.

Amir did not respond. He closed his eyes and enjoyed her touch. It seemed as if his world was beginning to close in on him and all of the tension and stress had settled into his body. For the first time in about five years, he had come down with a head cold. All of the benefits from his healthy living, nutritious eating and workout regimen seemed to be going out the window as he felt the pressure of the life changes he was trying to make.

He had told Tavares that as long as Tavares lived the life-style he was living, Amir could not be around him. He was out of the game. Unequivocally, no turning back—being around Tavares and the crew would undermine everything he had been trying to build for himself. Tavares had not responded, had simply hung up the phone. That was three days ago and he had not heard from his brother since. He had, however, received a visit from Sean, who had pulled no punches.

"What's up with you, man?" Sean had asked.

"What do you mean?" Amir replied.

"You know what the hell I mean. Tavares tells me from now on I've got to handle your business, permanently. I thought this was just a temporary thing, but apparently it isn't. He doesn't give any explanation...nothing. I question him and he tells me to leave it alone. He won't say nothing else. Doesn't want to discuss it. So I'm coming to get the story right out of the horse's mouth. What's up?"

There was no denying that Sean was hot under his collar and Amir was immediately thrown on the defensive. He appreciated neither Sean's visit nor his tone of voice, feeling that he didn't owe any of them anything. Yet he didn't want to make things bad for Tavares, and he knew that getting in Sean's face right now wouldn't be the best way to handle this. It would only cause more slack for Tavares. So he kept his cool and ignored the hostility in Sean's voice.

"Listen, man, it's precisely like Tavares said. I'm not going to be hanging around with you guys. I'm doing things on my own, in my own way and a complete break is what's best. When I first left, I was just trying to get my head straight, which I've done."

"Get your head straight? What is that supposed to mean? Man, look, I don't know what the hell is going on here, but what makes you think it's okay just to walk away...without even saying anything to anybody?" Sean said.

"Look, I spoke to Tavares. I had been talking to him ut my plans for a long time. I'm building a career for myself, something that I can be proud of, and I'm sorry if you've got a problem with it, but I don't owe you an explanation, Sean."

"Oh, is that what you think? Well, let me clue you in to something...your brother ain't running this thing by himself. I've invested a lot of time and energy to see this business grow, and I'm not about to let anybody jeopardize that."

"Would you listen to yourself. *Business.* You say that like you're selling real estate or something. What you guys are doing ain't no business, man. What you...what I was doing...that's nothing to be proud of," Amir said, his voice full of shame and regret.

"Man, go ahead with all that shit you're talking. Anything that makes money is a business. Oh, so you've developed a conscience now, and what, the rest of us are supposed to stop getting our pockets fat?"

"No, Sean, the rest of you are supposed to do whatever you need to do for yourselves. I hope my brother comes to his senses one day...you, too, for that matter, because eventually stuff catches up with you. I just know that I need to be able to sleep at night," Amir yelled angrily.

The muscles in Sean's lean brown jaw tightened as his eyes fixed on Amir's face. Amir's body immediately grew even tenser than it was, his gut telling him to remain on guard. Amir would hate to have to get into a fistfight with Sean, but he was prepared to throw down if he had to.

The two men squared off, neither one backing down. Finally, through clenched teeth, Sean spat out, "Tell you what, Amir. While you're doing all this *sleeping at night,* watch yourself. Don't go getting all self-righteous and start running your mouth, talking too much to the wrong people about us or else—"

"Or else what? Are you supposed to be threatening me, Sean? 'Cause if so, you might as well either back it up right now, or get the hell out of my face…and out of my apartment."

Sean glared at Amir for a moment longer before letting out a harsh chuckle.

"Whatever, man," he said as he turned toward the apartment door. "Just remember what I said. Me and the fellas are just trying to eat…same as everybody else."

"Yeah…right," Amir said after he'd slammed his apartment door shut behind Sean.

He couldn't believe that Sean and the others would think that he would do anything to harm Tavares. He had no intentions of causing any problems for any of them. The steps he was taking were about him and what he wanted for his life. He would never purport to judge someone else. He hoped that Tavares knew and understood that, even if the others didn't. Either way, he couldn't concern himself too much. He was devoted to trying to be a successful entrepreneur and an honorable man.

"Hello, Earth to Amir," Azure said, pulling him back to the present.

Her fingers felt amazing on his back; the hard knots that had kept his muscles at attention for what seemed like forever buckled beneath her touch. One by one, she eased away the rough spots, making him feel as if he was floating. If only things could be like this every second of every day.

In spite of his desire and his concrete efforts to move completely away from his old lifestyle, sometimes he worried that he wouldn't make it. He was on edge, and Sean's visit had done much to cause his anxiety to heighten. This was due in large part to the fact that he felt as if he were deceiving Azure. Once again, he wanted to tell her, wanted to lay his burden down at her feet and hope that she found it in her heart to understand him. His brain searched for the words, but nothing seemed intelligible to him. He sighed, feeling as though he were stuck in the check position in a never-ending game of chess. Checkmate was just a quick move or two away.

Azure gathered his locks in her hand, lifting them. She kissed the back of his neck tenderly.

"Baby," he whispered from the core of his soul.

He turned onto his side, pulling her slowly down beside him on the bed. He placed his palm on the side of her face, where the angle of her chin gave way to a graceful neck.

"I love you," he said plainly, as if he had said it a thousand times. In fact, he had shouted it in his brain and in his heart many times, the truth of it undeniable. Finally, when he had been seeking the words to tell her of his past indiscretions and to beg for her understanding, these were the only words that came out.

Azure considered his serious countenance and the depth of those three words was apparent. It was as if his soul had spoken to hers because the words were her own. Try as she might to convince herself that it was too soon to feel the way she felt for Amir, there it was, this overwhelming, all-encompassing feeling of being connected to another human being. She realized that her moment of truth had come. It was time to tell Amir about Jevar because if they had any hopes of moving forward, her past would need to be dealt with. She shifted her gaze from his face, momentarily afraid to look him in the eye. In that subtle movement, her distress was clear to him.

"Say something," he commanded, hope deepening his voice.

He wanted to hear from her own mouth that she did not feel the same way. He believed that would make things easier for him because if she did not share his feelings, he would not have to feel so guilty about who he was.

"I haven't been honest with you, Amir. You say you love me, but you don't really know me. There's so much… there's someone else," she breathed.

Her heart raced as she waited for him to turn away from her as she had expected. How could he not? What man would stay after confessing his love and finding out that there was another man blocking the way?

"I don't believe you," he said at length.

He couldn't believe that there was someone else because he had seen the way she looked at him. It was impossible to think that she could look at him the way she had, her eyes reaching into him and touching his soul, beckoning him, and also be looking at another man in that way. It wasn't foolish, manly pride that made him feel that she was lying. He wasn't that naive. No, it was more that his gut told him, and that intuitive feeling was strong enough to make him willing to stake everything he owned.

"Amir, let me explain. I don't mean that I'm seeing someone else. I wish it were that simple."

"So what do you mean?"

Azure sat up and attempted to get out of the bed altogether, but Amir clasped his fingers around her upper arm and held her in place. He didn't want her physically to move away from him as she told him whatever it was she was trying to tell him. He believed that as long as he could touch her and keep her within reach, the energy that flowed between them would be a strong enough force to keep what they had intact.

His eyes held hers, commanding her and at the same time pleading with her. She took a deep breath as if to expel the fear that she had been holding on to for so long.

"There was someone," she began in a low voice. "Someone who once meant...who means a lot to me."

"You keep going from the present tense to the past. Now I'm no English teacher but even I know that you can't use both at the same time. Which is it?" Amir asked.

Azure considered his question, looking deep inside herself to find the answer.

"It's both," she said at last. "This relationship never really ended...at least not in concrete terms. We met in high school...Introduction to Fine Arts class. I remember how we would argue about the merits of transcendentalism in art for hours. I thought he was the most opinionated jerk I'd ever met. But soon it became apparent to everyone around us that the reason why we disagreed so much was because we liked each other. By the end of our junior year, we were inseparable."

Amir remained silent, listening intently. That was one of the things she had grown to love so much about him, this ability to listen without interrupting. He listened with more than just his ears to everything she had to say, and he didn't judge, the only expression on his face one of concentration, as if what she was saying was the most important thing he'd ever heard. Only a person with great self-confidence was capable of this type of selflessness, because most people listened only long enough to find how what was being said related to themselves.

"We dated all through high school, and the summer

after graduation he asked me to marry him. His mom threw us a blow-out combination graduation and engagement party and even my parents were happy for us. Then in the fall, we headed down to Atlanta for college. Even though we went to different schools, we were less than an hour's drive apart, so we still saw each other all the time. I thought my life was so perfect. At a time when most people are still trying to find themselves, here I had found a man who I could spend the rest of my life with. We had it all worked out, and you couldn't tell me that things wouldn't be perfect for us."

Azure choked on these last words. She had been fighting so hard to hold it together and not to cry, but suddenly the unfairness of the fact that she had held such high expectations for her life, only to have them crushed without warning, cut freshly into her already wounded heart.

"What happened?" Amir asked gently, as he rubbed her arm.

"Our junior year...spring break," she said, forcing herself to regain control and continue. "A bunch of us decided to go to Cancún. The first few days down there were a blast. We partied, went rock climbing, scuba diving; you name it, we did it. By the fourth day, I was wiped out. Early that morning Jevar, my fiancé, and a few of the guys wanted to check out this spot they'd heard about from the locals. Supposedly, it was deep in this rain forest and they had fresh-water springs and some other really cool stuff. I told him I was too tired and that he should go ahead without me." She paused. "Those were the last words he and I ever exchanged."

Without saying a word, Amir pulled her into his arms. Her body relaxed easily into his as she wept. She had cried many tears over Jevar. Every time she thought that she had none left to cry, there they were spilling from her eyes, pulling at her gut, until she was lost in a sea of them. This time, however, it felt different. With each sob she felt as though she was letting go of something that had been holding her hostage for two and a half years. The more she cried, the emptier she felt and she welcomed that emptiness.

"Tell me what happened," Amir said after a long while had passed. He hated to push her, but he had to know. If he was, in fact, on the brink of losing her for whatever reason, then he needed to know up front.

"They rented some ATVs and rode up the side of a mountain. It was pretty treacherous terrain—narrow, curving roads. They said he hit a turn too fast and...his injuries were so severe they didn't think he'd make it to the hospital. But he made it, and I was there...by his side, for days. Finally, the hospital and the doctors said they had done all they could do for him. His parents had him flown back here and he was placed in one of the best facilities for coma patients." A sharp sniffle interrupted her.

"He stayed in a coma for three months. His body recovered from the injuries and there was significant brain activity, so we remained hopeful. I kept praying that he would wake up, and I truly believed that once he did, everything would be okay. I promised to see him through it. I kept promising that if he would just wake up, I'd be right there for him. And then it happened. He woke up...just like that. We were all so overjoyed. But he couldn't speak. He couldn't control his bodily movements or functions. Nothing. He just stared into space, his eyes expressionless, except for an occasional blink or tear. The doctors said that was as good as it would get. He had suffered extensive brain damage in all of the areas related to his motor, comprehension and language skills. He was seriously impaired and would spend the rest of his life that way."

"What about a second opinion?" Amir asked.

"Second, third, fiftieth. It didn't matter. They all said the same thing. I didn't believe them. I kept telling myself that they were all wrong. I refused to accept that this was happening to me…to us. We had so much to do, so many plans."

"I'm sorry, baby," Amir said softly, continuing to hold her tightly.

Azure pulled back from him.

"Don't be so understanding, Amir. Please…you should be angry with me. I didn't mean to mislead you. When I met you, I swear I wasn't looking for anyone. The last thing I wanted to do was get involved with someone. I tried to ignore it, but from the moment I met you, I wanted you. I wanted to be with you, to get to know you. That first night, when we talked, it was like a part of me opened up to you and all this stuff just came oozing out. It felt so natural, and looking back, I know that was selfish of me. I didn't want that feeling to end."

"There's nothing wrong with that. Baby, I felt exactly the same way."

"Listen to what I'm saying, Amir. I'm still tied to him. I don't know how to, or if I'll ever be able to let him go. I still visit him…and his family. And every time I do, I feel as though I should just lie down beside him and stay there forever."

Azure's words hit Amir in the gut, making him lose his breath for a moment. Could it be that he had lost her before he ever really had her?

"It was wrong of me to get involved with you and to let

things go this far when I know that there's a part of me that died the day I lost Jevar," she continued. "I don't think I can ever get that piece of myself back, and I don't have the right to ask you to take me this way…not when I can't give you all of me."

"Azure, don't you see that what you've given me so far is more than I ever thought I would have? I know you're not perfect and neither am I. But what would be wrong, baby, is if we lose what we've found with each other, because I don't think either of us will ever find it again. I'm sorry that you've gone through what you have. It sounds to me like you and Jevar were very much in love. While that should make me feel jealous, it doesn't. It makes me proud. You've stood by a man and your love for him even when there was no hope left. I could only hope that one day you'd feel as strongly for me."

"I do already," Azure said.

"Then why are you trying to run away from it?"

"I'm scared," Azure admitted in a whisper. "I can't go through it again. I can't lose like that again, Amir."

"Oh, baby," he said, showering her moist face with a dozen tender kisses. "You're not going to lose me…not unless you want to. I promise you."

"You can't promise that, Amir."

Azure searched his eyes, wanting to believe him in spite of the naysayer in her mind.

"Look, I'm not saying that it doesn't bother me at all, knowing that another man holds a piece of your heart. But I wasn't stupid enough to think that you didn't have a past, either. Let's just take this one day at a time and see what happens. You won't ever forget about Jevar, and you shouldn't—not completely. But maybe you'll find room for me, just a little," Amir said, pinching his thumb and forefinger together. He cocked his head to one side and smiled a weak smile, which prompted laughter from Azure. Through teary eyes, she smiled.

"You think you're cute, don't you?"

"Yeah, well, I do have a little something going on."

Azure shoved him playfully, glad that the weight of her secret was now off her shoulders. She didn't know what would happen in the future, or even if there was a future for them. All she knew right now was that she felt better than she had in over two years, and Amir had a lot to do with that.

She pushed him backward on the bed and covered his lips with kisses from her own. As she rubbed her soft body over his hard one, feeling him respond, she felt the emptiness within her slowly begin to fill. This time, while the passion between them remained as ardent as every time before, there was also an intimate sweetness as two souls comforted each other.

Chapter 25

Yanté sat staring at her computer screen, unable to focus on the report in front of her. She hadn't slept a wink the night before and her nerves were a little frayed. The secret admirer had struck again, and this time she was nowhere near being amused.

She had arrived home the night before and found a package waiting for her on her doorstep. At first she'd assumed it was a pair of shoes she'd ordered from the Internet, but noticed that no courier labeling was present on the box. It was wrapped in plain brown paper without a name and address for either the sender or the recipient. She picked up the box and shook it gently. The contents rattled, which piqued her curiosity.

She went inside and, without thinking, tore the wrapping off the package. The box was a plain white box like those used for pastries or for delicate objects purchased in specialty stores. She opened the box, peeled back a layer of tissue paper and gasped. Inside was a porcelain doll whose arms, legs and head had been separated from her torso.

A shiver went down Yanté's spine as she looked at the doll. She quickly pushed the tissue paper back into the box and closed the lid. She carried the box out back to her trash can and roughly tossed it inside. Back inside her home, she locked the door and stood with her back against it, trying to calm her racing heartbeat. She began to rationalize, thinking that maybe it was sent to her by mistake. Either that or the sender merely forgot to write her a note. None of that explained why the outside of the box bore no information nor did it explain the fact that the doll was broken into pieces. Had it just been damaged during transit, it was hard for her to believe that the torso would have been so perfectly separated from the limbs and head, almost dissected.

Just then she heard her cell phone ringing inside her purse. She snatched the purse off the table and retrieved the cell phone. The words Private Number were displayed. With a flip of her thumb, she opened the phone.

"Hello," she snapped.

"Didn't you like my present?" a harsh male voice whispered.

"Look, you jackass, I don't know why you're bothering me, but it's not cute and I'm certainly not impressed. So what you need to do is find somebody else to mess with 'cause trust, you don't want one of this. Now, either you leave me the hell alone or I will call the cops. Or better yet, keep it up, and I'll find you and kick your ass myself!" Yanté shouted.

The line went dead.

Now, as she thought back on the incident, she began to feel for the first time as though this situation was not going to turn out well. She thought again about telling someone, but changed her mind. She didn't like people to worry or fuss over her. That wasn't her style. She was the one who usually took care of other people. Besides, she refused to let this idiot think he'd gotten to her.

She went to work at her desk, blocking all negative thoughts out of her mind. Her cell phone rang again, causing her to tense up instantly. She looked at the display and recognized the telephone number of Carl, the doctor she'd been dating.

By the time she hung up, a smile had returned to her pretty face. Carl had been given tickets at the last minute to a play at a local theater that night and wanted to know if she was free to accompany him. Although she hadn't planned on going out, she eagerly accepted, grateful for the distraction. An evening out in the company of a refined, handsome man would surely rid her of all the ill feelings the mystery jerk had been bringing her.

Chapter 26

"He looked a little upset. Everything all right?" Azure asked Amir when he reentered his apartment. He had been out in the hallway talking to Raymond Cousins, who'd appeared on his doorstep unannounced and unwelcome. Cousins was one of the hired husbands who worked for Tavares. Already on his third marriage, Cousins believed this one would be more profitable than any of the others.

Amir shut the door and joined her in the kitchen area, where she was washing the dishes from the dinner of baked turkey wings, candied yams and steamed cabbage that Amir had made for her. In the few months when he'd lived with his grandmother as a child, he had improved on the cooking skills which his mother had already taught him. Later, when he and his brother and sister were on their own, it was Amir who prepared most of the meals while Tavares was out making money and Bridgette was busy with schoolwork.

"Uh…yeah. Well, he'll be okay. He, uh…it's just girl trouble," Amir said.

He had trouble lying to Azure's face like that, but he felt trapped.

"Aah, so he came to get advice from you, of all people?"

"Hey, what is that supposed to mean? I'll have you know I am well versed in the arts of love," Amir replied indignantly.

He pressed his body against her from behind, reaching his arms around her to cup her breasts. He kissed the back of her neck with feathery strokes. With a soapy hand, she reached back and stroked his cheek.

"Knock it off, buddy. We've got to meet Yanté in twenty minutes. Get yourself together."

"All I need is ten," he pleaded, continuing to rub his lips along the nape of her neck.

"Ha! Some expert you are." She laughed.

Amir gave her one last peck on the cheek and headed into the bathroom. He closed the door behind him, letting out a heavy sigh. Leaning on the sink, he peered at himself in the mirror. The five-o'clock shadow that he'd been toying with keeping did nothing to hide the two-faced man behind it. He could not believe that Raymond had had the nerve to come to his apartment. What's more, he couldn't fathom how the man even knew where he lived. Raymond had come to give Amir a message to deliver to Tavares and the crew. He said that he'd decided that he didn't need their services any longer and wanted them to consider their agreement null and void. Raymond claimed that he wanted the split to be amicable and that he figured that since Amir had always been the more reasonable of the bunch, it'd be best to talk this out with him first.

Amir didn't hesitate to voice his wrathful displeasure at Raymond's having come to his apartment.

"I don't know why you think you have a friend or an ally in me, but you don't. I can't help you. I'm not involved in my brother's business anymore and even if I was, I'm not a messenger."

"Come on, Amir, man. You're the only one who was always cool. Your brother…he's on some other level, man. Now, I don't want this to turn into something ugly—"

"Are you threatening my brother?" Amir asked.

Without being aware of it, Amir held his fists clenched and the veins in his neck grew taut.

"I don't believe in threats, Amir, but hey, a man's got to protect himself," Raymond had replied.

Amir stewed silently for a moment, fighting the urge to punch Raymond in his face. The only thing that stopped him was the fact that Azure was on the other side of the door. She had been the one who'd answered the doorbell, since Amir was in the shower. He'd come out of the bathroom to find Raymond chatting her up. He'd hustled Raymond into the hallway with barely an introduction.

He hated Raymond's smug face. Just because a man draped Armani suits and alligator shoes over his body did not make him less of a bum. The clothes on Raymond's back were just a covering, and his filthy heart was as visible as if he were transparent.

Amir moved in closer to Raymond, their faces separated by a mere couple of inches.

"Don't ever come here again. I have nothing to do with your situation, or any of that stuff for that matter. Not anymore. But I'm going to give you a little friendly advice for the road—don't cross my brother. It wouldn't be a smart move on your part, not smart at all."

"Now who's the one throwing threats around?" Raymond asked.

"No threat. Hey, man, it's your life and, frankly, I don't really give a damn. As I said, it's none of my business anymore."

Amir turned to go back into his apartment. Before he opened the door, he looked back at Raymond.

"Don't *ever* come here again," he repeated before going back inside.

It seemed ironic to Amir that just when things seemed to be going better than ever for him, something came along with the potential to screw them up. He had just received an offer to promote an album-release party for a pop singer, an opportunity that would help his new career really get off the ground. He'd also heard from the network that he'd planned a party for a while back; they would definitely be sending some work his way soon. He'd awakened in the morning feeling as though he was on that road to being the man he wanted to be, and it felt better than good. He and Azure were closer than ever, and she seemed to be growing excited about her upcoming art show. Why couldn't things just keep progressing without problems rearing up?

Amir knew the answer to that question even while he posed it. Everything that was done in the dark eventually came to the light. He and Tavares had been living a life that was bound to come back on them both—hard. He had thought that he could distance himself from it forever and eventually forget about it entirely. He had truly believed that he could make up for all of his bad deeds by doing good and by living a respectable life. He tried to tell himself that if and when something from his past came out, he and Azure would be so deeply in love that nothing could tear them apart. That was what he whispered to himself in that tiny bathroom, in front of the mirror that showed his two faces. Unfortunately, that didn't stop his stomach from churning. Still, he could not bring himself to come clean with her.

They spent the night at a jazz revue Yanté had invited them to at a trendy nightclub in the metro area. Musicians who had played for some of the legendary jazz singers of the era were there and they performed a medley of some of the unforgettable tunes that were still burning up the airwaves on certain radio stations. It was a lovely evening, and Amir momentarily pushed aside his doubts and his fears. It was also the first time Yanté and Amir had seen each other since she'd learned that he and Azure were dating. He had thought things might be slightly awkward, given the fact that she had been attracted to him, but she seemed to be happy for them.

"So, you and my cousin seem to be doing well," Yanté said at one point in the evening when Azure had excused herself to go to the ladies' room.

"Yes, things are going pretty good between us," Amir responded.

"I just want you to know that I'm happy for her...and for you. I haven't seen her this full of life in a very long time, so you must be doing something right."

Amir laughed. "I'd like to think so."

"I want you to take into consideration that she's been through a lot and she really deserves some happiness," Yanté continued.

"Happiness is all I'm planning to give her," Amir stated.

"Are you sure about that?"

"What are you trying to get at, Yanté?" Amir asked suspiciously.

Yanté was one of those beautiful women whom a man would underestimate, being taken in by her beauty, until it was too late. She was as sharp as a samurai's sword, and he didn't doubt that she could cut like one. Tonight, wearing a dress that flattered her amazing body, her hair done just right and her face flawless, she had men sneaking peeks at her over their brandy glasses while their wives sat chatting at their sides. But Amir knew that the surface was just that, and that inside was a woman who took no prisoners in the face of a threat to herself or someone she loved.

"I'm just saying, you're a very nice-looking man, I'm sure you know that. Women probably trip themselves up trying to get to you. But Azure is a one-man type of woman, feel me? She believes in monogamy, and I'd hate for her to have some hard-up woman stepping to her because of you. We don't do chick fights."

Amir looked Yanté squarely in the eye, measuring his words carefully.

"That's not my style, Yanté. Look, I'm in love with your cousin. She means more to me than any woman I've ever dealt with, and I have no intentions of losing her, especially not over some dumbness. Do you *feel me?*"

"Fair enough. I didn't mean to offend or insult you," Yanté explained. "I just shoot straight and let the chips fall where they may."

"No offense taken," Amir said, extending his hand to her.

Yanté shook his hand, covering it with her free one, just as Azure approached. Her smile was sweet, but the meaning in her eyes was clear. Yanté was mother hen and father bear all rolled up into one when it came to Azure.

"What are you two cooking up out here?" Azure asked.

"Nothing much. Just telling this man of yours that he'd better be taking good care of you." Yanté smiled.

"Oh, baby. She didn't frighten you, did she? Don't pay her any attention. She doesn't even carry the shotgun around with her anymore," Azure said, kissing Amir's cheek.

"I'm not that bad!" Yanté exclaimed.

The trio laughed, Amir understanding precisely where Yanté was coming from and respecting it all the same. It was nice to know that Azure had someone who had her back like that. He hoped, however, there'd never be another day when she'd need to be supported by anyone but him.

Azure spent the next few days planning for her exhibition, which was to take place at Joan Dartmouth's estate. Amir gave her the space she needed to get organized, assisting her whenever she needed him. However, while missing her every moment that she was unavailable to him, he also took advantage of the free time to make plans for himself.

He had been thinking a lot lately of his parents' home in Barbados. As children, he and Tavares had visited the sophisticated British Caribbean island with their parents once, before Bridgette was born. Their father's parents had left him a small piece of land in Bridgetown, which, at that time, was used primarily for sugarcane growing. Now that the land belonged to him, he had no idea what condition it was in, nor what it was being used for. If someone was, in fact, using the lands to raise crops, he was probably owed money for its use. In any event, he would like to at least see the area and find out a little more about where his parents came from.

Fortunately, Tavares had held on to their parents' documents. In spite of his desire to keep his distance from

Tavares and the crew, he needed to pay the brownstone a visit. He waited until evening before making the trip. He checked the block to make sure that none of their cars were in sight and, using his spare key, let himself in. In a closet in Tavares's apartment, Amir spent an hour poring through the two boxes of papers, until he found the deed to the land in Barbados. He also found his parents' marriage license and birth and death certificates as well as a host of old photographs and report cards from when he, Bridgette and Tavares were kids. He scratched out a quick note to Tavares that he had taken the papers and left it inside one of the now almost-empty boxes.

With a plan to surprise Azure in mind, he visited a travel agent and found out as much as he could about Barbados. After consulting Yanté about Azure's schedule, he booked a hotel suite in Bridgetown and made airplane reservations for them. Yanté was bubbling with excitement as she helped Amir prepare his surprise for Azure, but he was nervous to say the least. Obviously, he couldn't share this fact with Yanté because the thing that was eating him up was the thing that could break him and Azure up for good. In taking this trip he hoped to find the courage to tell Azure about his life, which now seemed a million miles in the past, and the things he had done wrong. Maybe while they were tucked away in their own private refuge, he wouldn't come out looking so bad. He could only hope that in a different atmosphere, some of the ugliness could be shaved away and Azure would still see him for the man that he was.

These were the thoughts that occupied his mind while love propelled him forward.

Chapter 27

As the driver pulled the car off the main road, Azure gasped. The driver leaned out his window and waved a pass card in front of the security box and a huge wrought-iron gate swung open slowly. The driveway leading up to the Dartmouth estate was half a city block long. The property was carpeted with acre upon acre of sprawling green and surrounded by a high stone wall on the east, west and south sides, the entrance gate at the north. As they approached the mansion, Azure saw tennis courts to her left and a salt-water pool accented by a ten-foot cascading waterfall to her right.

The mansion itself was a brick Victorian colonial with tall windows and a stately facade.

The anxiety she had been feeling all morning intensified exponentially as she climbed out of the car. Once again she was overcome by the belief that she was out of her league. Joan Dartmouth was loaded, and the types of people in her circle were equally as wealthy. Why Joan believed that they would travel out to this countryside estate to purchase artwork from an unknown little city girl was inexplicable. She kicked herself, silently wishing that she had never allowed Yanté and Joan to talk her into doing this exhibition. Just when she was contemplating jumping back into the car and speeding back to the other side of town, the front door of the house was flung open.

"Azure, you're here! Perfect timing. Those idiots we hired are making a mess of the showing. Come, come. You've got to get in there."

"What's wrong?" Azure cried, Joan's excited plea causing her to momentarily cast aside her own jitters.

"They're rearranging everything. Not following the map you laid out at all. Something about insufficient lighting and some other nonsense. I'm about two seconds from firing both of them."

"All right, calm down, Joan. We'll just see about this."

Azure followed Joan into the house, her head spinning to take in the sights in every direction. She was enthralled by the grandeur of the mansion. The foyer alone was the size of a large hotel lobby and equally as elaborate. Joan whizzed her down a long hallway and pushed open two oversize doors that led to a large room with vaulted ceilings, an oversize fireplace and an immense chandelier. Both the walls and the sheer curtains that adorned the numerous windows were a champagne color. The parquet floors gleamed, bouncing the sunlight that poured from outside in every direction.

The room was a breathtaking sea of activity, as several overall-clad men buzzed about. Azure spent the next hour overseeing the hanging of her paintings. By the time she had had items shifted, moved, raised or lowered, she was finally satisfied and she had less than an hour before the guests would begin arriving. As the caterers began rolling in tables, linen, chafing dishes and the like, Joan whisked her out of the room and upstairs. They traveled down a long corridor and into one of the guest rooms at the end. Joan left Azure alone to get ready, with a strong admonishment not to dawdle.

Azure sat down on the chaise lounge and took a deep breath. She couldn't believe all of this was happening. It was like being caught up in a whirlwind and being spun out of control. She had no idea where she was going to land and the thought made her dizzy. With sweaty palms she unzipped her garment bag and exposed the dress Yanté had picked out for her. It was a sleek evening gown with spaghetti straps from Versace. Azure had been reluctant when Yanté first selected the dress, feeling it was too racy for her and way too pricey, but after trying it on, she had to admit that it looked good on her. Against her dark-brown skin, the jade color gave off a romantic glow.

Azure took her time getting dressed, taking grateful sips from the glass of champagne Joan had sent up to help her relax. She carefully applied her makeup, wanting to have an evening look but not to appear overdone. Finally, when she was satisfied that everything was as perfect as it was ever going to be, she stared at her reflection in the mirror, attempting to convince herself that things would turn out just the way they were supposed to.

She had never believed in luck or destiny before. She believed that life was what you made it and anything good that came to a person was the result of hard work and determination. However, having gone through the trials and tribulations that had been thrown at her and having made it out on the other side had taught her that sometimes it didn't matter if you did everything right or everything wrong. There were certain things that were destined to be. For a long time she had been sure that Jevar and she would be together forever, and then that dream had disappeared like smoke. At that point she believed that having to bear that loss meant that she was set to live in darkness and solitude for the rest of her life. Yet when she'd least expected it, Amir had walked in and turned on the lights. She had not willed him to her, nor had she worked or planned her way into his life. There was nothing else to attribute their chance meeting and purposeful connection to but fate. Their paths were meant to cross and once that had happened, their souls connected. For that she was eternally grateful.

While it seemed Amir had touched the very core of her as a woman, her art represented who she was as a child of God. All of her hopes, dreams, pains and pleasures were represented in the brushstrokes that created the images which now adorned Joan Dartmouth's living room. For that, too, she was grateful. If she was meant to find fame and fortune through her paintings, so be it. More importantly to her, if what she had to say through her work could touch someone else's soul, then who was she not to allow that miracle to happen?

She took another deep breath as she prepared herself to go downstairs. A soft knock on the door captured her attention.

"Come in," she called.

A head full of light-brown locks adorning a sexy face leaned into the doorway.

"Hey, babe," Amir said.

He stepped completely into the room, shutting the door

behind him. Azure crossed the room and kissed Amir lightly on the lips.

"Hey, yourself." She smiled.

"Damn, girl, you look good," he bellowed, taking a step away from Azure to admire her fully.

"Why, thank you very much," she joked, spinning around slowly so that he could check her out from every angle.

He pulled her to him, kissing her deeply. She responded with every fiber of her being, still so enamored by him even after months of dating. She was amazed at the passion he inspired in her, making her feel like the most beautiful woman with his touch and his look, long before he spoke any words.

"I'm proud of you," he said when they parted at last.

"I haven't done anything," she said, smiling.

"You've got a steady stream of people coming through those doors downstairs, oohing and aahing, who I'm sure would disagree."

"What? Are people here already?" she said as she glanced at her wristwatch and realized that she had passed more than an hour in what seemed like only minutes. "Oh, my goodness. I'm supposed to be down there. Why didn't someone come to get me earlier?"

Azure's panic-stricken outburst prompted laughter from Amir.

"Relax, babe. You need to make a grand entrance. Trust me, those people are not going anywhere. Mrs. Dartmouth's got enough food down there to feed an army. There's music, chatter and somebody decorated the entire place with the most riveting artwork I've ever seen."

"Oh, you!" Azure smiled.

Amir kissed her forehead and she was immediately filled with a relaxed vibe.

"Thank you for being here," she said.

"Where else would I be? Now come on, let's go and greet your public."

Amir bent his arm at the elbow and Azure hooked hers in his. He escorted her down the spiral staircase and into the living room.

There was no preparation for what Azure saw when she entered the exhibition. The amount of people present was staggering. She recognized only a handful, including her parents, Yanté and her parents, local art dealers and a few friends. She was immediately whisked away by Joan and spent most of the evening meeting people, shaking hands and discussing her art education and background. It was a whirlwind of activity which made her giddy and almost lightheaded.

A couple of hours into the showing, Azure found Amir again. He was standing in a corner talking to a dignified black man, who Azure later found out was from a cable station that patronized the arts. Amir introduced them and informed Azure that Mr. Bishop was a producer who was interested in including her in an upcoming segment of a show titled *Art About Town*.

"I'm flattered, Mr. Bishop," Azure said.

"We would be honored to have you. I think our viewers can relate to a young artist from the area. And, you certainly won't be hard to look at," Mr. Bishop complimented.

Azure blushed, thanked Mr. Bishop and excused herself. Joan was waving frantically to her from across the room.

"Azure, dear, I'd like you to meet some very good friends of mine," Joan said when she approached.

And thus the evening progressed. When the room finally began to thin out, Azure realized that she had never introduced her parents to Amir. That had been her intention tonight, figuring that her mother could hardly be overly critical in a room full of people she didn't know. She spotted her parents standing with another couple near one of her paintings, *Sun Shower.* Taking Amir by the hand, she led him over to them.

"Excuse me, Mom, Daddy—"

"Azure, there you are. I didn't get a chance to talk to my own baby girl all night long," Nicholas Monroe said, laughing his deep, hearty laugh.

"Oh, Daddy," Azure said, lacing an arm around his waist.

"Sweetheart, meet the Johnsons. They're from our church," Vetta said.

"It's nice to meet you both. I'm so glad you could make it," Azure said, shaking hands with the couple.

"It is definitely our pleasure. I'm so glad that your mother invited us. She was just going on and on about her talented daughter and when they had us over for dinner, we saw the painting you did of their wedding picture. It was so lovely we thought we'd just have to see some of your other work. Your mother didn't lie—you are extremely talented."

"Thank you." Azure smiled. She shot a quick glance at her mother, who was grinning from cheek to cheek, and she couldn't help but wonder if the champagne had gone to her mother's head. This could not possibly be the woman she'd grown up under, afraid to be anything less than perfect for fear of hearing a never-ending litany of how she could have done it better.

"Well, thank you, Mrs. Johnson. I hope you find something here you like," Azure said, recovering.

"As a matter of fact, I was just saying that I'd like to have our wedding photograph done…you know, like you did for your parents?"

"All right. Why don't you come by the gallery one day next week and bring your photo album with you. I'll take a look, and we can talk about it. How's that?"

"That'll be perfect," Mrs. Johnson said. "Congratulations again, Azure," she added as they hugged her parents and said good-night.

"Guys, I'd like you to meet someone," Azure said, finally getting to the reason she'd come over to her parents in the first place.

"I was wondering who this handsome young man was, lurking about," Vetta said.

"Ma'am, sir, nice to meet you," Amir said, extending a hand to Nicholas.

"Amir Swift, meet my parents, Nicholas and Vetta Monroe."

"Well, well. I heard through the grapevine that there was someone occupying all my daughter's time, keeping her from visiting home. I suppose that would be you?" Nicholas teased.

"Uh…I—"

"Amir, don't answer him. Daddy, knock it off."

"Oh, I'm just teasing the young man. You can take a joke, can't you, son?" At Azure's less-than-amused expression, Nicholas put up both hands in surrender, and said, "All right, all right. Good meeting you, Mr. Swift."

"Amir, please. Just call me Amir," Amir said.

Azure smiled, shaking her head at her father's foolishness as well as at Amir's nervousness. He was standing up straight and tall, as though he was reporting for boot camp.

They exchanged chitchat for a while before duty called.

Azure reluctantly excused herself, not wishing to leave Amir alone with her parents. However, by the time she returned several minutes later, her mother had her arm looped in Amir's and was taking another stroll around the exhibit. Her father stood alone where he had been left, staring at the same painting.

"Dad? Is everything okay?" Azure asked, joining him.

"Better than okay. My little girl is a star." He shook his head slowly from side to side. "I just can't believe how good you are. This is really good work."

"Thank you, Daddy." Azure beamed.

"Your mother and I are very proud of you. Look at her— she's been clucking like a proud mother hen all night long."

"I've never seen her like this before. It's quite a shock," Azure said.

"Your mother loves you, Azure, and she's very proud of you. Even though she may not show it, she's always worshipped the ground you walk on. She just has a funny way of expressing her feelings, is all."

"If you say so, Dad."

"It's true. Don't be so hard on her, you hear? Besides, she's mellowing out in her old age."

Azure watched her mother walking and talking with Amir. Vetta was an attractive woman in an understated sort of way. She never wore makeup, not even for special occasions. Her dark-brown skin had a natural glow that made her look younger than her fifty-three years. She wore her hair pulled back into a bun most of the time, even though her husband often told her he liked her better with it down. At a solid size ten, Vetta was fit and in good health for a woman her age. She power walked with her neighbor every morning, ate no fried foods or red meat and rarely drank alcohol. Watching her now, Azure realized for the first time that she could be personable, even warm. This was something that she had not noticed when she was growing up. Maybe there were things about her mother that she disliked, but it seemed to her now that maybe she had never taken the time to get to know the woman behind all the criticism and negativity.

Azure and her father caught up with Amir and her mother near what she liked to call her Growing Pains collection. Much of the crowd was gone by then and the Monroes prepared to leave, as well. In yet another surprising move, Vetta put her arms around Azure and hugged her tightly.

"I like this young man," she whispered in her ear before letting her go.

"Me, too." Azure smiled.

Amir volunteered to see the Monroes to their car, while Azure saw the few remaining patrons out. As Azure had made plans to stay overnight in order to organize the packing of the paintings that had been purchased and to prepare them for delivery to the various guests, she and Amir said their good-nights at the door.

"I wish you were coming home with me tonight," Amir said.

He rubbed his lips softly across hers. Like a gentle breeze, the gesture caressed her and left her wanting more. For a moment she was tempted to follow him out the door, but knew that she would feel guilty about leaving Joan and Yanté to deal with all that needed to be done.

"I'm coming straight to your place tomorrow evening," she promised.

They kissed again, this time long and deep. The sensations that stirred within her were as explosive as the first time their lips had met.

Tomorrow couldn't come too soon, was her thought as she watched Amir's car depart down the long driveway and disappear into the night.

Chapter 28

"Girl, I told you you were going to be a hit. These folks could not get enough of your work up in here tonight," Yanté squealed, kicking off her slingbacks and plopping down on the lounge chair.

They were out on Joan's patio, wineglasses in hand. All three women were exhausted, the night having been much more of a success than any of them had imagined. After the exhibit, Joan had taken them on a tour of the sprawling mansion. Room after beautifully decorated room sent Yanté into a frenzy. The entire house was done in a classical European style, but it was not oppressive or stuffy in any respect. Joan had done much of the decorating herself and informed them that she had not changed anything about the house since William had died. She'd considered it several times, but had not been able to bring herself to do so. Now that she'd made the attempt to revitalize the hotel, she thought that she might endeavor to breathe new life into the house, as well.

After touring the mansion, Joan had her housekeeper bring wine and a light snack of imported cheeses, crackers and soda bread out to them.

"Can you believe this? This is insane. We sold almost every painting!" Azure screamed with delight.

"Yes, and you've been commissioned to do…what, three more?" Joan added.

"Yep. I cannot believe people paid this much money for *my* work," Azure said, as she fanned the stack of checks in her hands.

"I don't know why you don't believe it. Shoot, they probably would have paid ten times what you sold these paintings for," Yanté commented. To Joan, she added, "Next time, we are going to consider a major increase. If we leave it up to Azure, she'll lowball herself every time."

Azure ignored Yanté's slight, still coursing on the good mood of a magical evening. The women continued to chat about the success of the showing, the excitement providing a natural high.

"Now, you know the first thing you're going to need to do is to hire an accountant to incorporate yourself. This income needs to be kept separate from the gallery," Joan advised.

Joan stopped talking when she realized Azure had not responded, not uttered a word in several minutes. She was staring out into space, a smile playing at her lips.

"Azure, dear, whatever are you thinking about?" she asked.

"Huh? Oh, my goodness, Joan…I'm sorry…I guess I was zoning out."

"Zoning out, all right. You'll have to excuse her, Joan,

but she's in L-O-V-E, so it's difficult for her to stay focused these days!" Yanté exclaimed.

"Well, I'm extremely happy for you, dear, and I hope that the young man is understanding because you're about to become a very busy woman," Joan said.

"He's wonderful. But hey, I'm sorry. I didn't mean to take up your time like this. Joan, I hope you know how much I truly appreciate what you've done for me. I mean, I know that you're a busy woman and quite frankly, you've done way too much already."

"Azure, why can't you just accept help when it's given to you?" Yanté interrupted.

"I have accepted it, Yanté," Azure protested. "It's just that poor Joan here has gone above and beyond. Thanks to you, I might add."

"Yeah, thanks to me, because you certainly weren't going to make a move," Yanté retorted.

"May poor, too-busy Joan interrupt here for a second?" Joan laughed.

Watching Azure and Yanté go back and forth at one another was like watching a sparring match between professional boxers, but twice as entertaining.

"It *is* your house," Yanté chirped.

"Why, thank you. Now, Azure, you are absolutely right. I am a busy woman and I've got a lot on my plate with the hotel. However, helping a rising star soar to the heights she deserves is nothing remotely resembling work. Therefore, you're going to sit here and listen to the sage advice of an older…no, slightly older friend."

"Yes, ma'am," Azure acquiesced with a smile.

Joan continued, providing contact information for an accountant who was a close friend of hers. Azure listened intently, forcing all thoughts of Amir out of her mind for now. Yanté dozed while they made plans for going forward. Joan thought that Azure should consider hiring someone to help her at the gallery since she would be very busy in the coming weeks working on the pieces for which she had been commissioned. Azure had not really considered what would happen to the gallery if she started selling her own work, and the thought of not being able to work there did not sit right with her. She enjoyed discussing artists and their work with patrons and loved being able to search for new pieces and put them on display. The idea of giving all of that up had never occurred to her and she wasn't certain if that was what she wanted to do.

Later that night as she lay in one of Joan's guest rooms, she thought about how differently her life was turning out than she had envisioned. She had not gone to see Jevar since she'd told Amir about him, but that didn't mean she didn't think about him often. She tried to figure out what he would have done if the situation had been reversed, but she couldn't. It was difficult to determine what a person would do in a strange situation like this. Everyone would like to believe that their love would be never-ending and that they would stand by their mate no matter what. However, the reality was that you just didn't know until it happened. What good was keeping herself locked away, alone and lonely? It certainly was not going to make Jevar get any better, nor was it going to erase the tragedy that had struck. Maybe Yanté was right and she had lucked up and run into two of the ten people she was destined to meet. Whether her cousin was right or not, Azure decided that she owed it to herself to find out what lay ahead for her and Amir.

Chapter 29

The woeful cry of the trumpet rose up over the crescendo of the band. Amir's arm was tightly wrapped around Azure's waist, her right hand clutched tightly in his left. Their bodies were pressed together as close as two separate people could possibly be and they moved in time to the music, a slow grind which their bodies seemed to have danced forever. The magic their union seemed to be made of caused other couples on the dance floor to take a second look at them, envious of whatever it was that they shared. It was different, somehow, than the passion of new love because they seemed to have reached a level of intimacy that only couples who had weathered storms and survived years together possessed. Yet, like a shiny new penny, it lacked the complacency of old lovers, who had long ago forgotten the urgent ardor they once felt. It was both of those things, old and new, fresh and seasoned. It caused their steps to be light, as if they were floating on invisible clouds as they glided across the dance floor at the Savoy, a small nightclub on the island of Barbados, moving to song after song. For them, even in a crowd of hundreds, they were alone and all that mattered was each other.

"You must have been a dancer in another life. You move like music," Amir whispered in Azure's ear.

"You're just the perfect partner, is all," she responded, and she meant that sincerely.

Amir ran his hands along the sides of Azure's hips, loving the roundness of them. Slowly, guiding her body against his, visions of her skin blending with his danced in his mind. She stared into his eyes, as mesmerized by them as she had been the day she'd met him.

They danced the night away, until neither could take the extended foreplay any longer. Alone at last in their suite, Amir lit several candles and turned on the two ceiling fans. A warm breeze blew across the room. He crossed the room and stepped out onto the balcony, where Azure stood looking out at the calm waters below. She bent her head backward, exposing her soft neck. He reached out, touching her face and then traveling down her neck and across her breasts, ever so slowly. He gave each breast a firm squeeze, then kissed her softly on her neck.

The private villa Amir had taken her to was situated on a secluded beach. Their room was the only one that faced that area of the beach, leaving them to fulfill one another's every fantasy. With the stars, sand and ocean as their backdrop, they painted a sensational three-dimensional portrait.

Azure's colorful sarong, wrapped beneath her arms and tied in front, slipped away from her body with the slightest tug. Beneath, Amir found that she was wearing only a bandeau and bikini bottoms. He inserted a thumb on either side of the bikini and pulled it downward. Azure watched as his expression changed, immediately registering surprise as he viewed her bare womanhood. She had gone to the spa a couple of days prior to their trip and had opted for a Brazilian wax for the first time.

"Wow," he remarked.

"Do you like it?" she asked.

"It's different…it's cute." He smiled.

He slowly dropped to his knees and began kissing her belly button. Slowly, his kisses turned to laps as his head moved lower and lower. Her naked center tingled under the caress of his tongue as he nuzzled his face against her. She moaned, softly at first and then more loudly as he drove her to the heights of pleasure. She leaned against the balcony's railings to steady herself, grabbing his locks, tugging at them, helping to drive his tongue home. When her legs began to quiver beneath her, he stood, picked her up and carried her inside.

The cool sheets greeted their warm bodies. Hot tongue met hot tongue as they languidly kissed. He had not had enough of her taste yet and returned for more. He dined on her like a man at his last meal, responding to her commands for more or less, more or less. Finally, when she began to beg him to climb deeper inside her than his tongue could reach, he deftly rolled on protection and used his other instrument of pleasure to enter her. She contracted around him and received him with every inch of her being.

He turned over so that he could lie on his back and she could be free to ride him, which she did expertly. She squeezed her muscles together, providing enough friction between them to start a forest fire. Each time he neared climax, she would slow down to a delicate motion, teasing him. Her chocolate breasts, with nipples like missiles aimed and ready to fire, dangled before his face, begging to be licked. When she sped up and rode him hard, he felt ready to go out of his fevered mind.

"I love you…I love you…I love you," he whispered over and over again.

With her body she showed her love for him. It was all-encompassing and beyond reason, the way she felt for him, and she did everything she could to show him how much he'd come to mean to her. They climbed higher and higher, feeling as though they had left the planet altogether, inside one another's love.

The couple spent the next few days moving at a lazy pace. Lovemaking became like a food in this lovers' country. When they were not exploring one another, they toured the one-hundred-and-sixty-six-square-mile coral island, learning about the Bajans' rich culture and Caribbean flavor. At the Barbados Museum they discovered artifacts from the island's longstanding heritage. They also toured the Historical Society's magnificent homes built in the early eighteen and nineteen hundreds. Together they watched their first cricket match at the Garrison. Additionally, after several inquiries and visits to the town clerk's office, they were able to locate the land that belonged to Amir's family.

The land was barren, no longer being used for crops. It was just under three acres and ended at a pier which overlooked a small inlet from the ocean. It was the most beautiful place either of them had ever seen. Immediately, ideas began swimming around in Amir's head as he thought about numerous possibilities for the place.

"Maybe I could build a summer home?" he mused

aloud as he and Azure sat on the edge of the pier watching the sun set.

"How about a bed-and-breakfast? You could make some good money off tourists like us," she replied.

"That's not a bad idea. I still can't believe all this land has just been sitting here. I remember hearing my parents talk about coming home one day, when we were all grown up and on our own. I'm sorry they never had the chance to come back and do something with it."

"Well, maybe it was just waiting for you to come along," Azure mused.

Amir put his arm around her, pulling her close to him. He marveled at how she could be so supportive of him without having anything concrete about his abilities to go on. He bet that if he told her he wanted to build a time machine she'd hand him some tools and tell him to go for it. She believed in him based not on what he'd done, but on what she believed he could do. To receive that kind of blind faith from someone made him believe that anything was indeed possible for his life. He wanted so desperately to make her proud of him. At that moment, sitting on the edge of a rickety pier in Barbados, he decided that he would never tell her about his past. He did not want to ever see anything in her eyes but trust and faith in him. He also vowed that he would make it worth her while. She would be proud of him and one day, when the time was right, he would make her his wife, and nothing before that event would matter.

Chapter 30

"Girlfriend, please, just because you've got a man now, don't be trying to give me advice on love. When I need advice, I tune in to Michael Baisden on *Love, Lust and Lies*. Okay?" Yanté teased.

"Oh, yeah, listen to a bunch of screwed-up callers trying to be armchair psychologists instead of me." Azure laughed.

"Whatever. Shoot, if nothing else, some of those people keep me laughing."

Yanté was on her way home when she'd received a call on her cell phone from a restricted number. She'd answered it only to hear heavy breathing. Annoyed and slightly on edge, she had decided to drive over to Azure's house after calling to confirm that she was home. Having just put an early end to the date from hell, she was not in the mood to go home alone and field crank phone calls.

The guy she'd gone out with was someone she had met

at church, of all places. He was here from West Virginia, visiting his mother, who lived in the D.C. area. He seemed like an interesting person, worked at a hospital in the radiology department, enjoyed outdoor sports and was an avid traveler. That was what he'd said as they stood outside the church after the service. However, over dinner tonight she'd uncovered some pathetic truths. First, he was simply a clerk in the radiology department, enjoyed *reading* about outdoor sports but did not actually participate in any and he hadn't traveled farther than three hundred miles by car. *Boring* didn't begin to cover it, and much of the evening was spent with him telling her that if she loaned him a few bucks, he'd take her to a great hotel and casino over on the south side of town. She'd feigned a headache halfway through the appetizer and was now equally as hungry as she was pissed off at time wasted.

Yanté sauntered into Azure's kitchen and opened the refrigerator. The moment she did this, Bud raced into the kitchen, his nails clicking across the floor. He stopped near Yanté's feet and sat down, his tail swishing behind him. He peered up at Yanté, who ignored him. After several minutes of searching and not finding anything appealing, she slammed the door shut. The cabinets were equally bare, save for some boxed potatoes, a can of tuna and a couple of boxes of pasta.

"You have next to nothing in here to eat," she complained.

"Well, I haven't been cooking much lately," Azure explained.

"Yeah, too busy out trying to become the Love Doctor. All that dining and romancing you've been doing lately has got me jealous. Speaking of which, how was Barbados?"

Yanté returned to the living room crunching on a stale

cracker she'd found in a package on the countertop. Bud was at her heels. Yanté playfully shoved him aside.

"It was fabulous. I never knew what a beautiful island it was."

"Never mind the geography lesson. How was the lovin'?"

"Girl, you haven't lived until you've made love on a white sand beach with waves licking at your behind."

"Really?" Yanté oozed dreamily. "Wow!"

"*Wow* is right. We had such a good time—away from everything with just the two of us. We ate, shopped, went sightseeing and made love three or four times a day. I swear I didn't want to come home."

"Okay, that's just great," Yanté said, tossing a throw pillow from the couch at Azure, hitting her shoulder. "Now I'm really jealous. By the way, where is Mr. Swift tonight?"

"Working."

"And where exactly is it that he works again? I mean, homeboy certainly doesn't keep banker's hours."

"He does parties. You know that. If memory serves, wasn't it you who said he throws *the bomb* parties?" Azure said accusingly.

"Party, singular. I only attended one and I said that it was all right, I guess," Yanté retorted.

Azure sucked her teeth at Yanté. "Whatever."

"Anyway, are you trying to tell me that he makes a living off of that?

"Duh. You yourself said how packed that one party you went to was. Think about all of those people paying twenty dollars a pop. My man puts together nice affairs where people can get dressed up, shake off the workweek blues and have fun. People are willing to pay for good fun, you know. Did I tell you about that Stepper's Ball he sponsored a couple of weeks ago?"

"No, you didn't. But that's okay, I'm used to being treated like a stepchild."

"Oooh, did you miss a good party. I haven't danced like that in so long. And those folks were dressed up, head to toe. Black people sure do look good when they put their game on. They had both a live band and a deejay. It was hot, I'm telling you."

"Well, I'm glad you're having fun for a change. Mr. Swift seems like he's melted through the ice princess's frosty exterior and has gotten her all hot and bothered inside." Yanté laughed.

"Mmm-hmm, girl, you don't even know how right you are."

Azure and Yanté slapped hands and laughed. They went into the kitchen, where Azure whipped together dinner for the two of them, a minor miracle considering she had next to no groceries in the house. They sat around sipping wine and listening to music while they talked for the next couple of hours. Yanté's cell phone rang several times during the course of the night. She just looked at the restricted number with annoyance and finally, she turned the phone off altogether and tossed it into her purse.

"Is that the date you kicked to the curb tonight blowing up your phone?"

"No…actually, I don't know who it is. Someone keeps calling my phone and blocking their number."

"What do they say when you answer?" Azure asked.

"Nothing really…just some heavy breathing. Probably some jerk dialing random numbers," Yanté said dismissively.

"Can't you have the wireless company do something like block blocked numbers or trace it?"

"I don't know. I'm not worried about it. Whoever it is will grow tired of their little game eventually."

"Yanté, sometimes these whack-jobs don't stop at just phone calls. They keep going until you pay some sort of attention to them," Azure said with concern.

Yanté changed the subject, not wanting her cousin to know that she was, in fact, beginning to worry. She didn't need a safe to fall on her head to know that the flowers, the doll, the notes and the phone calls were all connected. Whoever this nut was, he was definitely fixated on her. She promised herself that if there was one more incident, she would contact the police. In the meantime, she tried to shrug it off and concentrate on all the good things that were happening for Azure. Try as she might, however, the nagging sensation of fear remained on the fringes of her mind.

Chapter 31

"Joan, are you all right?" Azure asked.

It was Saturday morning and she had come out to Joan's house to have breakfast at the latter's invitation. Joan also had received some correspondence regarding Azure's paintings that she wanted to share with her. They had spent a few evenings and lunches together and had grown very fond of one another. Joan was funny and engaging, and despite the fact that their backgrounds were vastly different, they found that they had much in common where it counted most. But now, seated in her sunny kitchen, it was apparent that Joan's mind was a million miles away from croissants and orange juice.

"Huh? Oh, Azure, forgive me. I…I just…oh, boy," Joan stammered.

"What is it, Joan? Come on, something is obviously

bothering you. It might help to talk about it," Azure said, regarding Joan's strained expression with concern.

"I feel like such a fool. I can't believe I've gotten myself into this mess," Joan said.

Suddenly a guttural sob escaped from Joan. She covered her face with well-manicured hands and cried into them. Azure sprang from her chair and ran around the table to Joan's side.

She put her arms around the tearful woman.

"Joan, shh, it's okay. Whatever it is, it can't be that bad," she comforted.

Several minutes passed in which Azure rubbed Joan's back, trying to soothe her before Joan was able to regain her composure. Joan dabbed her eyes with one of the pale-pink linen napkins from the table. Azure sat down again, holding Joan's hand as she continued to reassure her that everything would be okay.

"I'm sorry, Azure. I shouldn't be dumping this on you. You came out here to have breakfast and instead, I'm breaking down before you've even finished your coffee."

"Don't worry about all that, Joan. You're obviously upset over something, and even though we haven't known each other very long, I would hope that you consider me a friend. If I can help you in any way, I will."

"Thank you, Azure. That's very kind of you, but I'm afraid there's nothing you can do." Joan sighed, another sniffle escaping.

Joan was silent for a short while, and Azure didn't want to push her. She sat quietly, still holding Joan's hand and waiting to see if she would eventually be able to talk about whatever was bothering her. Joan was reluctant to talk, but realizing that she really had no one else to talk to and that the burden she was carrying was way too heavy to continue to bear alone, she sighed.

"When I met William, I thought that finally I had found the man with whom I was supposed to spend the rest of my life. We had so many plans, you know?"

Azure winced, nodding her head. She knew all too well what Joan was referring to.

"Together, we built one of the most fabulous hotels, not only in D.C., but on the whole East Coast. I believed that we were unstoppable, and I never once imagined myself without him. But then he was gone. Just like that," she said, snapping her fingers.

"It's hard to accept when things happen so suddenly," Azure agreed.

"At first I told myself, oh well, that's the end. For those first few days I thought there was no way that I could go on with business or anything else for that matter."

"But somehow you did," Azure reminded her.

"Yes, somehow. After a while, I was able to cope. I threw myself into the hotel and worked my butt off to keep the dreams I'd shared with William alive."

"There's nothing wrong with that, Joan. Sometimes we have to cling to whatever life preserver we can find just to get us through the bad times."

"I know, but it was very lonely. I would come home late at night after working all day at the hotel to a big empty house and I would cry myself to sleep. I thought I was losing my mind sometimes. Just when I thought I couldn't bear another lonely day, I met someone."

Joan gave a sardonic laugh. "I knew he was probably not someone I should get involved with. I figured we'd have a few laughs, some mind-blowing sex, and that would be that."

"So what happened?" Azure asked. She was completely surprised both by Joan's candor and by her admissions.

"Four months after I met him, we flew to Las Vegas, got wasted and got married."

Joan buried her face in both hands, crying again.

"Married?" Azure exclaimed. "Oh, Joan…so soon?" she said.

"I know, I know. It was stupid and reckless. That was six months ago, and I have spent the last five trying to get rid of him."

Azure was speechless. She couldn't believe that someone like Joan Dartmouth would make such a mess of her life. The Joan Dartmouths of the world were supposed to have their stuff together. That just went to show that anyone could be a victim of their own weakness, under the right circumstances.

Joan went through the entire sordid relationship, ending with a confession that this husband of hers was threatening to expose some secrets he'd uncovered about the Dartmouths. While she didn't give the specifics, she said that this man was blackmailing her and she felt as though she had to give in to his demands or else she would find herself in serious trouble.

Azure offered her a shoulder to cry on and tried as best as she could to convince her that everything would work out in the end. Joan admitted that when she had first found out what type of man she'd foolishly married, she'd felt as if she had been sucker-punched in the gut. She couldn't believe how taken she had been with the man's handsome looks and fake charm. She pulled a picture of him from her purse and showed it to Azure. This time, it was Azure's turn to be hit below the belt.

"That's him. Raymond Cousins, my darling young husband," Joan said with a wry laugh.

Azure stared into the face of the man who had come to Amir's apartment a couple of weeks ago. She remembered his face clearly, although he was much more handsome in the photograph than he was in person. At Amir's door, there had been a certain cockiness about him that made him not quite as attractive. He'd held an unlit cigar in his hand and had waved it about as he talked in a most flamboyant manner. Azure remembered how Amir had brushed aside the man's visit as merely being an acquaintance who was having girl troubles. If that was the truth, then Joan had to have been that *girl* and Amir must know that. A sickening sensation rose in the pit of her stomach as she contemplated Amir's connection with this man. *Could he be a part of an attempt to blackmail Joan Dartmouth? Why would he do that?*

Suddenly, Yanté's words returned to her mind, smacking her in the face. *And he makes a living off of that?* Maybe party promotions really wasn't enough to pay the bills. Azure shuddered, wanting to erase these thoughts from her mind. Not Amir, not her Amir. He couldn't do something like that to someone. While she could not make herself believe that it was true, she also could not shake the doubts that this information had brought to her.

"Joan, how did you meet this man?" she asked.

"He approached me at a party. A friend of mine was having an engagement party for her daughter at this swank club and I went, hoping to snap out of the funk I'd been in. It was in all the papers, the celebrity event of the year. At first I was reluctant to go because the guest list had been published, and I didn't want to be bothered with all the press people who were sure to be sniffing about. I had been hounded on and off since William's death, the big question being whether or not I was planning to sell the hotel. In any event, I went. I was sitting at the bar, waiting for the couple to be presented and the engagement officially announced so that I could make my departure, when Raymond approached. He bought me a drink, complimented my dress and the next thing you know…I remember getting the feeling that he had been watching me all evening, waiting for the chance to come over."

Hmmph, more like waiting for the chance to strike, I suppose, Azure thought to herself. To Joan she said, "Joan, what are you going to do?"

"Pay the man, I guess. What else can I do?"

The woman who had at one time seemed dynamic, even larger than life to Azure, now looked small and defeated. It hurt Azure's heart to see her like this. She tried to comfort her as best as she could, all the while thinking the worst of Amir. She knew that she had to confront him and hoped with everything in her being that what she suspected was wrong.

Chapter 32

"What in the world happened here?" Yanté shrieked as she entered her office at the hotel.

The room was a complete and utter mess. The desk was turned upside down, and papers were strewn everywhere. The high-backed leather chair behind the desk had been sliced with a razor or some other sharp instrument, three long gashes running from the back to the seat. The tiny two-seater in the corner of the room had also been cut and the stuffing was pulled out in several places.

"We don't know," answered the hotel security guard.

The concierge was on the telephone calling the police.

"When I came in this morning, your door was wide open. I thought you were here early because I knew that you'd closed it before you left last night. I stepped in and found this," the secretary said.

Yanté walked around the room, assessing the damage

as she went. Several framed photographs had been smashed. She picked up one and noticed that the picture had been removed. She combed her memory to figure out which picture had been in the frame and finally it came to her. It was a picture of her at her undergraduate commencement exercises a few years back. Immediately, her stomach began to churn. Why would a vandal break into her office, tear it up and steal a photograph of her?

"There were some kids running around the hotel late last night. They made a mess in the laundry room and the fitness center. I'd bet my paycheck that it was them," the security guard said. "I'm going out front to wait for the police to arrive."

"And I'll go and look up the family of those kids who were staying here. They checked out this morning," the concierge said.

"Yanté, is there anything you'd like me to do for you in the meantime?" her secretary asked.

"No, thanks. I've got a meeting to get to upstairs. Mr. Bryant, please let me know if the police need anything from me when they get here," Yanté said to the security guard.

"Sure thing, Ms. Lourde. I'm sorry about this," he said.

"Thank you."

Yanté exited her office and headed to the main elevator bank. She felt some relief that it was probably just kids who'd done this damage. She didn't allow herself to think about the alternative. She believed that the person who was sending her flowers was just a secret admirer. There was no indication that he'd had anything to do with what happened in her office.

As she entered the elevator, she never looked back. If

she had she would have noticed the man standing near the newsstand with a magazine in his hand. He was not looking at the periodical at all, but was staring at her, a sick smile plastered on her face.

Chapter 33

Azure paced the floor, little Bud yapping at her heels. He seemed to sense her anxiety and grew just as uptight as he waited with her. She glanced at the clock on the mantel and realized that only minutes had passed since she'd last checked the time, although it seemed like more than an hour.

Amir's car rolled into her driveway, spitting gravel from the tires as it approached. She was at the door, swinging it open before he'd come to a complete stop.

"Hey, babe," he greeted her as he climbed out of the car.

Azure stepped aside to allow him to enter without saying a word. His lips kissed a cold cheek. He looked quizzically at her stoic face and was immediately filled with a sense of dread. He was uncertain what he'd walked into, but knew instinctively that the romantic evening he had hoped for was not about to take place.

"Amir, I need to show you something…to ask you a question, and I want a simple yes or no answer," she began.

"Okay," Amir answered.

He waited as she walked across the room to the mantel and picked up a photograph. She returned to where he was standing and held the picture up to his face.

"Do you know this man?"

Amir's breath caught in his throat as he stared at the smiling face of Raymond Cousins, with his arm draped around an also smiling Joan Dartmouth. Amir looked from the photograph to Azure and then back.

"Is this not the man I saw at your apartment a couple of weeks ago? The guy you told me was just a friend having girl trouble?" she repeated, waiting, her countenance filled with trepidation.

Suddenly, Amir felt a great wave of relief washing over him. All these months of turmoil which he'd experienced were now over. He had been torn between telling her the truth about himself and the fear that she would leave him if she knew. Now, he didn't have to wonder what would happen anymore. His moment of truth had arrived.

"Yes," he said plainly.

Her face grew hard, then that look changed to the un-mistakable veil of disappointment.

"How do you know him?" she asked.

"Can we sit down?" Amir pleaded.

She followed him to her kitchen, where they took seats opposite one another at the dinette. Azure leaned back in her seat, her body language telling him that she was out of reach to him. He knew that he had to do everything in his power to change that. He also knew that he didn't have much time in which to do it.

"His name is Raymond Cousins."

"I know his name. How do you know him?" she asked again.

"We're business associates," he said.

"Business associates? Exactly what kind of business associates could you be with this man?"

"Azure, I'm not sure what Joan Dartmouth has told you, but…"

"But what, Amir? Don't worry about what she's told me. It's time that *you* told me something. Exactly what is your *business,* Amir?"

"Babe, listen, I do exactly what you think I do—I promote parties."

"Obviously that's not all you do, Amir. Joan says that this man tricked her into marriage and has been trying to milk her dry ever since. He's a con artist and now he's blackmailing her."

"Blackmail? Hold on, baby, I don't know anything about that," Amir defended.

"Don't you? You said you're a business associate of this man. Close enough for him to come to your home, so how could you not know what he's into?"

"Let me explain, Azure. Before you jump to conclusions, please let me explain, baby," Amir said.

He reached across the table to take her hand, which she snatched away. She folded her arms across her chest and leaned farther back into her seat, farther away from him.

"I'm waiting."

He began in a low voice. He went all the way back to the day he'd lost his parents. He talked about Tavares and how he'd stepped up and did what he'd had to do to keep the three of them together. She listened intently, waiting for him to get to the present day and his connection with Raymond Cousins. He tried to read her face, but he could not tell what she was thinking. So, slowly and carefully, he went on with his story.

He talked about the early days, when Tavares was hustling every way he knew how to make a buck. He talked about the days when they didn't have money to keep the lights on and how the social workers threatened to take him and Bridgette away from Tavares.

"They seemed to want to see us fail so that they could split us up and stick me in a group home somewhere. Bridgette was still young enough for somebody to want to adopt, but who would want an angry black teenage boy? And then Tavares would be all on his own. They said he could get welfare for a few months…maybe move into a men's shelter for a while. He refused to let that happen.

"Tavares found a way to keep us together. He got involved with the uncle of a friend of his in this marriage-for-money scheme, and, to his surprise, it worked."

Azure winced as her deepest fears were confirmed. Amir could not ignore the pained look in her expression as she stared incredulously at him.

"Before we knew it, he was making good money. I finished high school and tried to find a job, but I wasn't really qualified to do much. We wanted to make sure that Bridgette had everything she needed. We wanted to send her to college."

"So you joined Tavares?"

"Yeah, I did. He had done so much for us, for me. How could I turn my back on him?"

"And how could you turn your back on all that money?" Azure snapped.

"No, it wasn't like that," Amir began, but stopped. If he was going to be honest, then he need to be completely open. "Okay, maybe that was part of it. I liked the money, too. It felt good being able to go wherever we wanted to go and to keep Bridgette in all the latest gear that everyone else was wearing. We had a nice apartment, a full refrigerator and nobody was waiting to turn the lights or phone off. It felt good. But that's not all there was to it. I really felt like I owed Tavares, and he needed me in the business. I needed to have his back, just like when we were kids at the swimming pool. For the first time, I found something I was good at, a skill that somebody needed."

"Oh, and what skill would that be? Scamming women out of their money? Tell me, Amir, how many women have you deceived, married and then taken to the cleaners?" Azure's voice had risen. "Oh, God, you're probably married right now!" she yelled, jumping up from the table.

"Azure, no," Amir said, standing, as well.

Azure backed away from him until the stove prevented her from moving any farther away from him.

"Listen to me, baby, please. I'm not married to anyone and never have been. Tavares and I ran the scam, but I promise you I would never do something like that. These guys we hired…they're nothing more than prostitutes, and I could never sell myself like that."

"Oh, so if they're prostitutes, then that would make you and Tavares the pimps, right? Yeah, that's much better!" Azure exclaimed.

Amir sighed heavily, feeling like a man sinking into a lake of quicksand. He felt as though he was fighting a losing battle, but he was determined to go through it anyway.

"Azure, please try to understand. This was not a way of

life I chose. Sometimes in this life you have to do what you have to do. I'm not trying to justify it because I know that there is no justification. I set women up to marry gigolos and I profited from it. That's wrong and I know that. I did the research, located the targets and matched the right guy for the job. Don't you think I feel bad enough about myself without knowing how this looks to you?"

"Listen to you, Amir. Do you hear yourself? You say, *targets, research, job*. You throw these words around as though they are everyday duties in a normal, run-of-the-mill occupation. You're a pimp, Amir. Plain and simple. There is absolutely nothing mundane or ordinary about that."

Bud, who had long since grown bored with their conversation and was lying beneath the table asleep, suddenly perked up as their voices grew louder. He came from beneath the table, looking anxiously from one serious face to another.

"And I feel like shit for being part of it, Azure," Amir yelled. "There, now I've said it. Happy?"

He stepped closer to her, and Azure moved to get away from him. He grabbed her arm, afraid to let her walk away from him because inside he knew that if she did, all hope would be lost.

"Get off me, Amir," she spat, enunciating each word with strong emotion.

The puppy scurried beneath the table at the sound of her voice and remained there.

"Please, don't walk away from me, Azure. Please, let me make you understand. I know this is wrong. This is not the man I want to be. I want to be someone you can be proud of. Hell, someone I can be proud of. That's why I quit. I left Tavares several months ago. I walked away from all of it."

"I'm supposed to believe that meeting me was so real that you had this life-altering epiphany and decided to turn over a new leaf? Amir, please. I'm not that naive."

"That's not what I'm saying, Azure. I've wanted to get out of the business for a long time now. I tried to tell Tavares so many times in the past year or more that I couldn't do it anymore. I tried to convince him that we should both just walk away. Take the money we've made and do something legitimate with it. But Tavares, he can't see anything else. He's so into this life…this way of living and nothing I could say would make him change his mind. For the longest time, I felt guilty about wanting to leave him. I was confused and scared. I didn't want to lose my brother, so I hung on longer than I wanted to. It was eating me up inside, but I hung on. When I met you that day, I was so down and out I could barely think straight. I wasn't sleeping, hardly eating. I hadn't been with a woman before you in more than half a year. So yeah, if I wasn't strong enough beforehand to get out, I certainly knew from the moment I laid eyes on you that day at the gallery that I no longer had a choice."

Amir released her arm and backed away from her. Tears had begun to stream down her cocoa-colored cheeks and he wanted to reach out and wipe them away, but he was afraid to try to touch her again. She began shaking her head slowly, right to left, as if she were trying to erase everything that he had just said from her mind. He just stood there, waiting and praying. The thought of losing her had him gripped in a vise of fear, paralyzing him.

"I don't know who you are," she said finally. Her bottom lip trembled as she spoke.

"Yes, you do. It's me, Amir, baby. The man who's crazy

for you. I haven't changed, Azure. Maybe I'm not the man I led you to believe that I was, but that wasn't deceit. It was hope. You made me feel like anything was possible. Loving you is the most right thing I've ever done in my life. All I want to do is be the man that I'm supposed to be, and I don't know that I can do that without you. Please, Azure, please don't let this destroy us. Give me another chance, and I promise you, I will never let you down again."

Azure's body shook now, as the tears flowed steadily down her face. Her head felt tight, as if there was a rubber band around it, squeezing the oxygen out of her brain. Her lungs became thick, struggling to bring the air in and out of her body. She couldn't look at Amir, didn't trust herself to. He took a step toward her and she placed both hands up in the air, palms facing him as if ordering him to stop. He obeyed her silent yet unmistakable command. Azure pushed past him and walked out of the kitchen.

Amir placed both hands on his head and held them there. He, too, felt as if everything were being sucked out of him. The moment he had dreaded for months had finally arrived, and it was worse that he had imagined it would be. She was lost to him now, and he couldn't think of a way to win her back. He was afraid to follow her into the living room because he didn't know what awaited him there. Eventually, however, he had to.

Azure was sitting on the sofa, staring out into space. Tears no longer fell, but her eyes were red and swollen.

"Azure," he called. Her gaze moved slowly to where he was standing. "Can we talk about this?"

"No, Amir, we can't. See, I've been sitting here trying to understand how I can move past this. If we can find a way to get over this and get back what we had."

"We can…I'm sure of it," Amir said, a glimmer of hope in his voice.

"No, that is precisely what we can't do," Azure responded.

"Why not?"

"Because, Amir, we didn't have anything."

"Oh, baby, don't say that. We had so—"

"Stop!" Azure commanded, interrupting him. She slammed her hand down on the sofa cushion. "If we had had something so real, this would never have happened. I don't know you, Amir, nor do I know anything about you. I don't know what kind of person you are because everything you've told me is based on a lie. How do I know what else you conveniently forgot to tell me?"

"Azure, you know me better than anyone else in the whole damned world. I am the man whose soul you saw just by looking into my eyes. And you were right on the money with what you saw. I haven't changed. Yes, I've been through some things in my life, and I have had to learn some hard lessons. But I love you, and I know you love me. I'm willing to work hard to change who I was. I told you I'd take you no matter how much or little you could give me because I wanted you just that badly. Do you remember that?"

Azure let out a wounded laugh.

"I knew it was just a matter of time before you'd throw Jevar in my face. But news flash, Amir—there's a big difference between you and me. At least I was honest with you. As soon as I realized that you and I had moved to another level, I was honest. I gave you the opportunity to choose whether you wanted to stay or go. You could have told me and let me make my own choice. All these months you've pretended to be something you are not. What's more, what you've actually turned out to be is a lousy two-bit hustler. Joan Dartmouth is a decent woman who has helped me so much. How can I look her in the face knowing you're responsible for all the pain and suffering she's in right now?"

"I am not responsible for that. I told you that I don't know anything about her being blackmailed. I would never stoop to something that low."

"Wouldn't you?"

"No, I wouldn't. I'm not trying to say that my part in this is not bad enough. But you've also got to recognize the fact that these women have a choice. No one is holding a gun to their heads. They want the comfort and companionship these guys provide them with. What they give to these men, they give willingly."

"Yeah, and you willingly take a piece of the pie and your pockets get fat. Tell me something, Amir, when you and I go out…dinner, movies, that trip to New York…are you spending these women's money on me?"

Amir did not respond, but hung his head low.

"That's what I thought. I am so disgusted with you right now, I can't even find the words." She walked toward the front door, snatching it open angrily.

"Get out, Amir."

Amir started to protest, but the look in her eyes and on her face stopped him cold, making the words freeze in his throat. He walked to the doorway, stopped and turned to look at her again. He wanted so desperately to just wrap her in his arms and love away all this anger and disappointment. He continued through the door, which slammed shut behind him, causing the wind to blast against his back. He leaned against the closed door, pressing the tips of his fingers into it. If he thought banging on it, begging, screaming or pleading would do anything to change her mind, he would have done that and more.

Inside, Azure laid her body against the door. She wanted to call him back, but she could not. The pain of his deception was something she thought she would never get over. It reached the depths of her being, making her ashamed of herself for not seeing clearly who he was beforehand. A fresh batch of tears began to spill from her eyes, until heart-wrenching sobs racked her entire body. After Jevar, she had been so careful in avoiding this very thing, and now, here she was again—alone and destroyed.

Azure was not alone in her despair. Amir felt equally as desolate and torn up. He couldn't trust his legs to carry him to his car, so he remained standing outside of Azure's door for a very long time. Finally, when it began raining and his throat hurt from swallowing his sobs, Amir left.

Chapter 34

Amir drove aimlessly around the city, with nowhere in particular that he wanted to be. In the wee hours of the morning, he landed on his sister's doorstep. Bridgette opened the door to find her brother soaking wet from the rain and from the buckets of tears that he'd shed. She let him in, giving him a towel to dry off with and a set of warm clothes to change into. Over a steaming cup of green tea, Amir talked openly with her, telling her things which she had always suspected over the years, but which had never been discussed or confirmed. He told her the details of his and Tavares's business dealings, explained how they had supported her all those years and shared with her what it had cost him. She listened quietly, without uttering a word until he was finished. Once everything was on the table, he felt no better, nor any worse. Numbness had set in along with fatigue, and he thought that he would never feel anything substantial again.

"You know you have to make things right. Between you and Tavares, for this woman who is being blackmailed and…with Azure," Bridgette said at long last.

"I don't know how to do any of that. I feel so lost right now," he said sincerely.

"I know," Bridgette said, reaching out to take her brother's hands in hers. "We all make mistakes, Amir, and we all do things that we later regret. Tavares…well, Tavares has chosen the life he wants to live, and we can't do anything about that. We have to let him live his life, make his mistakes and, hopefully, learn his lessons."

"I'm worried for him, Bridgette. He acts likes everything is about the money. He doesn't even see the dangers of his lifestyle, and nothing I say to him seems to make one bit of difference."

"And it won't until he's ready to hear it. Look, Amir, I don't want to sound selfish, but I definitely have way too much going on to go chasing after a grown man."

Bridgette was quiet for a time, letting her words sink in with Amir. She felt so bad for her brother, for both her brothers for that matter. When their parents had died, she'd been very young, and, while she missed them terribly, Amir and Tavares had made her the best childhood a little girl could hope for. They became her mother and her father, giving her all the love and support that she needed to grow up. But for them things had been harder. There was no one to guide them and nurture them. No one to make sure they came in at a decent hour, ate their vegetables or stayed out of trouble.

"Amir, I could sit here and say that you were wrong and

that he was wrong, but for that matter, so was I. I never questioned where the money was coming from. You and Tavares took care of me and that was all that mattered. The time for regrets has passed, Amir. Now, we have to look forward. You are an honest, decent brother, who's made bad choices, but you're trying to make things right. Move on," Bridgette said.

"How?"

"Tavares loves you, and he will realize that that is more important than anything else…some day. From what you've told me, I doubt the feelings are one-sided between you and Azure. If she loves you, Amir, she'll come around, and she will find it in her heart to forgive you. That's the easy part, though. It is up to you to give her a reason to trust you again."

Amir soaked in all of his sister's wise words of advice and while he still felt hopeless, he was strangely comforted.

"When did you get to be so smart?" he asked.

"I got it from my big brothers," she replied, smiling.

By the time they finished talking, it was almost five o'clock in the morning. Bridgette insisted that Amir lie down in her bed for a while before heading home. She said that she was going to get some work done for the next hour and then hit the twenty-four-hour gym up the block before the early-morning crowd got there. Amir didn't argue, fatigue having weighed his bones down as if he had one-hundred-pound sacks of coal tied to his body. He slept fitfully, the unbearable nature of his predicament keeping him tossing and turning, feeling like a mouse trapped in a maze.

He slipped into and out of dreams until one dream in particular woke him up in a cold sweat. He was twelve years old again and Tavares was in their living room, answering the telephone. The caller said that their parents had been in a car accident and were in critical condition. When Tavares and Amir arrived at the hospital, their parents were sitting in the waiting room. Outside of a few minor scratches, they were fine.

"Mom, Dad, you're okay?" Tavares asked.

Amir ran to his mother and threw his arms around her.

"Of course we're okay, boy," their father said. "Listen though, we've got to go now."

"Go? Go where," Amir asked, frightened.

"Honey, your father and I have to leave you now," his mother said. "I want you to promise me that you won't get into any trouble. Be good and listen to Tavares."

"Tavares, you're the man of the house now. It's up to you to make sure your brother and your sister are taken care of."

"What are you talking about, Dad? How can I do that?"

"Figure out a way, boy. But just remember, stay out of trouble. None of that hustling and scamming that young brothers fall prey to out there in the streets."

His parents got up and prepared to leave. His mother gave both boys a kiss and a hug and then they walked off, down the corridor and through the swinging doors of the emergency room. They waved goodbye, their smiles big and bright as if they were just going away for the weekend. The two boys stood side by side, tears streaming down their faces, waving back.

Amir awoke, calling after his mother. Sweat poured down his face, mixing with his tears. He covered his face with his hands and shuddered.

"Goodbye," he whispered, over and over again. In this dream he got the chance to do what he had not been able to in real life. He said goodbye. Bridgette was right—it was time to move on.

Chapter 35

It had been almost a week since his breakup with Azure, but Amir was far from the point of moving on. He had written to her, apologizing again, and left her several telephone messages. One day, he'd stood across the street from the gallery and watched her arrive to open up for the day. He'd wanted to dodge the ceaseless traffic and snatch her into his arms, but he was more afraid of the certain rejection he'd receive than of being hit by a car. He left without making himself known, the image of her going with him. He paced around his apartment, feeling like a bird in a cage. His wings had been clipped and his heart could no longer fly.

Tavares hadn't called him all week, nor had he returned any of the messages Amir had left for him. He knew his brother was angry, but had hoped by now he would have come around. In the meantime, he had been receiving crank calls. The caller would just breathe into the phone after he'd answered, not saying anything, before hanging up. Amir was certain that only Sean would do something so childish, so he didn't let it bother him. Half of the time he'd look at the caller identification and if it wasn't Azure's home or gallery number or Tavares, he didn't bother to answer it.

Much of his last conversation with Azure reran itself through his mind. In particular, he thought about what she'd told him about Joan Dartmouth being blackmailed. At first he planned to ignore it and to stay out of the situation. But as the days passed, he thought more and more about it and about Bridgette's advice. He realized that he needed at least to make sure that Tavares knew that Raymond was acting shady. It was not only wrong, but it was extremely dangerous. What Raymond was doing would do nothing but bring trouble to the business, and that was something Tavares wouldn't tolerate.

As much as he despised the thought of going back to the brownstone and getting involved in any of the dirt that settled there, Amir decided to go and see his brother in person, not wanting to leave a message any more detailed than *call me back* on his voice mail. He hoped that Tavares would receive him well, and, if he had any luck, maybe Tavares could give him some advice on Azure. The past five days had been torture, and Amir was not sure how much more he could take.

He arrived at the brownstone and was immediately annoyed. Sean and Big Rick were sitting outside on the steps when he pulled up and parked. While Rick gave a slight nod of the head when Amir spoke, Sean's reply was an icy stare. Amir walked past them and headed inside to find his brother.

"What's up, Tavares? Didn't you get my messages?"

he said when he found his brother in his spare room lifting weights.

"Yeah, I got them. What do you want?" Tavares asked, never losing count of the arm curls he was doing.

Sweat dripped from Tavares's head; his red T-shirt was dark with perspiration. He did not look at his brother, but kept his eyes fixed on the floor in front of him.

"Come on, man. How long are you going to give me the cold shoulder?" Amir said, sitting on the empty bench next to Tavares.

"Hey, Amir, you're the one who broke out, remember? Not me. I'm still right here."

"Just because I left the business, Tavares, doesn't mean I left us. I'm your brother, man. We're more than this, any of this," Amir said, waving his hand around the spacious room with its thousand-dollar, state-of-the-art fitness center, stereo system with surround sound, plasma television and mirrored walls.

Tavares lowered the dumbbell to the floor beside his feet. Resting his elbows on his thighs, he clasped his hands together and silently cast his eyes downward. Amir sat watching a man who shared his blood, who looked as if he was contemplating a nuclear equation as opposed to whether or not to speak to his own brother. Part of Amir was angry that this was such a decision for Tavares, but he didn't have the strength to express that anger. The last thing he wanted was another fight on his hands. So he waited, if not patiently then at least with a certain amount of understanding. He knew that he had put Tavares in a bad place with the crew and for that, he was sorry.

Tavares looked up at his brother and a slow smile spread across his face.

"Man, why do you look like you're about to cry?" Tavares joked.

"Maybe I am." Amir smiled.

"Get outta here. You haven't cried since you were twelve years old."

Tavares stood up and grabbed his brother in a tight hug. Amir's grateful body relaxed for the first time in days as he hugged his brother back.

"I'm sorry about all this, man. I just want you to understand that it's not about you and me. We're always going to be thick as thieves. I just need something else for myself," Amir said.

"Forget it, man. It's all good," Tavares said, slapping him on his back heartily.

The men separated, Tavares playfully punching Amir in the arm.

"Man, I'm starting to think maybe you've got a point," Tavares said.

"What do you mean?"

Tavares went on to tell Amir about some of the problems he had been having in the past couple of weeks. Giovanni Vesnas had become a problem. The wife had cut him off and thrown him out with only the clothes on his back. Apparently, she had an uncle they had failed to uncover who had ties to the Italian Mafia. This uncle had paid Giovanni a visit and made him an offer he'd have been a fool to refuse. That didn't stop Tavares from wanting his money for the past two months that Giovanni had been dodging him. Finally, however, Tavares chalked it up as a lost cause, but he absolutely refused even to consider keeping Giovanni in the fold, leaving the man virtually friendless and homeless. Giovanni had come around a couple of times, making vague threats about exposing the business.

Giovanni was desperate and Amir knew that desperate men were usually dangerous men because they lost their ability to think rationally. He cautioned Tavares to tread carefully—maybe keep a low profile for the next few weeks. Taking on new targets or setups with Giovanni's threat hanging in the air was probably not a good idea. Of course, Tavares shrugged it off and Amir dropped the subject.

"Man, I was just joking with you. I'm not about to let *anyone* take anything away from me. I built this business out of nothing and a few minor setbacks won't stop me from making my money. Enough about all of this nonsense. What else is wrong with you?" he asked.

"What are you talking about?"

"Come on, Amir. You forget that I raised you? You look like crap…like you haven't slept in days, and I know it ain't just about you and me. What's up?"

At that point, Amir crumpled. He had had no one to talk to about the blowup with Azure besides Bridgette, and it was killing him inside. While he appreciated her advice and had taken a lot of what she'd had to say to heart, he felt he needed a man's perspective to help him sort things out. That was just one of the many things he missed about his father.

He told Tavares the entire story, not leaving anything out. His brother was right—he had not cried since he was twelve, when his parents had died, but lately he felt as desolate as he had back then.

"This girl has really got a hold on you, huh?" Tavares replied sympathetically.

"Yeah, man."

"All right, first things first. I'm going to personally put

my foot in Raymond's ass. He's finished in D.C., that's for sure," Tavares vowed.

"No, hold on a minute, man. Let me step to Raymond. I need to figure out a way to straighten him out myself. I feel like I owe it to Joan Dartmouth."

"Okay, that's cool with me. Make sure you tell him not to ever show his face around this town again because I don't know what I might do if I see him."

"You've got it."

"Tell me something, baby brother—do you think fixing things with Raymond Cousins will impress your little lady? I mean, that's not a bad idea, but do you think it'll be enough?"

"I honestly don't think there is anything I can do to win her back. She doesn't even want to see me or hear from me."

"So that's it? You're just going to let her go? Man, I guess she didn't mean that much to you, huh?"

Amir glared at Tavares.

"What? I just got through telling you how much I love that woman. Why would you say something like that?"

"Because if this were the bottom of the ninth, with bases loaded, two outs and the count was three and two, you sound like you'd be the batter who's already putting his bat away in the dugout. The game ain't over until it's over, baby," Tavares said. He smacked Amir across his behind with a hand towel. "I'm going to take a shower. Are you hanging around?"

"Nah, I've got to get going."

Amir left the brownstone, his head heavy with thought. First he needed to find a way to get Raymond Cousins off Joan Dartmouth's back. The only way to beat a snake is to use his own venom against him. One of the practices that Amir had instituted when he first got involved with the scam was to do background checks on the guys they used. He returned to his apartment and opened the locked file cabinet he kept in the corner of his living room. He retrieved the file he'd created on Cousins and read through it slowly. At first read, everything seemed to be in order. There were no red flags which stood out. Amir cursed, banging his fist on the table. He turned back to the first page and began reading again, this time even more slowly. Cousins was originally from a small town in Texas. The file said that he and his brother, Victor, who was a couple of years older than him, had grown up in a working-class family. They'd relocated to the northwest after Victor had completed college.

On the last page of the file the name Monica McFadden was circled in red ink. There was a question mark in the margin next to the name. Amir remembered the name having come up during his research as someone from the Cousins family's past, but nothing had ever come of it. He had not been able to find out anything about this person and, as it had been the only question mark in Raymond Cousins's background, Tavares had told him to disregard it. Now, however, he began to think that maybe it was something after all. Puzzled, he pulled out his laptop and connected to the Internet. He searched for hours, everything from the archives to local newspapers to some of the major papers from the Texas area. Finding nothing, he decided to make some phone calls. Among the people he reached out to was a guy he knew who worked as an insurance investigator. Two days later, Amir had all the information he needed. He set out to put a plan in motion to stop Raymond Cousins, once and for all.

Chapter 36

The park was shrouded in darkness by the time Amir saw Raymond Cousins approaching. He had been waiting for almost an hour. Alone in the deserted park, his despair grew hard in his heart, turning into a vile anger directed at Raymond's treachery. The situation he was in was no one's fault but his own, and he made no qualms about that. He accepted responsibility for not having been honest with Azure and for being involved in the lifestyle in the first place. However, he was angry at Cousins because his greed and sordid nature had put Joan Dartmouth in the position she was in, leading her to confide in Azure.

"What's up, man?" Cousins said in his most arrogant tone.

"I can't call it," Amir replied nonchalantly.

"Yeah, so, what can I do for you?"

"What's the matter, my man? Are you in some sort of a rush?"

"Well, you know what they say—I've got places to go, people to see. Besides, you made it clear that you don't want to have nothing to do with me."

"You're right," Amir said, a cold edge coating his words. "Let's get to the point."

"Let's," Cousins responded, equally as cold.

Amir reached into his jacket pocket and pulled a photograph out. He handed it to Cousins and watched his reaction. His face lost its cocky glow and the muscles in his jaw grew tight.

"Is this supposed to mean something?" he said at last.

"Well, why don't you tell me? I mean, I don't know about you, but my brother means everything to me. Doesn't yours?"

"What do you want, man?" Cousins snapped.

"I want the same things you want—to move on. The way I see it, that's precisely what you and your brother tried to do. You guys wrapped things up into a nice, neat little package, didn't you?"

Cousins glared at Amir, clutching the photograph. Amir was encouraged. The gamble he had taken paid off. He had hope that what Cousins felt for his brother was at least half of what Amir felt for Tavares. If it were, then he would do anything to protect him.

"Say what you've got to say," Cousins said quietly.

His voice had lost its self-assuredness and his face was stoic.

"Sometimes, Raymond, even when we think we've crossed all our t's and dotted all of our i's, we miss something. Some little detail gets overlooked and we're caught out there." Amir paused for effect. "You missed something, Raymond...and I found it."

Cousins let out a weak laugh, trying to maintain what

was left of his tough-guy demeanor, but it was apparent that he was nervous.

"I hear Victor is a front-runner for the assemblyman seat in…what's the name of that little town in Delaware that he lives in now?"

"Farmington," Cousins said softly.

"Yeah, that's it. I hear it's a nice little place. He's got a wife now, two kids, right? A perfect little family. He's poised to have a great career in politics."

"You'd better not mess with my brother," Cousins growled.

"That's real funny, man. That sounds like just what I told you a little while back, but you obviously ignored me. So I'm going to say it again—don't mess with *my* brother. The shit you're doing to Joan Dartmouth—that's going to mess things up for him and that's not cool. You were hired to do a specific job and you've taken it way too far. So here's what we're going to do—you're going to place in an envelope all of the information you have on Joan Dartmouth, sign the divorce papers and send a messenger to her house first thing in the morning. Then you are going to bounce. You're going to leave D.C. and never come near her again. That means no contact, no threats…nothing."

"Why should I do that?"

"Because you don't want to see your brother lose everything that he's worked for…just like I don't want that to happen to my brother."

"Your lowlife brother can't hold a candle to mine. Don't compare the two," Cousins spat.

"Oh, so now you want to talk about who's the better man? Whatever Tavares has done, that's for God to judge, not you. Besides, you two have got just as much to answer for, if not more. Wouldn't you agree? Let's see, falsifying information, stolen identities, fraud…shall I go on?"

"We did what we had to do," Cousins defended weakly.

"Really? Is that your story? You and your brother were nothing but juvenile-delinquent trailer-park trash. You both had an arrest record a mile long. So you reinvented yourselves. You went from being John and James McFadden, sons of Monica McFadden and father unknown, to Victor and Raymond Cousins. But, Raymond, why didn't you guys stop there? For crying out loud, your brother fabricated undergraduate and graduate degrees. Now he's in charge of making policy and local government when he's about as qualified as me! And by the way…he's still got outstanding warrants."

Amir pulled out a slip of paper from his back pocket.

"How'd you get that?"

"I've got my sources. What, you think you're the only one who's good at the blackmail game? The secret to longevity in this life, my man, is to make sure that you've covered your own dirt before you go digging through someone else's."

Cousins was silent as he glared at Amir with a look that could kill. Amir wasn't worried because he knew that no matter what despicable things Cousins was capable of, he was a chicken when it counted most. Murder took heart and that was something that Raymond Cousins certainly didn't have.

"What's it going to be?"

"You son of a bitch," Raymond grunted.

"Watch your mouth, Raymond. Let's not turn this thing uglier than it needs to be. Now, either you can play nice or I can make sure this story hits the front page of every major newspaper on the East Coast. Make up your mind right now," Amir ordered, his patience running thin.

Cousins stared at him with contempt and loathing. He considered his options for a fleeting moment, realizing that he really didn't have any. He could not allow his brother to go down for something that had happened almost a decade before. The past was long since forgotten and Victor had turned his life around, and now here was Amir Swift trying to ruin everything.

"You got it, man," Raymond conceded.

"Yeah, that's what I thought."

Amir turned and began walking away. Over his shoulder, he said, "You should consider yourself lucky that it was me and not Tavares who came to see you."

He kept walking, out of the park and, he hoped, away from his last duty of an old life that he wanted to forget had ever existed.

The housekeeper opened the door and signed for a package delivered by a messenger service. She turned the package over to a nervous Joan Dartmouth, who wondered what catastrophe had shown up on her doorstep now. In her study she tore open the package and found inside the documents Raymond Cousins had shown her, detailing William's evasion of several million dollars in taxes over the years. Also inside was a signed and notarized copy of the divorce papers she had served on Cousins.

She sat numbly staring at the stack of papers, trying to figure out how this could have happened. Tears slid down her cheeks as she said a silent prayer, thankful for whoever or whatever had conspired to free her from Raymond's clutches. She doubted seriously that he had had a change of heart because in those last few weeks with him, she had realized that he did not have a heart to be changed. He was a callous manipulator who didn't care who he hurt in order to get what he wanted. Something had to have happened to make him change his plans.

She had been given a second chance to do right by her husband. Whatever William had done, it was wrong to have his name sullied now, when he was no longer able to defend himself. She had been stupid and careless to allow a man like Raymond Cousins into her life and her home, and she prayed that wherever William was, he could forgive her. As much as she had learned to run the hotel on her own, she would have to use that same energy to learn how to live by herself. Until she was comfortable alone, she would never attract the right person to share her life with. That was a lesson that she'd just had to learn the hard way, and learn it she had.

Joan threw the incriminating documents into the wire mesh trash can next to the desk. She searched through her desk drawer until she found a lighter. It was a twenty-four-karat-gold lighter with the initials WD embossed on it. She remembered when she'd given the lighter to William one year for their anniversary. He'd used it every time he lit a cigar. Joan lit the envelope on fire, and dropped it into the can and watched as the flames and smoke shot up. She watched intently as past mistakes, hers and William's, turned into gray, meaningless ash.

Chapter 37

Azure shook hands with Philip Deveraux, the director of the Tate Gallery in the heart of a revived London, an excited smile plastered on her face. She had arrived in London earlier that day and had scarcely had a moment to breathe. Mr. Deveraux's assistant had whisked her away from the airport and driven through the busy streets at warp speed. She had been taken to a luncheon at a trendy American-style restaurant where she had met other artists whose work she used to gaze at on the walls of her own gallery. Seated side by side with some of the great impressionists of modern times was almost more than she could bear.

Nervously, she talked about her own work and eventually, with the aide of a dry wine and humorous company, she was able to relax. By the end of the meal she no longer felt out of her league and she knew that she was as enriched by meeting these people as they were by meeting her.

At the Tate she was taken on a tour by Mr. Deveraux personally. He showed her where her work would hang during the weeklong exhibit of contemporary American artists. They had three of her pieces on display. The first, *Peace,* was a revision of a portrait of a young boy that she had painted while she was still in college. She had refined it as she'd learned more about her craft and now it possessed the right balance of innocence and wisdom that she had been trying to capture. The second piece, *Freedom,* was a tribute to the African-American struggle as seen through the eyes of an elderly man seated in a rocking chair.

Her favorite of the three, *Love's Portrait,* was also the one she found the most difficult to talk about. It was an oil painting that she had done after the first time she and Amir had made love. The nude couple resembled her and Amir, though their features were blurred. His vanilla skin against her chocolate, her hands buried in his locks, everything about the painting exuded sensuality. The violet and lavender background set a warm mood which invited the viewer into their world. She was proud of the way the portrait had turned out and knew that the inspiration behind it was what made it so special.

London was nothing like she had expected. She had envisioned a quaint, romantic atmosphere but instead found that London was a dynamic metropolis as vivacious as Manhattan on theater night.

On the second day of the exhibit, as Azure stood near the back of the gallery sipping a glass of wine, she noticed a man staring at her. He was a tall, brown-skinned man with a smooth bald head. He wore a charcoal gray suit over a black fitted shirt. When he caught her eye, he raised his glass to her. She returned the gesture and offered a slight smile. He approached, as she'd known he would.

"Ms. Monroe, I apologize for staring, but you are the most striking woman here tonight," he said.

His heavy accent was French, but a come-on in any language was easy to pick up on.

"While I thank you for the compliment, I'm sure that is not true. French women are extremely attractive," she returned.

"I won't argue that. My mother is a lovely French woman. You, however, are leagues ahead of most. Allow me to introduce myself. I'm Vincent Davis," he said, extending his hand.

"Azure Monroe," she replied.

He raised her hand to his mouth and kissed it softly. She smiled as she took another sip of wine.

"At the risk of sounding like a groupie, I'd like to tell you that in addition to being the most beautiful woman in the room, your paintings are also quite fantastic."

"Are all French men as smooth as you, Mr. Davis?" Azure asked, without missing a beat.

"Ouch! Dare I say that the lady is jaded?"

"No, not jaded. I'm just from the tough streets of D.C. where if a sister is not careful she could extend a hand and lose three fingers in the exchange." She laughed.

Vincent Davis was quite the charmer. He was impressed by Azure even before he'd exchanged a word with her. Her artwork spoke volumes for itself and her wholesome beauty was something to behold. Once he began talking to her, however, he was completely smitten. He had dated women of all nationalities and walks of life, American women included. However, he found Azure's candor refreshing and welcomed the challenge of breaking through her reserved exterior.

After the exhibit closed for the evening, Azure accepted his invitation to see a little bit of London. He promised to have her in early as she had a good deal of business to tend to in the morning.

They rode the world's largest observation wheel, the London Eye, and it was unlike any other Ferris wheel Azure had ever seen in her entire life. It rose an impressive 135 meters above the ground on the South Bank, between Waterloo and Westminster bridges. From the top, Vincent pointed out the different parts of central London and beyond. Under the night sky the view was magical, making Azure feel as if she had been transported to another galaxy.

Vincent made Azure laugh, something she had not been able to do since her fight with Amir. He entertained her with stories of his childhood in London, of growing up with an eclectic mix of relatives. His mother was a French woman with Dutch grandparents, while his father had been born in Jamaica and had migrated to London as a teenager. Vincent spoke a variety of languages fluently: English, French, Portuguese and Italian. He told her that he was a sociology professor at the University of London, but was considering taking a job abroad some day.

Azure enjoyed spending time with Vincent and guiltily allowed him to take her mind off her troubles. She spent the next day meeting with different benefactors of the arts and was commissioned to do some paintings of what they termed "American Life" at a handsome profit.

The following evening Azure strolled along the River Thames with Vincent. He shared many more things about himself, including the fact that he had never been to America, but intended to get there one day soon. From what he'd heard, he did not think it was somewhere he would consider settling down, but he was intrigued by its reputation as a land where people lived uninhibited by social norms.

"Maybe you could be my guide?" he queried. "That is, if your boyfriend doesn't mind."

"What makes you think I have a boyfriend?" she asked.

"A woman as beautiful as you could not possibly be single. I'm certainly not that lucky."

Azure was flattered by Vincent's attention, but anything beyond conversation was not what she wanted.

"Look, Vincent, I've really enjoyed your company, but honestly, I've just come out of a relationship, and I'm on a bit of a hiatus from men right now."

"Well, he must have really done you wrong," Vincent said.

"Let's just say we both made mistakes. I look at it as a lesson learned," Azure replied.

"That's a healthy attitude. But you know, it is a proven philosophy that the best way to mend a broken heart is to jump right back into the ring."

Obviously, Mr. Davis did not give up quite so easily. She smiled without replying, and a short while later ended their evening in the lobby of her hotel. He kissed her on the cheek and walked her to the elevator. She knew that he was hoping for an invitation upstairs and was clearly disappointed when the elevator doors closed with him on the outside.

A couple of days before her trip was scheduled to end, they shared a picnic lunch in St. James Park. Over crepes and wine, Vincent pleaded with Azure to extend her trip. He wanted to show her more of his country, and he thought that if they spent a few more days together it would be good for her, as well. Ironically, he told her that he had been taken with her from the moment he'd laid eyes on her. It was reminiscent of her meeting of Amir, yet unfortunately in this case, the feelings were one-sided. She realized that despite her best intentions, she had led him on to think that he had a chance with her. She reiterated that she could not offer him anything more than friendship and politely declined his invitation. Lunch ended with a sad farewell as she realized that spending any more time with Vincent would be completely unfair to him. He gave her his contact information and implored her to keep in touch. She also gave him her address in D.C., and promised him that if he ever did decide to take that trip to America, she would willingly be as gracious a host as he had been to her.

It was refreshing to spend time with a man again, especially since she had no intentions of becoming involved. Part of her wished that she had consented to having a fling with him. She certainly knew that Yanté would chastise her thoroughly for not having experimented a little. But she realized that she could not replace the passion she'd had with Amir so easily, and that in the end, she would not feel good about sharing her body with a man so carelessly. Amir's touch was still fresh on her skin, and his scent still lingered in the air around her. No matter how hard she tried, she had not yet been able to exorcise him and the last thing she needed was to try to fake it with someone else.

After saying goodbye to Vincent, Azure spent her last couple of days in London on her own. She visited all the usual tourist attractions, including Westminster Abbey and Buckingham Palace. She lucked out and was able to witness the changing of the guard at the palace. The dignity of the ceremony was especially beautiful and inspiring. On a stroll through London streets she stumbled upon a weekend market on Portobello Road. The offbeat open-air trading post was right up her alley. She shopped endlessly, finding gifts for her family. She spotted several things which she would have loved to give to Amir and had to remind herself of the impossibility of that.

The entire visit was magnificent, but throughout she felt as though something was off. She knew that this was a once-in-a-lifetime experience and she could not help but wish that Amir was there to share it with her. He would have loved everything about London and the sheer joy of watching him enjoy himself would have made it all the more pleasurable for her. That was one of the many things she missed about him—his desire to experience things. He was as much of an explorer as she was and doing it alone just wasn't quite the same.

It would be a long time before she was able to go places and do things without thinking of Amir, but she felt that she had no choice. She had lost her trust in him, and she did not believe that it was possible to regain that essential element in a relationship once it had been destroyed.

She returned home with a renewed sense of pride about herself and her work. She had made valuable contacts and was slowly beginning to understand the far-reaching impact her art was having on the community at large. It was a good feeling to know that she could touch the lives of people she didn't even know just by capturing images on canvas. She threw herself into her work, painting feverishly at times. A week later she received a postcard from Vincent which made her smile. He'd signed it, *Your French friend,* and she relished the thought of having a man halfway around the world thinking about her.

Too bad her thoughts still lingered on another man, who was less than a fifteen-minute drive away.

Chapter 38

Amir remained at the back of the museum, watching Azure and the other artists. The exhibit was a benefit sponsored by the mayor and designed to bring the arts to the inner city. All of the proceeds from the sales would go to enrich an art partnership with the area public schools and the community outreach agencies. Azure was one of a dozen artists who had contributed works to be sold and she was on hand to sign autographs and be photographed.

She was as beautiful as ever. He noticed that she'd cut her hair very short, emphasizing her angelic face. The white silk dress she wore hugged her curvaceous body, inviting warm memories to the surface of his mind, memories which he had been trying to forget. He watched her smile and chat with people, and to the naked eye she appeared to be happy. However, despite the fact that so much time had passed, he could still read her, her heart and mind, like a book. Behind the smile and the conversation, there was a dullness in her eyes. She looked as though she were wearing a mask that covered up an unimaginable sadness. He hated himself for being the cause of that unhappy countenance. While she had changed his life for the better in the brief time that he'd known her, he wished that he had never met her. She would have been better off without ever knowing and loving him.

He took one last look at her before slipping out of the gallery's door. He'd wanted to have her picture embedded in his brain, for this was the last time he would see her. He was grateful for what she had brought into his life and knew that no matter what experiences waited for him, he would always treasure their time together. He only hoped that one day she would be able to move on and find a man who was truly worth her time and her love.

"Goodbye, sweetness," he said aloud.

He pushed the gallery door open and walked away. A single tear escaped from his steel gray eyes and he blinked it away rapidly. His heart was broken for what seemed to be the umpteenth time in his life, but this time he knew that he'd brought it on himself. Had he taken his chances and been honest with her from the very beginning, he might not have lost her. He'd taken a gamble, bet heavily and lost. He picked up his pace, walking faster and faster until he finally broke out into a full run. Finally, out of breath and feeling like an idiot, he stopped. It was no use anyway. He could never run fast enough or far enough to get her out of his mind, so he gave up trying. He would allow the memory of her to live in his heart taking solace in the fact that at least they'd had one chapter in the great storybook of life.

* * *

The door of his apartment had been jimmied. Scratch marks along the door and on the cylinder were a giveaway. Cautiously, Amir inserted a key into the lock. The apartment was dark. He closed the door behind him and cast his eyes around the dark apartment. A figure was standing near the window. Amir clenched his fists tightly, ready to pounce. Suddenly he was hit from behind, and a blow to the back of his head sent him to his knees. The person who'd hit him knelt on top of him, with his knee in his back. Dazed, Amir struggled, but to no avail.

The other intruder walked casually away from the window and approached them. While he could not see either of their faces, he could tell that the guy on his back was a large man. His heavy breathing gave away the fact that he was not used to much physical exercise. He pulled Amir to his feet, pinning his arms behind his back. The other guy stepped in closer, but before Amir's eyes could accommodate the darkness, he was punched in the face, once and then a second time. A jab to his gut caused him to vomit. The final blow, to his temple, knocked him out. His body sank to the floor like a sack of potatoes.

When Amir came to, he was alone. He opened his eyes, trying to get them to focus, and sat up, clutching his side, which hurt intensely. He crawled across the floor until he reached the switch for the track lights on the ceiling. By their light he was able to see what had been hidden from him in the darkness. His apartment had been ransacked. Books, CDs, papers and clothes were strewn from one end to the other. His television was smashed and the contents of the refrigerator had been emptied onto the floor.

He leaned against a wall, wiping the blood from his lip.

He didn't need to think for one second about who his late-night visitors had been. All he needed to do was to figure out how he would get back at them. He pulled his cell phone out of his pocket and dialed the one person he knew would have his back. Tavares answered on the first ring and Amir immediately felt that everything would be all right.

[faint text bleed from previous page, illegible]

Chapter 39

"Crap," Yanté swore as she pulled her car into the driveway of her house.

The motion-sensor light did not come on. Yanté placed the car in park and sighed. It had been a long day, and she was anxious to get inside, take a hot bath and crawl into bed. She hesitated momentarily, reluctant to approach the house in the darkness. She glanced out of the car's back and side windows, but saw nothing save her neighbors' quiet houses. Driven by fatigue and the comforting thoughts of her welcoming bed, she dismissed the absent light and got out of her car. At the door, she fumbled with her keys, unable to see the locks clearly. Muttering under her breath, she finally opened the door and stepped inside. Closing the door behind her, she reached over to the wall and turned the knob on the lights. Nothing happened.

"What the hell?" Yanté questioned aloud. She looked

out of the window at her neighbors' houses again and noted that there were lights on up and down the block.

"So much for a power outage."

She headed to the kitchen, dropped her purse on the table and continued toward the utility closet, which was located near the back door. Seconds before she reached the box, a hand grabbed her by the throat from behind. She gasped and was swiftly dragged backward. She stumbled and clutched the hand around her throat. She began scratching at it, trying to stop it from completely cutting off her air.

"Hey, baby," the deep voice attached to the hand whispered in her ear.

She tried to scream, but her voice was being strangled by the hand. She struggled against him, but he was too strong and she was too unprepared. When they reached the living room, the man roughly pushed her down onto the sofa. She immediately tried to jump back up to her feet, but a sharp punch to the left side of her face knocked her back down. Her head was spinning as her brain became clouded.

"What do you want?" she screamed.

"You, baby," he said again.

In a flash, he was all over her, pressing her down onto the sofa with his enormous body. His breath, which smelled like garbage, was all over her face as he panted heavily. His hands began roaming, roughly touching her legs, her face and her bruised neck. They felt calloused and scratchy against her skin. Bile rose in her throat as her stomach churned beneath him. Her mind felt foggy, as if she were in a dream. But this was no dream. She was filled with horror as she realized what was about to happen to her, and she felt powerless to stop it.

"Please, don't do this," she begged.

Blood was beginning to pool inside her mouth from the blow she had sustained. She tried to free her hands to wipe at her face but he held them tightly above her head. His fingers were now probing her underwear, trying to find the entrance to her womanhood.

"Do what, baby? You know you want me. You've been waiting for me to come, haven't you? Didn't I send you flowers? You didn't like the doll, huh? Huh? I can't hear you," he screamed into her face.

"No," she whispered.

"What's the matter, Yanté? Am I not good enough for you? Huh, you tramp? Answer me!"

Tears slid down Yanté's face as terror took control of her mind and body. She realized that this man was the person who had been stalking her. She kicked herself for not taking it more seriously and alerting the police. All this time he had been toying with her, playing with her and setting her up for the kill and stupidly, she had done nothing to protect herself. Suddenly, anger set in, crowding out the fear. She would not accept this. She refused to allow this person to do what he had planned to do to her. This was her life, and at that moment she decided to dig her heels down and fight for it.

"Nooo!" she screeched from deep inside the pit of her stomach.

At the same time she grabbed a section of the man's cheek and tried to tear it from his face. Momentarily stunned by her action, he reared back. With a kill-or-be-killed attitude, she used that second of opportunity to summon all of her strength and shove him off her. He fell onto the floor and Yanté leapt off of the couch. She snatched the mother-and-child figurine from the end table next to the sofa and swung it at him. He blocked her blow with his arm and grabbed her legs, pulling her down to the floor onto her knees. He punched her again, his fist glancing off her left eye. She winced with pain but did not allow herself to stop moving.

Still grasping the statue, she swung again, striking him on his right shoulder this time. The statue flew from her grasp and he swung back at her, punching her in the stomach. She doubled over in agony and fell onto her side. He grabbed her throat, pressing hard, and her eyes fluttered. For one moment, she felt as if the end was near. That moment was fleeting, however.

Full of fire and fight, Yanté reached out and grabbed his genitals, squeezing equally as hard. He let go of her larynx and tried to pull her hands from his privates. She held on for dear life. Reaching up, she punched him as hard as she could directly in his nose. He coughed roughly and backed away. Yanté began screaming at the top of her lungs. She jumped up from the floor and half ran, half stumbled toward the door, her shrill cries for help deafening to her own ears. Her only goal was to make it out onto the street and to haul ass. She didn't know where she would run to, but she wouldn't stop until she found someone who could help her.

She flicked the locks on the door and was turning the knob when he grabbed her shoulder from behind. She shrugged him off, moving deftly to the left. She ran to the kitchen, with him in hot pursuit, determined to get to her. He growled angrily as he reached out and shoved her hard in the center of her back, causing her to fall forward into the kitchen table. With her face level with the tabletop, the shiny metal of the bread knife that she had left there that morning caught her eye. She snatched it with her right hand, spun around and at the precise moment that he was less than one step away from her, rearing his hand back to hit her again, she leaned forward and, with all the force she could muster, plunged the knife into his abdomen.

He grabbed the protruding handle, staggering backward. The front door, slightly ajar from when she had turned the knob, was at that moment shoved open, and her next-door neighbors burst in. Simon Alberts, a high-school hockey coach in his forties, quickly sized up the situation and charged the invader. Putting the struggling man in a chokehold, he yelled for his wife to get Yanté out of there. Kelley Alberts took a shivering, still-screaming Yanté by the shoulders and half dragged her briskly out of the house.

By the time Yanté's screams had diminished to gut-wrenching sobs, the police had arrived and the perpetrator was handcuffed to a gurney and being loaded into an ambulance. A second pair of paramedics from the fire rescue team had also arrived on the scene and were attempting to see to Yanté's injuries. They called for another ambulance to transport her to the hospital.

"Wait," she said.

She walked outside into the now-awakened street. At the sound of sirens and the sight of flashing lights, her neighbors had come out in droves to see what the commotion was. She hobbled over to the gurney, holding her aching waist. She was determined to see the face of the man who had broken into her home and assaulted her. His eyes were closed, but even without seeing them, she recognized him immediately.

"Do you know this man?" a female police officer said to her gently.

"Yeah, I do."

The janitor from the bakery lay on the gurney, moaning. She thought about the way he would smile at her when she stopped for her coffee in the mornings and the times she'd looked up to see him checking out her body from head to toe. She remembered the day he'd asked her to go out on a date with him and how she'd told him thanks, but no thanks. She hadn't been rude or impolite about it. How dare he not accept her refusal as if she were not free to choose whom she did or did not want to date? She wanted to spit in his face.

"What did I do to you? Why me?" she yelled at him.

Kelley Alberts tried to pull her away from the gurney, but Yanté wouldn't budge. The wounded man opened his eyes ever so slightly and a crooked half smile formed on his lips. Yanté swung at him, but was quickly subdued by the police. She was carried away, hysterical, and placed in the second ambulance.

Chapter 40

Azure arrived at the hospital at approximately the same time that the ambulance pulled in. Kelley Alberts, who had met Azure several times in the two years that Yanté had been her neighbor, had called the gallery. Luckily, Azure was there painting. She had been spending most of her time at the gallery even though the memories of Amir were equally as vivid there as they were at home.

Kelley Alberts's frantic call sent Azure out of the door in a hurry, panic causing her limbs to tremble. When she spotted Yanté lying on a hospital bed in the emergency room, her heart virtually leaped out of her chest. One side of her cousin's face was swollen and purple, the eye socket puffy and the eye itself bloodred. The other eye had a large bruise above it that was quickly turning her light-brown skin purple. Her bottom lip was split, dried blood crusting in the corners of her mouth. The worst visible signs of her trauma were the deep blue-black finger marks around her neck. A nurse had placed a cold compress on the side of her neck, which she'd complained hurt the most. Azure cried out at the sight of her cousin.

"Yanté, what happened? Who did this to you?"

Yanté had stopped sobbing but at the sound of Azure's horrified voice, her tears renewed themselves. She reached out an arm to Azure, who immediately grabbed her and hugged her, while she cried.

It was a long while before Yanté was able to talk. Finally, she told Azure about the flowers, the notes and the phone calls. She laid out everything leading up to that evening and upon hearing the details of her harrowing ordeal, Azure felt an overwhelming sense of guilt. She had been so caught up in her own problems that she hadn't been there for her cousin when she'd needed her the most. She should have made Yanté take the phone calls more seriously or at least asked whether they had stopped, but she'd completely forgotten about them because she had been consumed with her own tragedies.

Yanté left the emergency room after a thorough examination and several X-rays. Three of her ribs were broken, but there were no internal injuries. Additionally, two teeth were loose and she would have to see her dentist the following day to determine if they could be saved. A rape crisis counselor spent some time talking to her and even though her attacker had been unsuccessful, the counselor explained to Yanté that she was still considered a survivor of a violent sexual attack. As such, there would be residual emotional issues that Yanté would have to deal with. She implored Yanté to come in just to talk sometime in the next few days, and Azure promised to bring her.

Azure took Yanté home with her. It would be a long time

before her cousin would feel comfortable going home again, if ever. She made Azure promise not to call her parents that night, saying that she would tell them herself the next day. Right now all she wanted to do was to sleep. The emergency-room doctor had given her a prescription of Xanax, which she took with a full glass of water and, despite Azure's protests, a shot of tequila. Within minutes she fell asleep in Azure's bed. Azure sat up for the remainder of the night holding her cousin and watching her rest. She stroked her back every time she moaned or cried out, willing her back to a peaceful place where the horrors of the past few hours could not harm her.

Silent tears fell from Azure's eyes as she thought about what her cousin had endured. She couldn't help but ask herself why people could do the cruel things that they did to one another, with no regard for other people's feelings. In no way did she liken her recent loss to the brutality Yanté had just suffered through, but her pain was still just as raw. As she watched Yanté snatch moments of uninterrupted sleep, she also felt empowered. If her cousin could get through this, as Azure knew she would, then she, Azure, could certainly get through anything life threw at her. As the sun crept into the sky, painting the world in beautiful shades, Azure allowed hope to be her salve—hope for love, hope for peace and hope for second chances. She refused to accept the notion that all life was meant to be was suffering and hardship. She, for one, had had enough of both.

Chapter 41

Azure approached Jevar's parents' home for what she knew would be the last time. Nothing had changed in the years she had been coming there nor in the recent months in which she had stayed away.

Mrs. Martin opened the door for her and was overjoyed to see her.

"Azure, honey, oh, it's so good to see you. You look wonderful, darling. I love the short hair," she said as she hugged Azure and led her inside.

"Thank you, Mrs. Martin. You're looking pretty good yourself. How have you been?"

"I've been just fine. My daughter Dominique just had the baby last month and, whoowee, if that ain't a chunky piece of cuteness. Come on in here and look at these pictures."

Azure sat with Mrs. Martin in the living room, looking through dozens of photographs of the new grandbaby. They caught up over tea and the sweet-potato pie that Mrs. Martin had baked that morning. Mrs. Martin told her of her recent visit to Atlanta where her daughter and family lived and informed her that she and Mr. Martin planned to take Jevar and move down there for good.

"Really?" Azure asked, surprised.

"Yes. It's something we had been thinking about for a long time and now, with the grandbaby, I really don't want to miss out on anything. My husband just retired from the post office a couple of months ago and there's really nothing keeping us here. I've been meaning to call you to let you know."

"That's okay. I'm sorry I haven't been coming around lately. I…I just…"

"Shh, baby. It's all right. I told you before that it was time for you to start letting go and moving on with your life. Sitting up here with me and with Jevar is no good for you. You're a young woman with a whole life ahead of you. Jevar wouldn't want to see you wasting away."

"It was just so hard. I kept thinking that if I hung in there with him, some miracle would happen and he would come back to us."

"I know, I know, baby," Mrs. Martin said, stroking Azure's hands. "But all the hoping and praying is not going to change things. Now some of the doctors have advised us to remove his feeding tube and let him go peacefully, but I'm just not there yet. I know he's not ever going to talk to me again or smile or be able to take care of himself. I accept that. However, I can't let him just die…not like that."

"I agree. That would be awful," Azure said.

"So, we're going to move down south and keep on

taking care of him. Even though he doesn't respond, I know he can feel our love. Maybe being around his sister and her family will be a good thing for him."

"I hope so. I wish things could have been different, Mrs. Martin," Azure said sadly.

"Hush up now, child. There is no point in wishing for things that can't be. All we can do in this life is live it. God's will may not always be our own, but we have to believe that things will work out just as he planned them for us," Mrs. Martin said. "Now, why don't you go on upstairs and see Jevar. Say goodbye, sweetheart. It's time."

Azure climbed the stairs as she had done for the past three years. At the end of the hall she turned the knob and stepped inside the bright, sunny room. The Martins had painted Jevar's old bedroom a vibrant yellow and the sun shone through the open shades. The windows were also open and a warm breeze sifted into the airy room. Jevar was seated in his wheelchair near the window. He wore a blue jogging suit. Safety belts were strapped around his waist and upper torso to keep him securely in his seat.

The home attendant was sitting in one corner of the room, reading a book. She had been working at the Martins' for the past year, helping with Jevar's care, including his bathing and feeding. In addition, a nurse came to the house every other day to clean his feeding tube and check his temperature and vitals. The nurse also worked the muscles in his arms and legs to help them from growing rigid and to keep the blood circulating.

The attendant smiled at Azure, set her book down on a table and left them alone. A radio playing in the background was the only sound in the room.

"Hello, Jevar," Azure said.

She crossed the room and sat down in the rocking chair that faced him. She touched his hand lightly and searched his face. There was no indication that he knew she was there. A white handkerchief was tucked into his collar. A bit of spittle had formed in the corner of his mouth and she wiped it away with the piece of cloth.

"I haven't been here in a while, I know. Oh, congratulations on your new niece. I saw the pictures and she is quite a little doll, baby. Your mom was just telling me that you guys are moving down to Atlanta to be near your sister. I think that's just great," Azure chatted.

Suddenly, she reached out and stroked the side of Jevar's face. He was still as handsome as he had been the day she met him. His face was slightly bloated now, a side effect of the numerous medications he was on to help stave off infections. It was also due to the fact that his body was virtually inactive. Other than that, he looked the same. His father cut his hair and kept his face neat and trimmed. His eyes, which were big and brown, stared vacantly into space, blinking involuntarily every so often.

Azure looked around the room. Other than the paint job, the bright coordinating bedding and curtains and the full-size mechanical bed with guardrails, the room had not changed much since they were in high school. All of the plaques Jevar had earned in high school for track and field and wrestling remained hanging on the wall, and the trophy shelf in one corner of the room was still there. Pictures of him and Azure and other friends were framed and stood on the dresser, next to his medications.

Azure remembered how they would sneak up and fool around in his bedroom when Jevar's parents weren't at home. They had never gone all the way in his parents' home, but had come pretty close. She could never completely relax because she was always afraid someone would come home and catch them. Of course, her house was definitely out of the question. Jevar wasn't allowed past the living room when they were teenagers.

She reminisced about the day that they did finally consummate their relationship. It was graduation night. After all the festivities were over, he picked her up in the brand-new Chevy Trailblazer that his parents had just bought for him. Azure told her parents that she was spending the night with Yanté and since she'd been doing that virtually every weekend since she was a kid, they didn't question her. Jevar had made a reservation at a Marriott Hotel in Virginia. They drove down and had dinner in the hotel's restaurant. Their first night together had been magical and filled with all the excitement of young love. She knew that for as long as she lived that day would be one of the most special days she'd ever have.

"I will always love you," she said softly to Jevar, hoping that even though he could not respond, he understood her. "Always and forever. I've missed you so much that it has stopped me from living. I've felt guilty about not going with you that day. Even though I knew there was probably nothing I could have done, I still felt as if I should have been there when it happened."

Azure was crying now as she dredged up all the raw feelings she had been holding on to. It was well past the time for her to let these emotions out, but that didn't make it hurt any less.

"A few months ago I met someone, Jevar, and I even felt guilty about that. I didn't plan to meet him, much less fall in love with him, but it happened. It's over now, but I learned something from it. I can't keep myself holed up in the gallery, painting and hiding. I finally realized that what everyone was trying to tell me was right on the money—it's wrong to waste what God has given."

She took his hand again and kissed him lightly on the cheek. She looked into vacant eyes, the sheer tragedy of it still too much to fully comprehend.

"Goodbye, Jevar," she whispered.

She held his hand for a moment longer and then set it back down on his lap. She rose and walked out of the room, not turning to look back. In fact, she erased all current images of him from her mind and remembered the old smiling, laughing, playful Jevar. She would cherish those memories for the rest of her life, but it was time to move on and make new ones.

Chapter 42

Amir approached the brownstone swiftly. He and Tavares had planned to step to Sean when the latter showed up one evening. It had been a week since Amir had been attacked in his apartment. When he'd told Tavares what happened and who he suspected it to be, Tavares was livid. Even Big Rick, who had been with Tavares when Amir had called him, was beside himself. Sean had been going on as if nothing had happened, but Tavares was not fooled by his act.

The injuries Amir had sustained had pretty much healed, only a slight dark spot remaining on his lower lip. He'd stewed all week long, anxious to get a chance to give Sean some payback of his own. He entered the brownstone using his spare key and called out to Tavares.

"Down here," Tavares said.

Tavares was in the recreation room, lying back on the

sofa. Rick was seated on his stool as usual, reading the newspaper.

"What's up?" Amir asked, looking from Rick to Tavares anxiously. "Where is he?"

"He's gone," Tavares said.

Amir looked at his brother quizzically for several moments, waiting for him to clarify what he meant.

"What do you mean, *gone?*" he asked when nothing further was forthcoming from Tavares.

"Just what I said—he's gone. Problem solved," Tavares replied coolly.

Amir turned to Rick, who glanced up from his newspaper. The hard stare in Rick's eye told him all that he needed to know. What was more, it was all that Tavares and Rick intended to tell him.

Amir hung around for a while, shot a game of pool with Tavares and then prepared to leave. He paused, wanting to know what exactly his brother had done to Sean, but immediately changed his mind. He didn't really want to know. He wanted to forget as much as he could of everything that went on in the brownstone.

Tavares watched his brother leave, happy that no real harm had come to him. He would never tell Amir precisely what had gone on with Sean. He would shield him from that knowledge as he always had, because he knew that Amir was not cut from the same cloth as he was. His heart was not callous and he certainly was not capable of inflicting harm on anyone. That was one thing that Tavares felt really proud about, although he knew that he could not take credit for it.

Chapter 43

Azure exited the taxi in front of her parents' home. After having been out of town and then, once she returned, very busy with her new successes, she had eagerly accepted their invitation to Sunday dinner, realizing that she missed them both. One of the most surprising changes in her life had been the onset of a much better relationship with her mother. The only way Azure could describe the change in Vetta was that she had finally had the stick removed from her behind. It seemed Azure had heard her mother laugh more in the past couple of months than she had during her entire childhood.

She opened the door, shaking her head at the fact that her parents still kept their door unlocked in the daytime. She would scold them about that for the thousandth time later.

"Hello," she called out to let them know that she was there.

"In here, honey," her father responded.

They were relaxing in the den watching a movie. She

entered and got the ultimate shock—her mother was reclining on one end of the sofa with her feet resting in her father's lap, and stretched across the carpet was Patrick.

"Patrick!" Azure exclaimed.

"Hey, sis, it's about time you got here," Patrick said, jumping up from the floor to kiss her.

"What are you doing here?" she asked, unable to mask her surprise.

"Patrick's been here since Thursday," Nicholas said nonchalantly, as if this were the most normal thing in the world.

"Will you guys hush up so I can hear what Denzel is saying," Vetta interjected.

"Sorry, Mom," Azure answered.

She took Patrick by the hand and led him out of the den and into the kitchen.

"What's going on?" she asked, one hand on her hips.

She searched Patrick's face for any of the telltale signs that he was drinking or using again.

"Nothing, sis. Why are you so suspicious? Look, I do listen to you from time to time, you know. You made a lot of sense. I went down to Maryland and worked things out with my mother. Well, sort of. You know how she is. But anyway, I decided that it was time to take some responsibility for my life."

"So what…did you go into a program?"

"Nope. Cold turkey. You know I can't get down with any of those group things…too much like a cult if you ask me. I've been shaking this monkey loose all by my little old self." He smiled.

Azure eyed him skeptically. Searching his eyes told her that he was actually telling the truth. He looked good, too. He had put on a couple of pounds and his skin didn't look dry and ashy the way it had the last time she'd seen him.

"All right, I'll bite. So you cleaned yourself up, made up with your mother…and what about the part that brought you here?"

"I figured Dad and Vetta can't be half bad if they raised a great girl like you. I wanted to take the time to get to know them…for real and maybe give them a chance to see that I'm not as much of a jerk as I acted growing up. I called Dad, and he and I talked, a little hesitantly at first. The more we talked the easier it got. We cleared the air about a lot of things and here I am."

"Wow! This is almost too much. I'm happy for you…for us," Azure said, tears forming and spilling from her eyes.

"Oh, stop it. Don't do that, sis. You're going to make me cry," Patrick said.

He hugged his sister and for the first time allowed himself to be hugged back by her. He knew that he had miles to go before he would truly be healed, but he no longer believed he was alone in his journey. She had always had his back, despite the fact that he had never really felt as though he deserved it.

"I'm proud of you," Azure said.

Those words were music to Patrick's ears, and he silently promised himself to try never to do anything else to lose his sister's faith in him.

Their father walked into the kitchen, Vetta on his heels, sniffling.

"What, has everyone in this house gone mad?" Nicholas asked, looking from his wife's teary-eyed face to those of his children.

"Mom, what's the matter?" Azure asked.

She reached over to rub her mother's back, still not

quite used to this softer, gentler side of her. Her father laughed, handing his wife a tissue.

"Nothing, other than the fact that her last name isn't Washington."

"Oh, Nicholas, stop it. I just can't believe that movie. That Denzel always gets me going. He just went all out for that little girl," she replied, blowing her nose.

They all burst out laughing at that. As they sat down to dinner Azure thought about how blessed she truly was. Despite the losses she'd had to come to terms with, she did not have any regrets. She truly believed that everything would turn out just as it was meant to, as long as she continued to believe in the power of love.

Chapter 44

"Are you sure you want to do this?" Tavares asked.

"Yeah, man, I'm sure," Amir replied confidently.

They were standing at the departure gates of Reagan International Airport. Tavares set Amir's suitcase down on the ground between them.

He studied his little brother's face for a moment, realizing for the first time that the boy he had been taking care of since he was twelve years old was long gone. In his place was a man. Tavares did not regret anything he had done for his family. He had stepped up when most young men his age would have balked at the responsibility. As the oldest, he could not admit how much he missed his parents. He had barely shed a tear at the funeral, trying to be strong for his brother and sister. He wasn't yet eighteen and nowhere near prepared to be a man. He'd watched his father take care of the family, be a loving husband and a stern but supportive father. When it was his turn, he'd doubted himself every step of the way. He'd had no one to turn to for advice, so he'd navigated the way on his own. No one could tell him that he hadn't done a good job, in spite of the way he'd done it. Bridgette was a beautiful, intelligent young woman and he knew that was because he had not allowed her to get sucked into a system that didn't work.

Maybe it had been wrong to allow Amir to join the business in the first place. At the time, he'd thought that by keeping his brother near him, working with him, he could continue to protect him from the traps society set for brothers. It was clear to him that Amir had become his own man and as much as Tavares had tried to prevent that from happening, it had. Standing outside the airport he understood why he was so resistant to Amir's leaving the business. He was afraid of accepting the fact that Amir did not need him anymore.

"I'm sorry I gave you such a hard time, man," Tavares said.

"There's no need for that, Tavares. I understand," Amir responded.

Tavares knew that Amir had, in fact, understood the meaning behind everything that had transpired between them. He'd loved Amir as a brother loves a brother and, perhaps, even more than that—as a father loves a child. Tavares also realized that the tables had turned and the time had come for him to learn from his little brother, the student becoming the teacher.

"You know there's no such thing as a one-way ticket. You can always come back," Tavares said, still clinging to what once was.

"I know, man, and thank you."

"No, Amir, thank you," Tavares said.

The two men embraced, each one unwilling to say the words but knowing that this was, indeed, goodbye. For Tavares, it was goodbye to the little boy he'd have fought tooth and nail to protect. For Amir, it was goodbye to a path taken which had never truly been his. Amir was sad to leave, but at the same time was encouraged that he had found the strength to go his own way. He was prepared to start anew and was excited by the possibilities which faced him.

"Maybe once you get settled and all the hard work is done, I'll come down and spend a few days with you," Tavares laughed.

"How about you come down sooner and help me out?" Amir responded.

Even as he said it, Amir knew that Tavares wouldn't get within two feet of the physical labor Amir was about to embark on. Tavares pulled a sealed envelope from his jacket pocket and held it in his hands. The gesture was one that Amir had known his brother would make.

"I've got everything I need," he said.

Tavares nodded, having known before he offered that his brother would refuse his money. Ironically, his feelings were not hurt by Amir's refusal. He was proud that his brother had turned out to be a good man, in spite of everything. He smiled, took one last glance at his little brother, turned and walked away.

Amir waited until he could no longer see Tavares's retreating figure. He couldn't help but wonder what things would be like the next time he saw his brother's face and that frightened him a little, but there was no turning back for him now. No matter what scary prospects the future held, the past was dead and buried. He picked up his suitcase and made his way through the sea of travelers milling about.

Seven hours later he landed in his parents' hometown
of Bridgeport, Barbados, now the place he hoped to call
his own home.

Amir had accumulated a meager nest egg of fifteen
thousand dollars from the parties he had arranged. He knew
that it wasn't a lot, but it was a start. He rented a small room
in a motel and immediately began working on his plans.
Before coming to Barbados, he'd had an architect help
him lay out designs for an eight-room bed-and-breakfast,
complete with a state-of-the-art kitchen, bar and lounge,
fitness center and indoor sauna. Outdoors, there would be
a tennis court, swimming pool and barbecue area. He got
referrals of local builders and stood side by side with them
every day. With the plans in hand he worked tirelessly to
see his dream come together, one nail at a time.

He applied for and successfully received a bank loan.
If there was one thing that Tavares had taught him, that was
the importance of maintaining good credit. Tavares had
made him file taxes since he had begun doing freelance
party promotions. With the seed money he'd brought with
him down to Barbados, he was able to watch his dreams
slowly and painstakingly turn into reality. He cut costs by
doing a lot of the labor himself, and he also did odd jobs
for people around the island to earn more cash. He main-
tained a small area of the property for raising sugarcane and
rented that space out to a couple of local farmers.

Working as hard as he was left him little time to think
or feel. He worked until his body was numb. His beard
grew in and his locks grew thicker. On the occasions that
he went into town to purchase supplies or file necessary
paperwork with the town clerk, he received interested
stares from women of all ages. Some of the bolder ones at-

tempted to engage him in conversation and while he was not blind to the exotic beauty of the Bajan women, he was not inclined to share more than a courteous greeting. His mind and soul were immersed in a desire to see his project to fruition and nothing else mattered. Besides, there was no room for romance in a heart that had been left in a small gallery in the metro area of D.C.

Chapter 45

"Hello?" Azure called. The apartment door was slightly ajar so she hesitantly pushed it further open and stepped cautiously inside.

"Yes?" a voice called from the living room. Azure stepped inside and was surprised to find a pretty young woman standing in the middle of the room, surrounded by brown boxes, bubble wrap, tape and other packing supplies.

"May I help you?" the woman asked as she peered at Azure. Slowly, a smile of recognition spread across her wide mouth. "Azure?"

"Yes, uh…I'm sorry, have we met?"

"I'm Bridgette—Amir's sister."

Bridgette recognized Azure from a photograph she had found in one of Amir's boxes. The photograph had been taken on the beach during their trip to Barbados, and he was standing behind her with his arms wrapped around her body. Madly in love was an understatement when describing the couple posed in that picture.

"Oh, goodness. Of course you are. I'm sorry…I should have recognized you. You look a lot like Amir."

"Yeah, we're like three peas in a pod."

Bridgette's hair was darker and wavy, and she wore it in a neat ponytail. Her complexion was a few shades darker than Amir's, yet her facial features were similar. In Amir's opinion, the eyes were the greatest difference between the two, Bridgette's being a warm brown. Still, they were unmistakably related.

Azure stepped further into the living room and looked around.

"Uh…Bridgette, I was…well, I just came by to…I was wondering if…"

"He's gone," Bridgette said softly.

"Gone?"

"He left a couple of weeks ago. He was kind of in a rush so I promised him that I'd clear out the apartment for him. I was just packing up some things to send to him. The other stuff, over there," she said, pointing to boxes stacked near the kitchen area, "those are things he wanted me to donate to charity. Do you have anything here? I mean, you could look through them if you wanted to."

Azure didn't know what to say. She shook her head numbly. From the moment she'd made the decision to come to see Amir and to apologize for her part in their breakup, she had never once considered the possibility that she would not get the chance to do so. She had waited too long, too wrapped up in the wrong she believed he had done her to think about the right things that had been there. When she'd found out from Joan that Raymond Cousins had suddenly done a three-sixty, backing off and signing the divorce papers, she knew in her heart that Amir had had something to do with it. Still, she allowed her pride to stop her from coming to see him.

Her heart sank into her shoes and her eyes began to burn. If she had not realized it before, certainly at that moment it felt like all the love she would ever be capable of sharing had rested with this man. Now, it was as if that love had died a thousand deaths right before her eyes. She felt heavy, the weight of her broken heart wearing her down. She wanted to turn and flee—to get away from his place, his sister and any reminder of him, but she couldn't make herself move. So she stood there, feeling like an imbecile but unable to escape.

"Listen, Azure, I was real sorry to hear about you and my brother…you know, breaking up. I mean, I know for a fact that he was really into you."

"Yeah, well…I guess it wasn't meant to be," Azure mumbled, humiliation making her voice sound molasses-thick.

"I don't think you really believe that," Bridgette said gently.

The women's eyes met and held, Bridgette's soft and concerned and Azure's full of pain. All Azure could do was to shake her head, not trusting her voice to speak for her again. Bridgette experienced déjà vu as she saw the same anguish on Azure's face that she had seen on her brother's. When Amir had announced his plans to move to Barbados, she was disappointed. On the one hand, she'd felt as if he was running away. However, on the other, she understood his need to have a change of scenery. She hoped that he would spend some time there and his heartache would be healed.

"He's hurting, Azure," Bridgette said plainly.

"Me, too."

The first tear fell as Azure admitted the agony she was in. It was time to shove her pride aside and at least acknowledge that she was feeling the loss of Amir.

"What are you going to do?"

"I don't know," Azure admitted.

She had come there hoping that Amir would be there and that they would meet one another halfway. Obviously, she had been hoping for more than he. He had packed a bag and skipped town to parts unknown without so much as a goodbye. It seemed as if that pretty much limited her options at this point.

"He's a good man, Azure…as good as they come. Don't give up on him," Bridgette said.

"Looks like he's the one who's given up," Azure responded weakly.

"He had to go. I don't necessarily understand all of his reasons, but I do respect the fact that he felt like he needed to leave. My brother has the most beautiful spirit I have ever had the pleasure of being around, and I'm not just saying that because he's my brother. But what he's gone through… is going through, I know that it's causing his soul to suffer. That's why I say that if getting away from here was the only way for him to find healing, well…he had to go."

Azure nodded, at a loss for words. She turned and began walking toward the door. She paused, biting her bottom lip as she chose her words carefully.

"When you talk to him, tell him…just tell him I said I wish him nothing but peace."

"I will, Azure. And just in case you still want to know— he's gone home…back to our parents' home."

Azure closed the apartment door behind her and walked down the hallway, the *click-clack* of her heels reverberating off the walls and creating a loud echo that did little to drown out her sobs.

"Where do you want these?" Yanté asked, motioning to the dozen picture lamps that she had just finished wrapping with plastic bubble wrap.

"Uh…I think there's a box of those…somewhere. Here," Azure said, pointing to an oversize box marked Fragile near the door.

They had been working in relative silence for over an hour. It was early in the morning, and the last vestiges of summer hung on defiantly. To Yanté's happiness, she was helping Azure prepare to move her studio out of the back of the gallery. Azure had hired someone to run the gallery for her on a day-to-day basis so that she could concentrate on her own work.

For the time being, the plan was for her to work out of the house. It was obvious that Azure was sad to be leaving the gallery, but Yanté knew that she had much more than that weighing her mind down right now. Yanté couldn't help but feel as though she was partly to blame. She had been pushing Azure so hard for so long to break out of her cocoon and meet someone. How many times had she chastised her for staying holed up in this place instead of hitting the clubs or the nightlife with her? Now it seemed that in following her advice, she had chosen a path which had ended badly. Or had she?

"Ashes, how about a penny for your thoughts?" Yanté asked gently.

"I don't know, girl. Sometimes I feel like no matter

what I do, it's just not going to work out for me. It's like I've got some sort of dark cloud hanging over my head," Azure said.

"That's just downright ridiculous," Yanté stated emphatically. "You can't really be blind to how blessed you are. I know you're hurting, but you have to see how lucky you are. There are people who have gone through and are going through far worse trials and tribulations than you. They keep on keeping on."

"I'm sorry, Yanté," Azure apologized, realizing how insensitive she was being. Considering what Yanté had just gone through herself, she had no right to be feeling self-pity. She could kick herself for her thoughtlessness. Yanté had just come out of a life-and-death situation with a few bruises and her sanity intact.

"No, Azure," Yanté said, sensing her cousin's guilt. "I'm not talking about me. Yes, that whole thing was the worst nightmare I've ever been through and I wouldn't wish that experience on my worst enemy. However, that's not it," she said. "Listen…when you lost Jevar, there was nothing you could do about it. He is gone and that's something that it has taken you three years to face."

"I know. It was just so hard to let go," Azure said.

Yanté set down the box she had been holding and walked over to where Azure leaned on the desk. She took a spot beside her and laced her fingers through her favorite cousin's.

"Who said you have to let go? You and Jevar had your time, your season together and there is nothing wrong with remembering that and cherishing it forever. But you have to move on."

"I did move on. A fat lot of good that did me," Azure said.

"Okay, and so it didn't go as smoothly as you would have

liked. Nothing ever does. Sometimes it's a battle and you have to fight to hold on to it. What have you got to lose?"

Yanté squeezed her cousin's hand and then let go, leaving her last words hanging in the air. Azure was tired of crying and tired of feeling sorry for herself.

"What about you, girl? Are you doing all right?" she asked.

"I'm doing just fine. I'm still staying at my parents' house, as you know, but that's getting real tired, real quick. They mean well, but you know how hard it is living at home once you've been on your own. I think they're secretly hoping I move back in permanently."

"You can't do that, Yanté. You can't let him win like that," Azure said.

"I know. I just had a new security system installed and I'm thinking about getting a dog or something. Maybe a vicious pit bull or a Rottweiler."

"Uh-uh. I won't be coming to your house anymore if you do that!" Azure exclaimed.

"Shoot, me, neither." Yanté laughed. "Anyway, I was thinking about going back home at the end of the week."

"Have you heard anything from the police?"

"Yeah, that nutcase is expected to plead guilty to a few counts, including assault and battery, attempted sexual misconduct and some other equally vile things. Apparently, he's done this sort of thing before and was registered as a sex offender. He wasn't even supposed to be living in the D.C. area. The prosecutor said he's probably looking at ten years, which is not as much as he deserves, if you ask me."

"I'm glad you're okay. I don't know what I would do without you." Azure smiled.

"I know what you'd do—you'd turn into an old maid who has forty-five cats and a house full of plastic-covered furniture," Yanté joked. "Seriously, though. What *are* you going to do?"

"I'm going to take a chance on life."

"Now that's what I'm talking about. That's what I've been trying to teach your blockhead all of these years. Take a chance. So what's the plan? What can I do?" she said eagerly.

"Slow down, speedy, I got this. I know what I need to do."

"Well, whatever it is, I hope it involves some white sand beaches and butt-licking waves." Yanté giggled.

Azure swatted Yanté's hands, laughing with her. She didn't tell her that she was hoping exactly the same thing.

Chapter 46

Amir sat on the edge of the pier, the nylon sweatpants he wore rolled up to his knees and his bare feet glancing across the water's surface as he swung his legs to and fro. The sun had made its ascent in the sky only a short while ago, bringing with it the light of a new day. The beauty of the water and the scenery around him still amazed him after having been there for almost a month. Each morning he made his way out to the water's edge to watch the sun rise and each day his breath caught in awe at what nature could do.

He had made the right choice in going there, of that he was sure. He could not remember a time in his life, since the day his parents died, that he had felt so connected with himself and with his spirituality. He was unclear as to what the future held for him, but that was okay. A burden too heavy for the strongest man in the world to carry had been lifted from his shoulders and now almost everything seemed right in his world. The house was coming along nicely. He had taken pictures just that morning and sent them via e-mail to Bridgette and Tavares. He couldn't believe how successful he had been at bringing his vision to life. Things were almost perfect, yet he couldn't pretend that there was not one element that was missing.

He shook his head, trying to stop himself from remembering the one thing that was wrong. The one thing that would never be right again, or so he believed. Try as he might, dedicated as he had become to living a life that was worthwhile and honorable, he could not go more than a day, not more than an hour without thinking about her. He prayed to the heavens above for her happiness and well-being, but he dared not have the nerve to pray for her forgiveness. His heart still ached for what he'd lost, but he believed that he had no right to feel sorry for himself.

The love he felt for Azure was something he would carry with him until he closed his eyes forever and the image of her would continue to dance through his mind. He closed his eyes now and saw her, sitting on a little stool in front of a blank canvas. She winked at him, a simple smile lighting up her beautiful face. He inhaled, wanting to smell the sweetness of her skin as he pressed his face into the fold of her neck. It was an elusive yet magnificent dream, which he was powerless to stop. She would haunt him for the rest of his days because he had loved her more than life itself.

"Amir."

He opened his eyes as a soft voice pulled him from his daydream. He looked out at the water, afraid to turn around because he did not believe in the impossible. But he felt her presence. It was all around him, enveloping him in such a way that even though he didn't believe, he had to turn around to see for himself.

"Hey," she said as his eyes traveled up her body, from her thong-clad feet, honey brown legs, bright orange halter dress and finally to her face.

Their gazes locked, his changing from disbelief to relief in an instant. Amir pulled his legs up onto the pier and stood. They were less than five feet apart, yet neither made a move. He couldn't because his body was paralyzed from the shock; she was equally unsure of herself.

"How?" he asked.

"Your sister," she replied.

He searched her face, looking for some clue as to what she was thinking.

"I've missed you," he risked.

"Me, too," she admitted, her eyes cast downward.

Looking up at him again, she added, "You owe me an apology."

"I'm—" Amir began. Before he could finish, Azure had taken several steps forward, closing the space between them. Standing inches away from him, she placed one finger on his lips.

"Show me," she whispered.

Amir began to breathe again. He closed his mouth over hers and devoured her. He drank her in as if he'd been lost in a desert for the past few weeks. All the sorrow that had made a home in the bosom of his soul seeped from his body at that moment, and he finally felt that he was truly at home.

A chance meeting in an art gallery was what brought them together. The connection of two souls, bound by destiny and fate to be together was what brought them to the place they would call home for some time to come. Yet they both believed that it was faith that had sustained them through the roughest of times. She had faith in his ability to be a man of his word. She believed that he would be the powerful man he was destined to be and would make the world a better place through his thoughts and deeds. For him, she was faith. She was the beauty this world needed, the peaceful spirit and forgiving heart that made the crazy seem sane. Together, they would paint portraits that were magical, and they would design a place where people could feel nothing but love.

Amir never fully understood why God had thought him worthy enough of another chance, but he vowed to spend the rest of his life being the man that she deserved. His parents would be proud of the man he'd become, and he could already feel their approval shining down on him as he held the woman of his dreams in his arms on a tiny pier in their homeland.

Epilogue

"May I have everyone's attention," Amir said, tapping his champagne flute with a fork.

Dressed in an ivory linen shirt and pants and brown leather sandals, his locks tied back and falling to the middle of his back, Amir addressed the crowd. His million-dollar smile warmed the entire room as he looked around at faces he'd known for years and those who were relatively new to his life. This gathering was a multifaceted celebration and every time he thought that his life could not get any better, it did just that. He was so grateful for all that he had been blessed with and not a day went by that he did not fall to his knees and thank God for seeing him through the darkest hours.

"I'd like to thank each and every one of you for coming and being with us. It means more than you can know. There's one person I'd like to thank especially. She is the guiding force behind everything I do, and I truly believe that without her by my side, I could not have accomplished all this," Amir said, waving his hand around the lavishly decorated room.

Sunrise Inn was celebrating its fifth anniversary. The inn, a modern bed-and-breakfast, had become one of the most visited resorts on the island of Barbados. It was known for its ambiance, decor and stylish furnishings. The waitstaff pulled out all the stops to make guests feel pampered and comfortable. The thing that held it all together, however, was the overall feeling of love and commitment exuded by its owners, Amir and Azure Swift.

"Baby," Amir said, holding out his hand for Azure, who was seated beside him, three-year-old Amir, Jr., perched on her lap.

She smoothed her son's unruly dusty-brown hair and kissed his forehead, the color of warm buttermilk. With eyes the same shade of gray and with the same tiny specks of brown as his father's, he looked up at his mother with a delighted smile. She placed her son on the seat next to her and stood, her protruding belly almost touching the table. She was six months pregnant with their second child, a girl this time, they believed. She took Amir's hand and moved closer to him.

"I love you more than you'll ever know. You are the best thing that's ever happened to me," he said, amidst oohs and aahs from their guests.

"And me, too," Amir, Jr., squealed.

Everyone laughed as Amir lifted his son into the air. Azure looked around the room at the smiling faces of the many wonderful people in her life. There was Yanté seated next to her husband, Dr. Carl Howard, looking as beautiful and happy as ever. Yanté had gone through a couple of rough patches when she'd relived the attack over and over again in her mind. She and Azure had spent countless hours on the phone, with Azure talking her through the bad moments and keeping her laughing about the good memories. She did this no matter what time of day or night it was until it was no longer necessary. Soon it was Carl who was there to chase the nightmares away and finally, there were no more bad dreams for Yanté.

Across the table from them were Azure's parents, who had recently retired, and who now spent the winter months divided between their homeland of St. Croix and here in Barbados, with Amir and Azure. Aunt Melissa and Uncle Marvin were also there, having the time of their lives on this, their first visit to the island.

Patrick, once a tortured soul hell-bent on self-destruction, hadn't flown in for the celebration—he was already there. He had been living on the island for the past three years and working at the inn. Patrick and Amir had become very close friends, just as Azure had hoped. They'd recently celebrated his fifth year of sobriety and, with positive thinking and sincere soul-searching, Patrick had grown worlds away from the angry boy and man he once was.

Joan Dartmouth had even made the trip to celebrate the inn's anniversary. She was still single—happily at last—and said that she was cautiously dating. She had been traveling more and was in the early stages of opening a second Dartmouth Hotel, in Italy, no less. Her corporation was a success and she now felt as though she had honored her late husband's memory. Although they came from different worlds and their lives were on different paths, Joan and Azure had become lifelong friends. That was the funny thing about friendships—sometimes people come into one another's lives unexpectedly but right on time to provide something that was missing. When that happened, beautiful liaisons could form, creating bonds that surpassed all differences.

Joan was never told about Amir's involvement in the Raymond Cousins situation—not the beginning of it nor the resolution. None of that mattered anymore for any of them, for they had all reached a position of strength and empowerment in their lives through the hard lessons learned.

Azure gazed into her loving husband's face, marveling at how far they'd come in a relatively short time. He was all the man that she had believed he could be, and she couldn't fathom that she had almost let him get away. She again gazed out into the sea of faces and saw Tavares seated beside Bridgette. Tavares had bought into a fast-food franchise in D.C. a couple of years back and had officially retired from hustling. Seeing Amir finally free from the constant worry his brother's former lifestyle had filled him with was a reward in itself. Once Azure got to know Tavares, many of her preconceived notions about him faded away and she found that beneath his tough exterior, he was not a bad guy. She did not approve of the things he had done nor did she condone the fact that he had roped Amir into following in his footsteps. However, she realized that it was not her place to judge him and as long as he was living a positive life, he would always be welcome in her home with his brother.

Amir popped the cork on another bottle of Dom Pérignon, the champagne oozing over the top and down his hands. Cheers rang out amongst the happy partygoers, with even little Amir getting in on the act. He laughed and clapped his tiny hands, raising his fruit smoothie in the air to click glasses with his father. Azure made the first cut into a five-foot-long sheet cake decorated with a replica of a painting she'd done of the inn. She had not painted since becoming pregnant for the second time, not wishing to subject the baby to the fumes, and was anxiously awaiting the opportunity to return to her passion. While the success she had reached through her artwork was phenomenal, the reward still came from the doing and not the showing.

Later on, when all was quiet and they were alone on their pier, Amir would wrap his arms around his ever-expanding wife and whisper in her ear. She would giggle and the baby in her stomach would kick her arms and legs at the sound of their loving.

Dear Reader,

We did it again! Thank you all for coming along on this journey of self-discovery. Despite their imperfections, Amir and Azure were able to elevate themselves to a higher level through love and forgiveness. They are proof positive that it is never too late for second chances, as long as you are courageous enough to take the first step.

I sincerely appreciate your readership. To those of you who take time out from your busy lives to send me e-mails sharing your opinions of my work, I'd like you to know that you are truly the inspiration that keeps me creating. I continue to strive to entertain you and, hopefully, provoke thought.

Next on my list is a romantic comedy that will surely tickle your funny bone and turn your thermostat way up!

Yours truly,

Kim Shaw

KIMANI
ROMANCE

**Bestselling author
Brenda Jackson
introduces
the Steele Brothers
in a brand-new
three-book miniseries**

Solid Soul

by **Brenda Jackson**

COMING IN JULY 2006
FROM KIMANI™ROMANCE

Love's Ultimate Destination

KIMANI
ROMANCE

"PLAY WITH BAD BOYS, BUT DON'T TAKE THEM HOME."

Jen St. George has always
lived by this one simple rule.
Will fast-moving bad-boy,
Tre Monroe, prove her wrong?
Is true love possible in...

FLAMINGO PLACE
by Marcia King-Gamble

COMING IN JULY 2006
FROM KIMANI™ ROMANCE

Love's Ultimate Destination